Steadfast
Will I Be

by

Susan Leigh Furlong

Steadfast Will I Be

Cover Art by *Abigail Owen*

The Wild Rose Press, Inc.
PO Box 708
Adams Basin, NY 14410-0708
Visit us at www.thewildrosepress.com

Publishing History
First Tea Rose Edition, 2019
Print ISBN 978-1-5092-2578-1
Digital ISBN 978-1-5092-2579-8

Published in the United States of America

Robin swung his knife out into the dark sea of fists and feet and heard a yelp of pain every time he made contact. He swung his knife again, but this time someone sliced his arm with a dirk on the inner side of his wrist. His knife fell. A swift blow to the back of his knees with another branch buckled his legs and sent him flat on the ground. The strikes intensified, as if knowing that he was down gave his attackers courage.

Blow after blow rained on his back, his legs, and his head. He scrambled to reach out for whatever he could, and several men fell on their backs after he latched onto their ankles and pulled. The pounding against his body was relentless.

Eventually, two of the assailants tugged on his arm, found his hand, and stomped on it until the bones in his hand shattered. His ribs cracked, his eyes swelled shut, and blood ran from jagged gashes on his legs, forehead, and cheeks. They rolled him onto his back, and the pummeling continued.

Suddenly the shouting stopped, and a familiar voice said, "We meet again, Sassenach! This time ye winna be ordering us off yer land! And we will be leaving with something of yers."

Robin felt a tug on the top of his right ear and then a sharp sting of pain as a knife sliced through the skin. The crowd cheered as the man kicked him facedown again.

Dedication

I am always amazed at the inspiration that comes to me
in the middle of the night and on long walks,
and I dedicate this book to my husband, Greg,
my son, Luke, and my granddaughter, Allison,
who never laughed at me for
spending so much time writing stories.
To my dear friends who read my drafts, offered advice,
and encouraged me to keep it up,
and to my book editor, Eilidh MacKenzie,
who saw potential in the manuscript
and helped me get it ready to publish.

Where I have chosen, steadfast will I be,
Never to repent in will, thought, nor deed.
*~a fifteenth-century poem from
the Findern Manuscript*

Chapter One

Northern England, 1518

The boy crouched under a solitary tree by the side of the road in the Pennine Hills. His lanky, battered, and bloodied legs had taken him this far and no farther. Shivering from the rain cascading off the nearly bare branches, he might not make it through the night without drowning. He turned his head at the sound of a horse coming down the road, splashing mud with each step, and closed his eyes as if praying for the rider to pass by.

"What are ye doing here, chiel?" asked the stranger on the chestnut stallion.

The boy's eyes flew open.

The man's thick brogue betrayed him as a Scot, one who risked being caught alone on the English side of the border. Discovery would mean a quick death at the hands of Englishmen who had had their fill of defending themselves against Scottish raiders.

The boy looked up at him through miserable dark-blue eyes surrounded by heavy purple bruises. "Nothing, milord. I will be on my way." As he started to stand, his ragged oversized tunic fell off his shoulder, exposing raw stripes on his back.

"Who beat ye, chiel?" the Scot asked gruffly.

Quickly, the boy pulled up his tunic. " 'Tis

nothing, sir. I will be gone."

"Are ye going back to the man who did it?"

The boy stuck out his chin and narrowed his eyes. "Nay!"

"Then ye will go with me." The man on the horse tossed the boy a piece of dry bread, which he caught and stuffed into his mouth all in one bite.

"Hungry, chiel?" the man asked.

The boy did not answer but swallowed the bread as quickly as he could.

Astride his stallion, the man towered over him. He had a chest like a bull, long copper locks, and a rugged face with a thick jagged scar running down his forehead and across his eye on the right side of his face. The man, despite his menacing appearance, had a kindness in his deep, rumbling voice.

The man reached out his hand and hoisted the bewildered boy onto his horse's rump behind him. Quickly, the boy slid up against the raised back of the saddle to keep from falling off. The man, unfastening a section of his woolen plaid from his belt, handed the edge of the long cloak to the boy, who draped it over his head, sheltering them both from the rain. Then the man took a thin slice of dried meat from his pack and handed it to the boy.

"Why are you helping me?" asked the boy, stuffing the meat into his mouth as fast as he could between words.

The man smiled, and his wide mouth tugged his rough red beard up nearly to his eyes. " 'Tis a long sad story that I am hoping will end better than it began." Then the smile left his face. " 'Tis only me to claim my family land. I have lost everything I love in the battle for Scottish freedom that I now ken winna ever end, so I am going home, ne'er to return to England, ne'er to wield my sword against another man. When I saw ye by the road, I thought ye might want the same, ne'er to have a weapon raised against ye again. Am I right, lad?"

"I mean no disrespect, milord," the boy said as he chewed, "but I am a stranger."

"Ye ride on my horse, so ye're a stranger no more. I am Bretane, Laird of Makgullane."

"I am Robin."

****

Southern Scottish Highlands, 1530

Robin slumped on the filth-encrusted floor of the prison wagon taking him to Caerlanrig, south of Edinburgh. The enclosed wagon, barely bigger than a cart, let in the lone hint of fresh air through the small barred windows at the back and at the door. He had only been a prisoner for a couple of hours, but already his iron shackles had scraped his wrists and ankles raw. The rusted chains dangling between his feet and his hands clanked every time he changed positions.

"Well, ye bloody Sassenach, how do ye like being on yer way to the noose?" snarled one of the two other prisoners. "Being English winna help ye now!"

Robin scowled at the gap-toothed man named Tinker. "It does not look like being Scot is helping you much, either," he said darkly.

The prison wagon hit yet another rut on the notoriously bad roads of Scotland's Southern Highlands, and Robin bounced against the wall where a skelf of splintered wood pricked his back. He twisted away from it.

The wagon continued to toss its three prisoners around in the tight quarters until Tinker lost his balance and fell into Robin. The man had a bushy beard, stringy ginger hair, and breath that would shame a thummurt.

A hard shove from Robin sent Tinker back into the opposite corner with a thud and a painful groan. The other prisoner, Ronald, scooted out of the way into the other corner.

"Ye think ye're the Lord High and Mighty Himself," Tinker said, struggling to sit upright again, "but ye're no better than the two of us! Talk like a bloody Sassenach all ye want, but yer neck will stretch just like ours!"

How true!

The people on the Makgullane estate, where he had lived for the last twelve years since Bretane had brought him home, ignored the English accent that marked him as an outsider as much as did his English looks. For the most part, Highland Scotsmen grew into brawny men with square jaws, thick beards of various shades of ginger, and hearty laughs. But Robin, although tall and broad shouldered, had narrow hips and an oval face with a straight nose and wide-set midnight-blue eyes—all traits of a man born south of the River Tweed.

Bretane, just as he said he would, had put away his sword and now fought the battle for justice in the courts and the legislature in Edinburgh, and over the last two years had been away on government business for long periods. With Bretane's blessing, Robin took his place and became the highly respected reeve of Makgullane.

Estates the size of Makgullane ran smoothly only if the manager or reeve took charge of every aspect of making it so. Robin made certain that the estate's people stayed fed with enough left over to sell or barter to provide income for all the things that could not be grown. He had to plan for the crop rotations of oats and barley and oversee the runrig system of planting. He supervised sheep, pig, cattle, and horse breeding, and all the building maintenance as well as dealing with the unexpected—insect infestations, crop failures, livestock diseases, and the like. He also managed the responsibilities and workloads of every person on the estate. Although most of the people had lived there for generations, Robin had the authority to hire workers and to dismiss lazy ones no matter what their ties to Makgullane. Everyone agreed that Robin's judgments were reliable, honest, and fair and also that his word was final.

Over the years, the people had listened to many insults directed at Robin for being English, but Robin had made it clear that he would deal with any such slurs on his own. More often than not, he chose to remain silent or walk away, although this went against the grain of many of the strong-tempered Highlanders. None thought him a coward; they had seen him stand up to many a bully in defense of others, but as he had told them, an injured man can do no work, and they had too much work to do to waste time nursing wounds. Words disappeared in the wind, but a broken jaw did not.

Today in the prison wagon, Robin didn't care a whit if he broke jaws or even if his jaw ended up broken. He had made his choice, and if the noose was the consequence for his choice, then so be it, but he didn't have to go willingly.

All at once, a rank smell rose up, and Robin's gaze darted toward Tinker pissing in the corner. Just before the man finished, he swung in Robin's direction, sprinkling him with drops of urine.

Lunging like a wild boar, Robin grabbed Tinker by the arm and jerked him to the floor. While pushing his face hard into the still-wet wood in the corner, Robin growled, "Do that again and your cock will be out that window before you can lower your plaid!"

Just as Ronald made a move in Robin's direction, Robin grabbed him by the sark and threw him on top of Tinker, shoving his face into the same wet corner. "It goes for you, too! Do we understand each other?"

Both men tried to nod, but they could only grunt and squirm. Robin took that as agreement.

Hunching back into his corner by the door, he scowled at Tinker and Ronald as they tried to find a clean spot on their plaids to wipe their mouths. They'd leave him alone from now on.

Robin fingered the hard edges of his most prized possessions that he carried in the leather pouch tied around his waist. His mother had given him a metal token embossed with a dog that she had found on the road, the only thing that remained of his life in England. Bretane had given him the other, a silver shilling, because a man should never be without coin. Robin only had half of it now.

Years ago, Robin and the woman he loved had split the coin as a sign of their friendship and loyalty. Today, the split coin symbolized their devotion and forever love for each other. She carried one piece, and he would carry the other until his dying day, which would be much sooner than he had expected.

He remembered the first line of the poem they had said to each other when they had exchanged the halves, first in friendship and later in love. *Where I have chosen, steadfast will I be, never to repent in will, thought, nor deed.*

He would never see her again, never see her long hair the color of a tarnished sunset or her eyes the deep green of moss on the side of a tree, never hear the whistle with which they had greeted each other since the day they had met. Three short puffs and one longer puff a note higher.

He whistled it now.

"Ye trying to call for help?" mocked Tinker.

Robin straightened up, stiffening his shoulders, and immediately Tinker put his hands up in a gesture of surrender. "No offense, but if ye are, call some help for the two of us, will ye?"

Robin leaned back against the wall and closed his eyes, wishing for a memory that would take him away from this prison wagon. The day he met Suann floated into his mind. He had only been with Bretane for six months, and he had made a terrible mistake that could have cost him everything.

He and several other lads had plotted to play a prank on their teacher, Father Bernard, a man as dull and dusty as the road to Edinburgh. He insisted they do all their studies in three languages, English, Gaelic, and Latin, and any mistake earned them a sharp rap on the knuckles.

They'd brought an old mare into Father Bernard's room, where they planned to make a great noise causing the animal to leave a mess on the floor. However, as Robin slammed down the chair, the animal keeled over dead. Everyone else ran, leaving Robin alone to take the punishment from Bretane.

Robin had reached the top of the stairs in the manor house and turned to go down the dimly lit corridor toward the small study at the end of the hall, where Bretane waited. An open window let in a sweet-smelling breeze. He sucked in a deep breath, but it did nothing to ease his churning stomach. The wind blew his thick, curly dark hair across his face, and he pulled at a strand to tuck it behind his right ear.

She perched on the top step in the shadows, waiting for him. Younger by maybe three or four years, she had long blond hair that hung down her back past her waist. He'd seen her around the estate, but he never paid her much mind. Once she had thrown a rock at his feet to stop him from stepping into a rabbit hole, but she'd run off before he could say anything. He didn't even know her name.

She whistled softly to get his attention—three quick puffs followed by one long note a pitch higher.

"What are you doing here?" he asked roughly.

"Ye shouldna be alone, no' at a time like this," she said. "I came to be with ye."

He shook his head to flick his hair out of his eyes again and tucked the loose strands behind his ear. "Run along. I do not want you here."

She leaped up and scurried over to him. "Oh, Robin, dinna be saying that. 'Tis the first time Laird Bretane has punished ye, and ye need someone to be standing with ye so ye winna be afeared."

"I am not afraid!" he said, even though his voice quivered a bit as he said it. "I am not afraid of a thrashing."

She put her small hand with its slim fingers on his arm. "I ken, laddie, that 'tis no' losing bits of your hide. 'Tis losing Bretane, but dinna worry. He winna send ye away. I promise ye."

"You cannot know what will happen," he said gruffly.

"Aye, I can. My mama's clear-eyed."

"Your mother can tell the future? Is she a witch?"

The girl straightened her shoulders and put her hands on her hips. She said, "Ye winna call her names! She is my mama, and she is a fine woman who helps people. She doesna tell the future for herself or for evil design. Ye winna speak of her as if she were a clootie!"

He shrugged at the unfamiliar Scots word. "What is a clootie?"

"A devil—and my mama, Thalassa, is an angel to me!" She kicked him in the shin with her slippered foot.

"Ow!" He rubbed the spot although it didn't really hurt.

Speaking with exaggerated respect, he said, "Forgive me. I did not know how important Thalassa is, but I do now. Your mama is an angel sent to lighten my load on this earth."

The girl leaned back on her heels as her tone sharpened. "Ye have a quick tongue, laddie. It wouldna be wise to use it when ye go into Laird Bretane."

"Robin!" bellowed Bretane from the room at the end of the corridor.

Today, in his mind, he could still hear Bretane's voice, sounding like a bull in a thundering storm while Suann's sounded like a tinkling bell.

Back then in the hallway, Robin had taken a deep breath. "I have to go. Who are you, anyway?"

"I am Suannoch."

"Susanna?"

"Nay, Soo-aunn-och," she said, pronouncing each part of the word slowly and distinctly. "Most people call me Suann."

"Soo-anne?"

"Nay, 'tis like the name of the beautiful bird with the long neck. 'Tis almost, but not quite like swan."

"Suann," he imitated.

"Aye." She smiled.

"Robin!" Bretane shouted fiercely from the room at the end of the hall.

Robin stepped through the doorway to find Bretane standing behind an ornately carved mahogany desk, one of his most prized possessions. To him it represented culture in the otherwise rustic Highlands. This room also held the largest collection of books in the Highlands, over fifty volumes. Seeing so many books stuffed onto the shelves had amazed Robin. He didn't know that many books had been written!

Robin hung his head and wished the floor would swallow him up.

"I dinna ken what to do with ye," Bretane said. "Many say that an English lad will ne'er find a place in the Highlands. Look at ye. Ye willna even wear the plaid, only trews and sark."

"I want to be covered up. I do not like the wind up my legs."

"A Scot is proud to feel the wind!" Bretane roared. "Ye're hopeless! Ye're a great deal of trouble, chiel. Too much trouble!" He threw up his hands.

"Please, Bretane, I want to stay here with you!"

"Ye maun learn that there are consequences for bad

choices. Ye made a verra bad choice in bringing that mare to Father Bernard, and it died. I canna let ye think I dinna care about that lost animal or that disrespect to yer teacher. I ken how ye suffered at the hands of yer da, but I want ye to ken that a thrashing is a lesson to learn and is different from a brutal beating for no cause."

"I will do whatever you say, but, please, do not send me away! I beg you!"

Bretane's forehead furrowed. "I am no' sending you away, but when we are done here, ye will go to the stable to learn to take care of the horses. All animals have value, and their lives are important if to no one but themselves. Ye maun learn that."

Relief flooded Robin so much, he had to lean against the wall before he could draw in a full breath. Then he remembered what else lay ahead for him.

Ordering him to the desk, Bretane bent him over it and raised his belt. After a dozen hard strokes that Robin would remember for a long time, Bretane left him there, saying, "When ye're ready to face the world, come to the stable."

"Aye," said Robin with a catch in his throat. He lifted his hands from the desk and turned to look out the window. Makgullane would be his home from now on, and Bretane would be his father in every sense but by birth. This time the breeze on his face brought him overwhelming relief despite his throbbing backside.

Suann's face appeared in the doorway.

"He is not sending me away," said Robin.

"I told ye so. Next time ye will believe me."

"Aye, next time."

On the stairs, she took his hand. He looked at her

curiously but did not let go. She walked with him out to the stable, and for the next twelve years they grew up together as the best of friends.

Now, knowing that Suannoch was safe comforted him in what little time he had left on this earth. Still, if wishes were keys, he would unlock his shackles and jump out the wagon door and run straight to her.

He flicked the loose curl of his black hair out of his eyes and tucked it behind his right ear, but immediately it fell back on his face. Then he remembered the real reason he ended up in this prison wagon. A cruel man with a wine-red stain on his face had cut away his right ear.

The wagon stopped, and soon the door swung open, and two soldiers grabbed Robin's ankles and dragged him out. He bumped down the wooden steps and landed face down on the ground with a grunt.

"Prisoner, what is yer name?" demanded the captain after Robin had been hauled to his feet.

"Robin of Makgullane," he said through his now bloodied lip.

The captain pointed back up the road. "Then, Robin of Makgullane, who is that following us? They have been behind almost since we left Makgullane. When we stopped, they stopped."

Robin stepped out of the shadows and squinted in the sunlight at the horse and three riders behind them.

Recognizing them, his heart twisted with equal amounts of happiness and fear.

Chapter Two

Three months earlier

'Twas a rare day in the Highlands, sunny and breezy, and warmer than it had been all spring. The grass grew a fragrant green, and the cloudless sky sparkled a glorious blue. Everyone knew it would be a delightful day at Makgullane!

The yard around the manor house was alive with activity. Two young men, Darby and Shane, enjoying the warmth of the sunshine on their faces, hoed the herb and vegetable gardens. Churning up the soil sent a pleasant musty aroma into the air.

Darby, a gangly, stoop-shouldered young man of eighteen, rested his arms on his hoe as he told a joke he had heard at the tavern last night. "It goes like this. A shopkeeper lived in Dingwall with his wife and family."

"Me kin live in Dingwall," said Shane without looking up. Although five years older, he didn't have his friend's lively personality. He spent contented nights on his cot, unlike Darby who basked in his nights as the Merry-Andrew of the tavern.

Darby wrinkled his nose in annoyance at the interruption. " 'Tis not about any of yer kin. So, this shopkeeper had thin and lanky children while those of his neighbor grew healthy and hardy. One day his

13

neighbor asked him why his children were so spare and of such a weak constitution, it being the contrary with his own young ones."

"Me kin is fat and hardy," said Shane, looking up.

" 'Tis not about yer kin!" Darby repeated. "So, the shopkeeper says, 'The reason is easily given. I work alone at the manufacture of my children, but you have quite a number of assistants in the making of yours!' "

Darby laughed like a mule being let out to pasture. Shane pondered the joke for a minute before he gave his own breathy chuckle. "Heh, heh."

The cook's assistant, Clive, as short and round as a stump, stood beside the nearby fish pond and overheard the joke. He smiled a lopsided grin as he dangled his hook in the water, hoping to catch enough of the small but tasty perch for the night's supper. He shouted out, " 'Tis a glorious day, lads!"

Two maids called greetings to each other as they flapped the dust out of rugs and blankets from the upstairs windows of the manor house.

The two-story stone house with a gray slate roof nestled between the craggy hills of the Southern Highlands. The four large rooms on the first floor consisted of a gathering area, a massive kitchen, a dining room, and Bretane's living quarters while the rooms upstairs housed Bretane's study and the sleeping rooms for the dozen maids and workers who did not live in their own cottages around the estate.

In season, sturdy grass and heather bordered the house, but a well-trampled dirt and gravel yard surrounded the stable and large barn. Just beyond the barn was the road that took Bretane to and from Edinburgh and brought other infrequent visitors from the east. No true road ran beyond Makgullane leading west, only a path that brave souls could walk or ride to the next gap in the hills.

"Have ye seen Robin this morn?" asked Maggy as she beat the blanket against the side of the house. "Does he look as fine in the morning sun as he did last night in the moonlight?"

"Finer!" replied Glynnis from the nearest window. "He is a braw and buirdly piece of manhood, that ward of Laird Bretane. I saw him walking toward the stable just now."

"Aye, he is a fine-looking man. Are his kisses fine?"

Glynnis closed her eyes and took in a slow breath. "Aye, his lips are like—"

Just then a sharp third voice shouted, "Glynnis! Ye winna be talking of that man's kisses! Yer da and me have chosen a MacLeod for yer guidman. 'Tis a good match and ye winna be fashious about it!"

"Aye, *a'mhàthair*," she said loudly. "I will accept a MacLeod. They are fine men." But to Maggy she whispered, "But it winna stop me from dreaming of Robin even in a MacLeod bed!"

A beautiful day at Makgullane!

Ten strangers also agreed that it was indeed a beautiful day when they wandered into the Makgullane yard. Two more rode in on horseback. The bedraggled bunch wore tattered clothing and had the gaunt faces of starvation. If not for the horses, they would immediately be recognized as sorners, sometimes called masterful beggars. Although solitary homeless beggars had existed in Scotland since the beginning of time, in recent years they had come together in groups or, as they liked to claim, clans. Makgullane had seen many such mendicants over the years, often taking pity on them with food and occasional shelter.

But these sorners seemed out of the ordinary because two of them rode horses that could only have been stolen. Could they be reivers, thieves who traveled along the Scottish and English border stealing, pillaging, and harassing whomever they came upon? The emblems on reiver bonnets, and on the padded armor on their chests called jac o'plaites, could easily be changed from Scottish to English depending on changing loyalties or location. Reivers often posed as beggars, so they could reconnoiter possible places to raid. Such thieves rarely came as far north as Makgullane, but that was no guarantee they hadn't exhausted the resources of regions farther south and had come looking for new places to pillage.

Over their rags, two of these men wore colorful silk coats, obviously stolen from who knew where, and two limped in on makeshift crutches. The dingy scarlet skirts on four of the women announced to everyone they would sell their bodies for the right price, and from the sorry look of them, that price might only be a slice of bread. A young girl dragged in a boy of about ten years with a dirty face who shook off her grip, planted his feet, and crossed his arms.

All pleasant chatter on the demesne stopped at the sight of them.

"Robin!" shouted Shane and Darby in unison. "Robin, come quick!"

Maggy and Glynnis flapped their blankets loudly against the wall as they, too, called out, "Robin! Now!"

"What's going on?" said Robin as he ducked his

head to step out the stable door. The youthful smoothness of his face when he arrived at Makgullane twelve years ago had been replaced by the strong features of a man. He had chiseled cheekbones and a strong jawline, which he preferred to keep clean shaven. His eyes still shone a twilight blue under thick dark eyebrows. His hair had darkened to a shadowy black, and the loose curls hung below his shoulders. He stood taller than many of the men on the estate, and hard work had given him the strength only a few could match.

Robin stopped short, first at the smell and then at the sight of yet another increasingly unwelcome sight in this part of the Highlands. The Gordon estate to the south of Makgullane had been overrun a month ago and their entire pig herd driven off. Then the Kilbride house had been burned to the ground after a reported fifty raiders had looted the storage barn and attacked the family, severely injuring Jack Kilbride. So far no one had been held responsible for these crimes.

The motley group arriving at Makgullane numbered only twelve, but Robin suspected more of them might be nearby, making them as a group unpredictable and dangerous.

Thinking it better to treat them as the beggars they seemed to be, Robin called to them, "I am the reeve here at Makgullane. We have no work for you. Move on!"

One of the men stepped out of the cluster of the woebegone. "My name is Keenan Gray. This is my wife, Elissa," he said, as he pointed to a stringy-haired red-skirted woman. A dark port-wine stain covered the left cheek and neck of Keenan's pasty gray face. His narrow eyes were an unsettling yellow color, and when he spoke the tip of his tongue peeked through the wide gap in his front teeth. "And my bairns, Hugh and Mercy."

The girl, too young yet to be put to work as a prostitute, pulled the boy forward. She curtsied, and after a shove to his back, the boy bowed.

Keenan continued. "Ye can see we mean ye no harm. We are only looking for work to feed our bellies. We are all able-bodied, just disheartened and abused by the cruel hearts of yer neighbors." He then, too, bowed deeply.

"We can have ye arrested!" called out Maggy from her window.

"Ye canna!" Keenan shouted back to her. "The law says ye canna arrest us if we say we will work."

"Saying and doing are two different things!" replied Maggy.

Keenan started to shake his fist at her, but his wife pulled his arm down and shook her head.

Robin kept his eye on two of the strangers when they wandered away from the group toward the barn and stable. They leaned on either side of the sliding barn door, crossing their arms. The boy also slipped out of the group, walking casually in the direction of the house until Robin moved closer, put his hand on the lad's shoulder, and turned him back the way he came.

At the same time, all the Makgullane men in the yard left their chores and formed a cluster behind Robin with their hoes and rakes in their hands. Maggy, Glynnis, and her mother stood just outside the manor house door, all holding brooms in front of them.

"I tell you again," said Robin, his voice rich and

full and carrying authority in its timbre. "There is no work for any of you on this land. Move on."

Keenan smirked and waved his hand toward the Makgullane men. "Do ye let a Sassenach speak for ye? Are ye such cowards that ye submit to English rule? Or have we walked so far that we have left the proud Highlands and tramped into bloody England?" He spat on the ground.

Robin stared silently at Keenan. Most times his silence made the accuser so uncomfortable, he backed down just as it did now. While the other men thought Keenan deserved a punch in the face, they followed Robin's lead, and when no one responded to Keenan's words, the man spit another large glob of brown phlegm into the dirt.

Robin said, "I will do one thing for you before you go. All of you sit right where you are, and I will see that you get some oatbread and a slice of cheese. Then you will all be on your way, and you will not stop until you have crossed out of Makgullane land. The border is about three miles to the east. You can easily make that by midday. Should any of you be found on our land again, the sheriff in Kirkcaldy will have you arrested. Now sit right where you stand."

After a long moment, Keenan motioned for everyone to sit on the ground, and that hesitation put Robin on alert. "Ralf, ride into Kirkcaldy and tell Sheriff Duncan that these sorners are coming his way so he can be on the lookout for them." As Ralf ran into the stable to saddle a horse for the hour ride to the village, Robin pointed to the beggars and said, "You have been warned!"

Keenan snorted, and again his wife put her hand on

his arm and shook her head.

Shane, stepping closer to Robin, said quietly, "Beggars and thieves like these are everywhere in Scotland now. They are dangerous. Why can naught be done?"

Clive spoke up. "I have heard tales about the famous Border reiver, Johnnie Armstrong. He and his gang raid all around on both sides of the border. There are great legends about how vicious he is and how rich. Ye dinna think these are some of them?"

In a whisper, Shane said, "Did ye see, Robin, that they carry dirks on straps around their waists and try to hide them with their cloaks? They are reivers for certain."

Robin shook his head. "These are only beggars so far."

"Do ye think Sheriff Duncan will come in time?" asked Shane, chewing on his lip. "We canna be left to fight them alone! Where is the law to help us?"

Shane and Clive had only heard stories about the politics and law in Scotland from travelers who may or may not have stretched the truth for their own purposes. Bretane was always a reliable source of information about the government, but he rarely shared the political doings with anyone other than Robin. What Bretane thought about the breeding of sheep or the building repairs interested the workers on Makgullane more than what the Privy Council argued about.

Putting his arms around both men's shoulders, Robin said, "Here's what I know about it. You've heard of the Wardens of the Marches, haven't you?"

Both men nodded.

"When King James IV was the king in Scotland, he

chose landowners on both sides of the border to keep order. The Wardens kept the peace, but then the king agreed to marry the twelve-year-old sister of King Henry VIII of England."

Shane's eyebrows shot up. "Now I'm no' against marrying a young lass, but twelve is more a wee bairn than a lass!"

"That doesn't matter if you're a king," said Robin. "But he may have loved another who died, and he grieved too much to take his child bride to bed until they had been married many years. James IV had hoped that by simply marrying her, it would unite both countries and keep the peace, and it did for a while. Eventually, she delivered a son."

"Aye," said Clive. "I remember when a royal crier came around all of Scotland to tell everyone about the new prince. By the time he got here, his voice was as raw as tree bark!"

"So, why all the trouble now?" asked Shane.

"Well, despite all James IV's plans, the peace did not hold, and he died at Flodden battling, of all people, his wife's brother, King Henry. The queen and mother of the eighteen-month-old prince, a weak woman, chose to marry Archibald Douglas instead of being her son's regent, and the clan Douglas is nothing but ruthless and greedy, allowing the lawless to live without consequence."

Shane pulled a face. "Isna James V a man by now? Canna he be king?"

"The problem is that now his stepfather holds him prisoner in Falkland Castle in Fife, and no one has seen him in a long time. Bretane says that he must be about sixteen years old, but he's a doitit by all accounts. They

21

say he cannot read or think because Douglas refuses to educate him."

Just then the women came out of the manor house with trays of oatbread and slices of hard cheese. They handed the trays to the Makgullane men who passed them among the crowd sitting on the ground. The beggar men pushed their women aside to grab as much as their hands could hold. Anything they couldn't seize fell to the ground, and the women scooped it up and stuffed it into their mouths. One woman handed part of her bounty to the girl, leaving the boy empty-handed.

Stepping into the melee, Robin grabbed bread and cheese from the overstuffed hands of one of the men, and when he protested, Robin shoved him hard to the ground. None of the other men dared say a word, especially not Keenan, who spat again.

"Here you go, lad," said Robin, handing the boy the food. "What are you called?"

The boy stuffed as much of the bread as he could into his mouth and mumbled, "My name is Hugh."

He had dark eyes, long black lashes, and hair with a tinge of auburn streaked through it. He wore dirty rags like the others, but over his shirt, he had a dark-blue vest with gold braid around the edges. Far too big for him, it hung almost to his knees, no doubt another piece of stolen bounty.

"Hello, Hugh. My name is Robin."

Hugh swallowed. "Thank ye, sir." He took a big bite of the cheese, chewing it noisily.

"Hugh," said Robin, "is Keenan your father?"

The boy shook his head. "Me only family is whoever will give me something to eat."

"Listen carefully."

The boy stopped chewing and looked up at him.

"My name is Robin, and this place is Makgullane. If you ever need me, come here and find me. I will help you. Can you remember that?"

The boy nodded as he stuffed another piece of bread into his mouth.

Suddenly, a strong odor of smoke filled Robin's head. It was an old memory from the day when he was fourteen and he'd needed help and there was none.

Until that day, all he'd ever known from the unpredictable madman called his father had been hunger and savage beatings that left him bruised and bloody, the scars of which, inside and out, still remained. The only softness came from his mother, who struggled all her life for survival and endured the worst to keep her three children alive. Since Robin had been old enough to lift a rake, he'd done the best he could to keep them from starving, but often it wasn't enough.

That day he had left early in the morning to muck out the stables of a nearby lord to earn a loaf of mealy bread and a head of cabbage for their dinner, but on the way home he spotted the pillar of smoke. Terrified, he started running, and when he arrived at their hut, it was on fire.

His father stood there growling at the flames. When he spotted Robin, he grabbed him by the neck and began beating him with the iron fire poker in his hand. " 'Tis your fault, you worthless piece of shite! You could have stopped it!" Bringing the still-hot iron bar down on Robin's back and legs over and over, he did not stop until the sheriff pulled him away.

Later when Robin could sit up again, the sheriff

spoke in a matter-of-fact voice. "I am sorry," he said. "Your da burned the house with your mother, brother, and sister inside. We tried to put out the fire, but 'twas too far gone. He is hanged, so you do not need to worry about him coming back to do you more harm. Have you anywhere to go?"

Robin shook his head.

By the time darkness fell, everyone who had come to help put out the fire had gone back home, none of them offering to take the boy with them, not that he expected them to. They wouldn't risk bringing home the son of a madman. He sat there alone until he saw the moonlight reflected off a small circle of metal in the dirt, about the size of a flattened walnut. The token, embossed in the center with a dog with a bushy tail, was worthless except that his mother had found it on the road and had given it to him. Picking it up, he ran off just as it started to rain.

A flurry of noise and movement among the beggars jolted Robin back to the present. Some of them pointed, and two women started to wail. Robin turned his eyes to the narrow path leading into the yard from the west to see what could cause such a stir.

He grinned. It was Thalassa, a familiar sight at Makgullane, but if he hadn't known better he, too, would have thought that the woman had been born in a cauldron filled with toads' eyes and bats' wings. Uncommonly tall as well as broad shouldered for a woman, her unkempt coal-black mane of hair had three wide stripes of white that began at the hairline and flowed down her back. She had a wide mouth with full lips, and under her arching eyebrows sat round eyes of violet, a color that gleamed in the sun's reflection. Her abundant bosom mounded above the cut of her cloak and overdress made of alternating panels of rich green and black.

Thalassa kept to herself in a cottage about a mile down the path from the demesne because most people feared her. They believed her to be clear-eyed, meaning she could tell the future, although Robin rolled his eyes every time someone said that. Her fortune-telling skills amounted to nothing more than keen observation and common sense, but people feared she might expose some deep, dark secret of theirs. Still none of that mattered to Robin because the woman was the best healer in the area, and many folks and animals on Makgullane lived longer, better lives because of her knowledge of herbs and treatments.

"Look! Coming down the path 'tis the clootie we have been hearing about for miles!" shouted one of the men who had walked in on crutches. He stood up and started to run back the way he had come. The two men in silk coats grabbed the reins on the horses and took off running, as well. One by one the other beggars followed, Keenan herding them as he went. Lastly went Hugh, who, just before he ran out of sight, waved to Robin and shouted, "I will remember!"

"Do ye think we have seen the last of them?" asked Glynnis, taking Robin's arm and pulling it around her waist, her plump fingers tugging him close.

"Nay, but Ralf is on the way to Kirkcaldy to tell Duncan. As sheriff, Duncan will be on the watch."

"I am afeared," said Glynnis as her biscuit-brown eyes roamed up and down his body. "I thank ye for keeping us safe." Her long pale eyelashes fluttered as her round, soft hips cuddled up to him familiarly.

Robin only nodded because he knew what she was after, but he would not be bedding her again tonight.

Just then Thalassa came near enough to be heard and said, "A nasty bunch, them. I came to see the colt ye call King Glory."

Stepping out from behind Thalassa's ample body, first came a young boy of about seven and then Thalassa's daughter, Suannoch, who looked nothing like her mother. Tarnished-sunset hair lay gently down her back. She had delicate facial features, but her lean, muscled body was clearly strong. Her heart-shaped face held round eyes of deep mossy green, and she had a smile that could light a moonless night. Today she wore a yellow kirtle with a pale-green overdress, both very becoming colors on her.

Robin smiled at the sight of her. When he had first met her, he had thought her a pleasant-looking child despite her willful personality, but poets blissfully wrote about her beauty at age twenty-two. In Bretane's collection of books, he had come across a poem by William Dunbar, King James IV's beloved court poet. It described Suannoch perfectly, although he would never tell her. She would take his head off!

Sweet rose of virtue and of gentleness,
delightful lily of youthful wantonness,
richest in bounty and in beauty clear
and in every virtue that is held most dear—
except only that you are merciless.

"Merciless" might have been a bit strong, but she could be as stubborn as an unbroken horse, and she had no qualms about expressing her opinion. Over the years, he had learned when to give her an argument, when to agree with her, and when to just nod in silence.

She also learned when to do the same with him. Her warning sign was the knot tightening in his jaw.

The other women on the estate, like Glynnis, scurried around him, vying for his attention. They admired his good looks and high position, and he didn't shun that attention because, after all, he had needs. He was a man, not a priest! The women gossiped among themselves and compared nights spent with him, and in many ways, he enjoyed that they did, but the reality was Highland women married Highland men. He knew that, and they knew that. Nothing lasting would ever come with any of them, not that he ever intended it to.

A night in bed with one of them, most recently Glynnis, meant nothing more than a night in bed, but he and the daughter of Thalassa had something much more important. For twelve years, the two of them had shared things, profound things. They knew each other's hopes, dreams, and secrets that no one else on the estate knew. But the one thing Robin valued the most was their shared laughter. He looked forward to every joke, prank, and teasing minute he spent with her, and the strong, deep connection between the two of them meant everything to him.

Robin moved away from Glynnis, who reluctantly let him go, tugging on his sark until he pulled free. He whistled three short puffs and one longer one, but Suannoch did not return the oft-used greeting between them. Instead she said, giving Glynnis a cold eye, "Hallo, Glynnis. 'Tis a fine morning to be out talking with Robin. Have ye naught else that needs doing besides hanging on the man?"

"*Haud yer wheesht!*" barked Glynnis.

Taking a step closer, Suann hissed, "Dinna tell me

to be quiet!"

Robin stepped between the two women.

Glynnis, knowing that Robin would not approve of her snatching out all of Suann's hair, said with a grimace, "Robin kens all I do around here. I canna be idle and take a stroll with my *màthair* whenever it suits me fancy." With a quick turn of her head, she strode back to the manor house.

Robin put his hands on his hips and said to Suann, "If you are expecting me to apologize for talking to Glynnis, I will not. I speak to who speaks to me."

Suannoch glared at him from under her eyebrows. "I am thinking that 'tis not talking she is after." They had had this discussion about Glynnis before. Suann claimed that she was just looking out for him, and he claimed that he did not need looking after.

"Thalassa," said Robin, "your daughter is trying to stop me from finding a woman of my own."

"Aye, that is exactly what she is trying to do," said Thalassa in her low-pitched voice.

"Do I have to put up with that?"

"Aye, ye do."

Before Robin could tease Suann anymore, she whistled the three short puffs and one longer one. He smiled, and a deep dimple appeared in each cheek before he returned the whistle.

"So 'tis all forgiven," said Thalassa. "I came to tend to the colt. Have ye seen him yet?"

"The colt? Nay," said Robin. "I just got to the stable when that sorry bunch of beggars arrived. What is wrong with him?" He followed her into the stable and over to King Glory's stall. Bits of hay drifted down from the loft just inches above Robin's head, and with a toss, he shook the straw off his hair.

Thalassa knelt by King Glory's stall and opened her cloth bag. The odor wafting out of the bag from the herbs and salves surrounded her and at times even announced her coming. " 'Tis a brushing wound on his right fore fetlock," she said.

King Glory, a newly foaled colt sired by a neighboring laird's black racing stallion, already displayed his sire's racing blood. However, the dam from Bretane's stock had not done well after the birth, and she refused to suckle her colt. This meant around-the-clock attention to ensure that the animal thrived. If he stayed healthy, he could be trained to run like the wind and be the winning stallion Bretane bred him to be, but not with a brushing wound like this one!

Obviously, the colt had been taken for a run, and with his still unsteady gait, his left hoof had brushed against and cut his right foreleg. The injury meant that he had been left unattended, and this did not stand well with Robin.

As soon as he saw the blood dripping down into the hay, his voice took on all the authority of the reeve. "How did this happen? Who took him out and did not walk with him properly? Thomas? Ralf? They will suffer for this!"

"It wasna Ralf or Thomas. Fergus has something to tell ye." To the boy cowering in the stable door beside Suannoch, Thalassa said, "Go ahead, lad, speak the truth."

Suannoch gently pushed the boy forward. A small lad even for his age, probably about seven or eight, he had dark-red hair and a smattering of freckles across his cheeks. Suann kept her hand on the young one's shoulder to give him the courage to face Robin.

"Fergus!" said Thalassa sharply. "The sooner told, the sooner 'tis done." The sternness in her voice startled the colt, who whinnied until Thalassa calmed him with a touch of her hand on his neck.

The small boy trembled as he looked up at Robin. "I just wanted to see him. He is so fine. I wish I had a colt like that."

Robin narrowed his eyes and raked his fingers through his hair. "Do you know how he got hurt?" He asked the question although he probably knew the answer.

Clutching his stomach and hanging his head, Fergus said, "He, he wanted to be outside. I...I...led him out to the parrock. I swear we stayed inside the fence, but he wanted to run."

"So, how did he scrape his leg?" asked Robin.

Fergus did not answer.

Thalassa spoke sharply again. "Fergus!"

"I shouldna taken him out," said the boy quickly. " 'Twas my fault."

Robin stepped closer to the boy. Fergus had to tip his head almost onto his back to see the man's face. "Then what did you do?" Robin asked.

"I...put him back in the stall, and I ran home." Tears filled Fergus's eyes.

"Lad, King Glory is a valuable animal who is in pain now. Do you think there should be punishment for taking him out without permission?"

"Aye," said the boy in a quavering voice as he dropped his head again.

"And what should it be?"

Suannoch interrupted. "He brought Thalassa here

to tend to the colt. Fergus should be given some mercy for that. He is verra sorry for what he has done."

Robin looked at her. "Sorry is not enough. The colt is hurt because of him. Every beast has value if to no one but itself and should not suffer because of negligence. I cannot have Fergus think that I do not care about that. This boy knew he did wrong."

He turned his attention back to Fergus. "Again, lad, what do you think the punishment should be?"

Fergus took a deep breath before saying very softly, "Ye could thrash me."

"All right, I will."

Suannoch gasped and pulled Fergus closer to her.

Robin went on, "But before I do, for the next month you will be here at the stable by sunrise to muck out the stalls and feed the horses. Ralf will show you what to do, and you will do everything he says. You will change King Glory's brushing sock every day. Ralf will show you how to wrap it and tie it closed, and you will work with the colt until his gait is proper. 'Tis your responsibility. If you are late or you do not do good work, I promise you a sound thrashing, one you will not forget, but for every day that you do well, you will earn a penny. Now go tell your mother that you will be working in the stables, starting today."

A grin nearly swallowed the lad's face. "Thank ye, sir!" said Fergus over his shoulder as he ran out into the yard before Robin could change his mind.

"Ye're a good man," said Suannoch. "Ye turned a bad situation into a boon for the boy. The penny will feed him and his *màthair,* Dorry. She takes in mending, but 'tis ne'er enough to feed them. It has been hard since his *athair* died."

31

Robin nodded. Being rescued by Bretane had changed his life, and Robin repaid that godsend in any way he could, any time he could.

Thalassa started out the stable door. "Ralf and Fergus can take care of the colt from now on. Suannoch has something to tell ye. Stay and listen to her." She stepped into the yard and started up the path toward her cottage.

"What is it, Suann?" asked Robin as he stroked King Glory's neck. The colt tossed his head as his way of showing thanks.

Uncharacteristic of the proud girl he knew, Suannoch kept her eyes on the ground while twisting a corner of her yellow kirtle. "I dinna ken how to tell ye this," she began slowly. Then she stopped and turned away from him.

She licked her dry lips, reluctant to say the words.

He touched Suann's shoulder to turn her around. "You can tell me anything. You know that." They had had each other when no one else would have them, and the loneliness had made their bond strong.

She sucked in her breath and reached into the small blue cloth pouch tied around her waist. Taking out one half of a silver shilling, she held it up. "There is no way to tell ye this but to say it quick. I have to give this back to ye. I am to be wed."

Robin felt a rock drop into his stomach. "Wed?"

Suannoch had given her favor to a Scot! But who? What man could mean more to her than he did? How could she do this without telling him? He might be the Sassenach, but how could she marry without giving him a word of warning? How could she give back the keepsake of the friendship they had shared?

He untied the brown leather pouch on his own waistband and took out the matching half of the same coin. He held it out.

She pressed her half into his hand. "Please be happy for me. Are ye happy for me?"

Robin choked on the only word he could say. "Aye."

He watched her walk away, too stunned by her announcement to move. Wed? Why hadn't she talked to him about it? How could she make a decision like that without him? How could the betrothal already be arranged before he knew about it?

He couldn't let this happen!

"Suann! Suann!" he called as he sprinted after her to where she stood on the path that led out of the yard to the cottage she shared with Thalassa. "Suann, wait!"

Chapter Three

She turned to face him with her arms akimbo and her hands balled into fists. " 'Tis done!"

"You cannot do this," he said, "not this way."

She gave him a withering stare. "Ye canna tell me what to do. Ye had yer chance, and ye didna take it!"

As she brushed off a windblown strand of her hair, she looked into the eyes she knew so well. She loved their deep bluish color that she imagined the sea looked like, although she had never seen the sea, and in those eyes she saw how the news of her marriage hurt him. Gone was the twinkle that always brightened her days, replaced by what she could only describe as shadow. She never wanted to hurt the one she loved so much.

He had been her best friend since she was ten years old, and they had spent time together nearly every day. Sometimes she sat by him while he did his chores. Often, she brought him a slab of bread slathered with butter from the kitchen, and they talked while he ate, and sometimes he helped her tend Thalassa's vegetable garden. It made her chuckle to remember the two of them chasing chickens around the yard, hoping to get a fat one for dinner. He could catch a bird before she could, but he could never wring its neck without getting pecked and scratched until his hands bled, and he had a worse time plucking feathers. Thalassa said that a Robin-caught bird was a special treat. Every bite came with feathers!

Now because of his responsibilities as Makgullane's reeve, they only saw each other occasionally, and she missed him so much, her heart ached. But at the same time, being apart was a good thing. The way she thought about him had changed since she had grown into a woman and Robin had grown into a man, a strong, broad-shouldered man with rippled muscles and cords in his neck.

When he repaired fences or sheared sheep, he often went shirtless, his chest tanned to a fawnlike brown. She found herself having delicious thoughts about licking the droplets of sweat off his neck and off the flat muscles of his stomach. When his curls clung in wet strands, she wanted to be the one to tuck them behind his ear to keep them out of his eyes. These thoughts and many others sent ripples of urgency through her body and between her legs, and sometimes at night she couldn't sleep because of her visions of him. Those notions had to be dismissed. She and Robin were friends, the best and deepest of friends, and she should not have these kinds of thoughts about her only friend at Makgullane, especially when he didn't feel the same way about her.

Suann saw how he flirted with other women, and she had desperately hoped that someday he would act that way with her, but he never even hinted that he might. Suann had seen him put his arm around other women and walk to a secluded place, and she knew what he and the woman did together. So many nights she wished that woman would be her, but Robin did not choose her.

She shared with Thalassa how things had changed

for her concerning Robin; she shared everything with her mother, and Thalassa had said that Robin must choose her. Either he would, or he wouldn't, and so far he had not. Last month, Thalassa had announced that Suann deserved a home and a family of her own, and reluctantly, Suann agreed to a betrothal. No more waiting.

Bretane agreed with Thalassa, and because Suann had no father to choose for her, he started looking for the right man. Yesterday, he had sent word from Edinburgh that he had found someone who lived in Stirling, and he would be bringing the man to Makgullane in a fortnight for everyone to meet. Suann resigned herself to the fact that if Robin could not be hers in every way a woman could belong to a man, then she had to leave Makgullane.

With that decision came anger, along with the realization that Robin, just like every other man she knew, was thick-headed! How could he no' ken how their childhood friendship had matured into grown-up love? As a full-grown man, he should ken these things! Did he think her too ugly for his bed? The other women on the estate fawned and giggled over him and agreed with everything he said, but when she thought about being such an *òinseach*, herself, her answer was a resounding *nay!* He had to choose her exactly the way she was. Today she had an almost overwhelming urge to smack him in the head and rattle his brain.

Still, she had to play the game to convince him that this marriage was for the best. She couldn't leave him any other way.

" 'Tis no' up to ye to tell me what to do!" she said crossly as they stood on the path. She lifted her foot off what felt like a stone digging into her boot, but the ground was smooth. The irritation did not come from her foot.

Robin turned his head away for a minute. When he turned it back, he asked in a voice as hard as iron, "Do you even know his name?"

"Of course. 'Tis Angus Gladstone," she said mimicking his gruff tone. "He is a master weaver in Stirling. He isna a rich man, but he makes a fine living, one that will keep me happy and well-fed. Ye maun not worry, Robin. I am grateful that Bretane has found a guidman for me."

"Why go all the way to Stirling? Is there no one here at Makgullane?"

She rolled her eyes. *Thickheaded!* "Ye ken as well as me that no men in the Highlands will have me because they say Thalassa is a witch. Most of them treat me like a bizzem who offers herself to men for free, and they winna consider me for a wife. Some say that I am the dochter of a clootie, but 'tisna true!" Her green eyes blazed with fury. "My *màthair* isna evil! She is good and loving!" She buried her face in her hands.

Robin gently pulled her slender hands down into his callused ones before he asked, "But what if you do not like him? It will not be a good marriage if you do not like him. Bretane cannot force you into a bad marriage."

" 'Tis so like ye to want to protect me, but this is how marriage is done. I have no father, so Thalassa asked Laird Bretane to stand in his stead. He doesna take this responsibility lightly. I trust that he has made certain that the man will treat me well. Bretane wants what is best for me."

Robin closed his eyes, took a deep breath, and exhaled slowly. He used this familiar gesture whenever he was upset and wanted to calm his racing mind to deal with the problem.

"But you have been planning your wedding for years," said Robin evenly. "You should not be made to give up your plans. Have you asked Mae Towdy to put the embroidery on your dress yet, the flowers and the love knots? Surely two weeks is not enough time for her to finish it."

It surprised her that he remembered something so trivial from so long ago. She had been twelve and he sixteen when she'd told him about how she imagined her wedding.

Robin had been repairing the slanted roof on the stable. Although not as high as the one on the storage barn, it still needed to be sealed properly to protect the hay and straw from rain. The chore had to be done frequently because of the strong winds that buffeted through the Highlands, tearing the wooden shingles off.

She had been sitting beside him on the gable while he hammered pitted iron nails into the shingles as she chattered on and on about her wedding. She knew just how she wanted it to be.

"My dress will be red and blue with a yellow chemise underneath, and it will be trimmed with green and red embroidery of flowers and love knots because the man I marry I will love forever, never-ending just like the thread on the knots." She looked skyward and sighed as if she could see the man in the clouds. When her thoughts came back to earth she said, "Mae Towdy does the most beautiful stitching. I will ask her to do it for me. I might have to ask her next year so that it will be done in plenty of time."

"You are getting married next year?" he mumbled through a mouthful of roofing nails.

"Nay, *amadan*! It will take her a long time to do the stitching, so the sooner I ask, the better."

He hammered the last of the nails from his mouth into the roof. "Do not call me foolish! I am not the one wanting a wedding dress while I am still a baby. Hand me some more nails."

She pulled a face before reaching into the leather pouch balancing on the gable between them and handed him some nails.

"So, who are you going to marry in this beautiful dress?" he asked, wiping sweat off his forehead before continuing his work.

"I havena decided yet. It maun be a braw buirdly man."

"Oh, a handsome strong man like me!" He winked at her.

She did not speak for a minute or two, and he kept nailing shingles. Then she said, "Aye, he will be like ye."

He looked up from his task. "Just like me?" he asked seriously.

With a quick nod, she said, "Aye."

"A man like me, but you mean a Highlander?"

She hesitated again before answering. "Mayhap 'twill be a Highlander, mayhap no', but it winna be an *amadan* like ye!"

He laughed before looking in the nail pouch and finding it empty. "I have to get more nails. Stay where you are, and I will be right back." He slid down the roof on the soles of his boots and jumped to the ground.

"Nay," she said, "I am tired of watching ye hammer." She drew herself up from a sitting position to squat on her feet. She started sliding down the roof like she had seen Robin do, but her apron caught on a broken shingle, stopping her mid-slide. Her feet flew out from under her.

"Robin!" she screamed as her dress, still captured on the shingle, tore, and she slid recklessly off the roof, arms and legs flailing. "Robin!"

Just as her feet came over the edge and she plummeted toward the ground, he was there, and she was in his arms, still screaming his name.

"You are safe now," he said as she flung her arms around his neck and sobbed wildly. "I will not let you fall."

"I was afeared!" she cried.

"Trust me, I will always be there for you. I will never let you go. I promise."

Today as they stood on the path, Robin said, "You need to have the perfect dress with all of Mae Towdy's stitching. Surely you see that."

"This wedding dress winna need love knots on it," said Suann quickly, "because we willna marry for love, at least no' yet, but Bretane says I can have all the time I want to get my bridal chest ready. I winna marry before I am ready."

Robin dropped his shoulders in frustration and started up with yet another argument against her marriage. " 'Tis a dangerous time in Scotland with no strong king. The countryside is overrun with reivers and beggars just like the ones that came here today. It could be dangerous for the man to travel here and for you to go back to his home in Stirling. Do you think a marriage now is wise?"

She blinked. Could this be her excuse to give Robin more time to choose her? "Mayhap ye're right, and I shouldna go to Stirling now. Mayhap it would be better to wait until law returns to Scotland."

Then, with a heavy exhale, she accepted that she had already agreed to the betrothal. It wouldn't be right for her to go back on her word, especially since Robin still hadn't chosen her or even hinted that he would. "But Laird Bretane has it all arranged. The bargain has been set. He is coming for me." Her voice quavered as she brushed dampness away from her eyes.

Robin didn't want his concerns about this marriage to frighten her; that was the last thing he ever wanted. "I am certain that Gladstone is a fair-minded man. Bretane would not have it any other way. You are a fine woman, worthy of being a wife. Is Thalassa pleased with his choice?"

"Aye," she said, "but I think 'tis ye who is no' ready for me to marry. Are ye no' happy for me?"

He hesitated before answering. In two weeks she would be gone, and he would never see her smile again. Suannoch had been his shelter and comfort in the strangeness of the Highlands from the first day they met on the steps, and he might not have survived without her. He certainly would have been dreadfully lonely. She and Bretane were his lifelines, his anchors.

However, in the last few years, the girl who had made him feel like he belonged in an unfamiliar place had grown into a beautiful young woman, and it troubled him that in his daydreams she had become the one he imagined lying next to him. Almost every night he dreamed of how her firm body would meld into his as he pulled her close. He could almost feel his fingers gliding over her skin from her neck to her legs and then between her legs. He imagined himself moving within her sweet softness. These thoughts troubled him and pleasured him at the same time.

Nearly every day Glynnis made sexual overtures to him, but Suann never had, and he would never insult Suann by thinking of her in the way he thought of Glynnis. He didn't care about Glynnis. He was friendly with her—never wanting to hurt her or make her feel abused—but she was not his friend, and he couldn't risk losing the most important part of his life, his friendship with Suann, by making those kinds of advances, however subtle, toward her. She had rebuffed men on the estate who had tried, and they had slunk away like beaten dogs.

Deep in his soul, in the place he never spoke of, also lingered a fear he had carried since the day he had lost everything and everyone he ever knew and loved in England. The only consistencies in his new life were Bretane and Suann, and he feared that they could vanish in an instant because of a fire or a windstorm or even a misplaced word, and today his worst nightmare had come true. She was leaving him!

Robin took a step back, breathing slowly out his nose. Then he lied to her. "I am happy for you. You should have a husband. All I want is for you to be happy. Are you happy?"

She smiled gently and nodded.

He gave their whistle and sent her on her way to the cottage while he went back to the stable. How could he stop her from making a big mistake? How could she marry someone she didn't even know? How could she leave him alone and miserable?

Suann could be pigheaded and stubborn, and once she made up her mind, she rarely changed it. If she did, it came with great reluctance, and she made certain that he knew the sacrifice she made, usually with a pout and a stomp of her foot. Sometimes he chuckled at how often he had manipulated her into doing what was best for her. If he put his mind to it, he could do it again, and she would stay at Makgullane where he wanted her to be, where she was supposed to be.

His first line of attack had to be Bretane and Thalassa. Since Bretane would be in Edinburgh doing his work for Parliament for two more weeks until he came home with this usurper of a husband, Robin would start by talking to Thalassa.

Three days passed before he had a break in his work schedule to visit her. His duties as reeve included all the jobs he himself had to do as well as supervising tasks done by others. He also had the nightly chore of recording in the ledgers everything bought, paid for, and owed, how well the crops were growing, and how close the livestock was to market. Missing even one entry resulted in hours of extra work to correct the situation; so, just as Bretane had taught him, he never neglected keeping his records up to date.

On the third day, right after the midday meal, he walked down to Thalassa's cottage. The sturdy house, built of stone, had two large rooms, one used as a living space and kitchen and the other as their sleeping quarters. A low stone wall surrounded the small yard.

Thalassa stood tossing grain to the chickens outside the coop in one corner of the yard.

"Suann isna here," she said without looking up at

him.

"I know. I want to talk to you," he said.

"I wondered when ye wad come."

He got right to the point. "Why are you forcing her to marry?"

This time Thalassa looked at him. "I am no' forcing her. No one is forcing her, except mayhap ye."

Robin blinked in surprise. "Me? I am not forcing her! I do not want her to leave Makgullane."

Thalassa put down her bag of grain, took his hand, and led him to the stone wall. She sat down and patted the stones beside her for him to sit. "We all ken that ye dinna want to lose Suann, but ye have done naught to keep her here. She canna live alone for the rest of her life just to please ye."

Brushing a loose curl of hair out of his eyes and tucking it behind his ear, he wondered how anyone could think she lived to please him! "What do you mean? Suann does not do anything just to please me. In fact, she vexes me more often than not."

"Ye think like a man!" Thalassa shook her head. "Open yer eyes, lad, and yer heart. If ye dinna do it soon, she will be gone and ye will be the one alone."

"What should I do?"

Thalassa drew her eyebrows into a scowl, sighed in disgust, and stood, picking up her bag of grain. She went into the house without saying another word.

He felt like a fox caught in a trap. First because Suann was leaving, and second because Thalassa would not help him make her stay.

Just then Suann appeared on the opposite side of the wall. "Robin, how can ye take time away from yer chores to talk to me *màthair*?"

"Not much of a talk. She did not answer with anything that made sense."

"Ye have to ken how to listen."

"She said I think like a man." He raised an eyebrow. "How else could I think?"

Sighing just like her mother, Suann said, "What did ye want to ken from her?"

He stood up and walked over to her. "You are making a mistake getting married to a man you have never met."

" 'Tis no' yer decision to make." She turned her back on him and crossed her arms over her chest.

"You are so stubborn. Can we at least talk about it? Please, just hear me out."

She uncrossed her arms. "All right. Walk with me. Ye ken the spot where we can talk."

He did know that spot.

Neither of them said a word until they reached a small grove of trees twisting across the side of the hill. Both knew exactly where within the copse of trees, bushes, and shrubs that an aged tree bent down and formed the perfect nesting place against its trunk. They used to come here to get away from people and chores. Hidden by the overgrowth, no one could see them from the path, and if they spoke quietly, no one could hear them either. It was their private place.

When they reached the tree, Robin lifted her up onto the substantial, low-hanging curved branch that he had spent hours sanding and smoothing. They used to be able to sit side by side on the branch, but now Suann sat and Robin stood, leaning his back against the trunk.

Leaves rustled in the wind, softly and then louder, making that special music that only nature could create.

The *rat-a-tat-tat* of a spotted woodpecker searching for bugs sounded in the bark of a nearby tree. Farther off a goldfinch and a crested tit called out as Robin and Suann waited for the other to start the conversation.

Robin spoke first. Even though it stung inside, he wanted to reassure her that he did want the best for her. "I am sorry if I sounded angry before. I know that most girls your age are married with children by now, and I want you to be happy. I do."

She reached over to stroke his cheek with the back of her hand. "I ken that ye do, and I want ye to be happy, as well. That is what I have wanted from the first day I met ye. Do ye remember that day?"

"Aye," said Robin, his eyes widening with the memory. "I was scared down to my boots that Bretane would send me away."

" 'Twas a foolish thing ye had done."

"Aye, that prank on Father Bernard with the mare. I had never had any schooling before, never learned to read, but he treated me as if I were doitit. He rapped my knuckles for every mistake!" He rubbed the backs of his hands as if they still stung.

"Ye may not have been a good student then, but ye are verra learned now. I think ye have read all the books on Bretane's shelves, and ye can add the figures for the sale of the wool faster than anyone else at the market."

"When I was a lad, lessons had no purpose except to torture me, but now I know that there will always be more to learn."

Bretane had spent hours every evening keeping the records for the estate, and since Robin liked being with him, he had often sat on the floor and waited until Bretane finished. Eventually, he got bored enough to pull a book off the shelf and look through it. Bretane helped him with the words he didn't know, and before long Robin became fascinated by the stories within those books. He learned about faraway places, read essays about the Bible and on farming, and enjoyed volumes of poetry, even a few novels. He especially liked the tales by Chaucer. Often, he read parts aloud, and he and Bretane shared a laugh. Over the years, Robin read all fifty books plus the new ones Bretane brought back twice a year from Edinburgh.

"Do ye remember when ye taught me to read?" Suann asked. "We sat here in this tree almost every day until it got dark while I stumbled over the words. And ye taught me to write by scratching letters in the dirt with a stick."

"I remember. You were a worse student than I was!"

She ducked her head and peered at him from underneath blond eyelashes. "I have a confession to make. I already kenned how to read. Thalassa taught me to read and write and do figures."

He cringed. "So why did you have me waste my time teaching you?"

Her laugh bubbled out like a brook splashing over the stones. "It wasna a waste of time. It gave us a reason to be together. Besides, ye brought me books from Bretane's shelves, and ye let me read other books than just the Bible. Most women ne'er get to read anything else."

"My biggest mistake was letting you read *The Education of a Christian Woman.* Bretane wanted me to stop giving you books after that one."

"I loved that book!"

"Because it said that women are equal to men."

She sat up straight, her green eyes flashing. "Well, are we no'?"

He'd seen less angry polecats. "You, milady, are equal to any man." When she didn't calm down, he added, "And the more men who realize that about women, the better off we will all be." He raised his eyebrows. "Better?"

"That's better," she said, resting her back against the tree again. She saw his grin and gave him a playful poke on his chin.

Shifting her position on the tree, she added, "Thalassa sent me to ye that first day on the stairs. She said ye needed someone to be standing with ye. I came to tell ye not to worry. Bretane would keep ye."

"That's when I first heard about Thalassa being clear-eyed, and the first time I ever heard the word *clootie*."

Suann pulled away from the trunk of the tree again and glared at him. "Ye winna call my *màthair* a devil! What she does is for the good, ne'er the evil! She sees the future to help people!"

Putting his hands up in surrender, he said, "Whoa, Suann! Others might call her a clootie, but not me. I know Thalassa is a good woman, and you would defend her against anyone to the death!"

"I would! To their deaths!" This time she punched his arm harder than the playful poke at his chin.

"Ow!" He rubbed the spot, remembering how she had kicked him in the shin twelve years ago.

He stood straight, then crouched down with his hands out in front of him. "I channeled that anger of yours when I threw the caber at the games last year. I clenched my teeth and tightened my muscles the way you do when you think someone has insulted your mother." He straightened up quickly with a loud grunt as he tossed his imaginary caber. "I outthrew Bretane."

Suann pursed her lips. "I hope I dinna make that awful noise."

"Nay, that is a manly sound."

She reached out and tried to straighten a few of his curls falling into his eyes. "Your hair is as curly and shaggy as ever. Do you even own a comb?"

"I do, but trying to pull a comb through it just makes it bushy. I use that wooden three-pronged pick you gave me. That helps some, but men do not worry about their hair the way women do."

Nestling her fingers deeper into his hair, Suann gave it a tousle. "Well, ye should."

He smiled, and those dimples that Suannoch loved so much sank into his cheeks.

"It could mean trouble for you if you marry this Angus Gladstone. He may not be as open-minded as I am. I want you to be happy, and I do not think Angus will make you happy."

"What do ye think will make me happy?" she asked in all seriousness.

He hesitated for a long time before saying, "I can make you happy. Stay here, and I promise we can spend more time together like we used to. I can make time for you every day."

She rolled her eyes. "Is that what ye think I want? More time to spend together as friends? Is that all ye think I am? A pal to whittle away the hours with? Is there nothing more?"

"More?" A light flashed in his mind, opening a

door to things he had never thought clearly about before. Like a clap of thunder, it came to him what she meant by "more." *More* haunted him at night with visions of Suannoch lying beside him. He felt *more* every time he was near her and every minute he was away from her. *More* was why he so desperately wanted to stop her marriage. It hit him like a shovel swung at his head.

At last he understood why other women meant nothing to him other than fulfilling a physical need. He never wanted to stay with them, never wanted to walk in the moonlight or hear about their ideas or beliefs. Only with Suann did he want those things. No other woman filled his heart the way she did. That was it! She filled his heart!

After clearing his throat, he announced, "I do not want you to go to Stirling to marry this Angus Gladstone." He took a slow deep breath before going on. "I want you to stay here with me."

Shaking her head in frustration, she said, "So 'tis still all about ye? All about what ye want? Is there naught in that manly brain of yers about what I want?"

"I think about what you want," he protested. "I can take care of you. I can build you a house big enough for us and for Thalassa. I can give you anything that the man from Stirling can."

"So ye think 'tis only a house I am wanting? Ye maun think me a right *fèineil* lass that I wad marry just to get me own house!"

Why did she make it so hard? "Nay, you are not selfish. Oh, Suann, I do not know how to say what I want to tell you!"

In that voice she used whenever she set him

straight, she said, "Here is what I have to say. I will only marry for love. Do ye love me, Robin? As a man should love a woman? I used to pretend we lived together in a stone house, and I would cook and sew yer clothes, and we would play games like Nine Men's Morris. Ye wad sit in a rocking chair by the fire and read to me. I was a child then, but as I got older, I imagined how we would share a bed the way a man and woman do."

She looked over at his startled expression. "Aye, a grown woman can have thoughts like that! And I am a grown woman! I want ye to look at me...the way ye look at Glynnis. But if ye dinna love me like that, all that, then I will wed the man from Stirling and make my life with him."

Robin raised himself up to his full height and stiffened his gaze as well as his tone of voice. "I will never look at you the way I look at Glynnis. You mean much more to me. You have meant everything to me for so long, but you were a child..."

"I am no' a child now!" she said in a voice that cut him like a whip.

Reaching into the pouch he carried, he felt around inside, first fingering the metal token with the dog on it that his mother had given him. When he found the two halves of the silver shilling, his and the one she had given back to him at the stable, he pulled them both out. "Bretane gave me this shilling a long time ago, and I have always carried it with me, or I have always carried at least half of it. We are like this coin. We are each half, but together we are a whole. I cannot keep both halves. You have to take yours." He held it out in his palm.

Slowly, she picked up just one piece and folded his fingers over the other piece of the coin. "Do you remember the poem ye told me when we decided to break the coin and each keep half? I was fourteen, and you were eighteen. The first lines are 'Where I have chosen, steadfast will I be, never to repent in will, thought, nor deed.' "

He answered with the second verse:

Your desert can none other deserve,
Which is in my remembrance both day and night.
Before all creatures you I love and serve
While in this world I have strength and might,
Which is in duty, of very due right,
By promise made with faithful assurance,
Ever you to serve without variance.

" 'Tis a verra pretty verse about love and promises," she whispered.

He leaned in close to her and murmured, "Then, we did not think this coin meant anything more than a symbol between friends. It did not mean what it does now. I am sorry that I was not smart enough to realize…to understand what changed between us. We were friends for so long, I thought it was wrong to think about you as a man does who wants…who loves a woman, but I do want you in that way. I want you in every way a man can love a woman."

She touched his hand. "Ye werena wrong. Fault was mine for no' telling ye what I wanted."

Laying his hand over hers, he said, "Now I understand this coin is a promise of love, love between a man and a woman, one that I should have said a long time ago, so I do it now. I do love you and I want you to be mine…forever."

She took her half of the coin and leaned forward to gently rub it against his cheek. "This means everything to me." Before he could answer, she whistled their special pattern, and he returned it.

They looked into each other's eyes, his blue and hers green, for a long moment as the importance of what they had just said to each other sank in. She swung her legs over the side of the branch in front of him, and at the same time, he placed his hands on either side of her face. Slowly, he leaned in between her knees until his stomach touched the tree limb, and their mouths were close enough to breathe the same breath. "We have been friends when no one else would have us. We are each other's other half."

He yearned to kiss her, yearned to seal the promise they had made, yearned to taste her as he never had before. Suann quivered. He leaned in even closer. His lips were almost on hers when she whispered, "Robin, I canna. Bretane has signed a paper making the promise to Angus. A betrothal, a contract, has been made. If I maun wed and go to Stirling…" She pulled back, swallowing tears. "Your whistle, our whistle," she said. "If I marry, I will no' hear that whistle again. I will miss it more than anything else!"

Without warning, she threw her arms around his neck and the tears she had been holding inside burst into sobbing. "I canna live a life without our whistle. Ahhhh," she howled in frustration as tears streaked her cheeks. "Bretane canna make me marry another! Not now! I love ye and only ye! I winna do it! Please, dinna let me go!" She fell against him as her shoulders shook with her crying.

He held her close. He felt her heartbeat against his

chest and soon his own heart beat in unison with hers.

"I will always be there for you," he said.

"But the contract."

"I will never let you go."

While he comforted her, a thought flashed through his mind that he might be moving too quickly, that the words of their commitment of love came too easily. Since coming to Scotland, he had learned to order his life, to plan ahead, but this change had come without warning and so quickly.

Had both of them had enough time to fully consider what it meant? Feelings were one thing. Living the reality was another. Could Suann, his cherished friend, become his cherished lover in the few minutes it took to say the words? Had his body made a decision that his mind and his life were not ready for?

Nay, they had known each other too long and too deeply. They may not have said it in words, but they had made their commitment of love to each other a long time ago. He stroked her hair and made soothing whispers.

She soaked his shirt with her tears, and her sobbing gradually dwindled to small gasps and sniffles. Wiping the back of her hand across her cheeks, she pushed away the tears and snorted a loud sniff to clear her nose. Robin chuckled at the sound, and a few seconds later she joined him in laughter.

With his sleeve, he finished drying her face. "Are you ready to be mine?"

"I have always been yours," she said.

Gently with his fingers, he tipped her head back and leaned in again until his lips skimmed across hers.

Arching toward him, she opened her mouth ever so

slightly, and he felt her trembling as she whispered, "Robin, at last."

Their lips melted into each other, soft and unsure at first, but soon a jolt of energy raced through him, and nothing else mattered as much as the two of them together. All the emotion they had both been holding deep inside flooded to the surface, and years of unspoken passion engulfed them both.

He deepened the kiss, gently pushing her lips apart with his tongue. She moved her tongue to meet his and urged him deeper, their embrace tightening at the same time. His arms encircled her, pulling her soft breasts into his chest.

Splaying her fingers across his back, her hand moved up to his neck to where the breeze ruffled his hair against her fingers. She tugged him closer.

He pressed into her, and she accepted all his mouth had to give. The kiss deepened with desire, giving and taking, wanting and needing. He craved her with a power greater than he had ever felt, and she made it clear with sounds deep in her throat that she wanted him in the same way. They said in their kiss what had never before been spoken.

He lifted her off the branch and set her on her feet, all the while never letting her lips leave his.

Just then a deep voice said, "Look what we found, lads. Might ye share the lass?"

Chapter Four

The birds that had been so noisily chirruping fell silent.

Robin swung her behind him with one hand. "Who are you?" he asked the three men standing on the other side of the tree.

Their clothes were threadbare and dirty, and they smelled worse than rotting meat. One had a black rag tied around his head covering his right eye. Another's nose fell off to one side like it had been stomped on by someone's muddy boot. The third man, the one who spoke, had a red stain across his face and a silk coat over his rags. He carried an axe, while the arms of the other two were laden with small logs and branches that could be used for firewood.

"Who are you?" Robin repeated as he gave them a warning look. "You do not belong here."

The man who had first spoken spat out, "Sassenach! Ye dinna remember me? I am Keenan Gray. Ye sent us away three days ago with naught more than some bread and cheese. Ye could have spared more and ne'er missed it, but ye didna, so I am thinking ye might share what ye got in yer hands right now to even things up."

Robin glared at them.

"We are three and ye are one, so this time ye will be the one walking away empty-handed!" He pointed his axe at Robin. "Ye may go, but the lass, we wad like ye to stay."

Drool dripped down the chin of the man with the eye patch as he said, "What do ye think, lass? Three real men, Scots bred and born, instead of this English lubberwort. How about it, lass? Ready for a good ride?"

Before Robin could stop her, Suannoch stepped out from behind him, put her hands on her hips, and said, " 'Twill be a short ride! I dinna think any of ye could keep it up for verra long."

All three men snarled, and Keenan Gray spat.

Robin, looking down at her with eyes that shot daggers, said, "What are you doing? Let me handle this."

" 'Tis me they are after. I winna take it without a fight."

With a nasty smile, Keenan grabbed his crotch. "We like it better when ye fight, lass." Lifting his arm, he threw the axe directly at Robin, who grabbed Suann and jumped with her behind the protection of the tree trunk. The axe lodged in the bent limb of the tree with a loud thwack.

Slipping under the limb, Robin started to jerk the axe free, but before he could release it, Keenan and the man with the eye patch charged at him, knocking him face first into the trunk. Robin hit the tree with a grunt as the two men, so proud of their small victory, grinned, revealing blackened and missing teeth. "Do ye see that the odds are no' in yer favor, Sassenach?" growled Keenan. He let out a menacing laugh.

Robin was not amused.

The third man with the broken nose ducked under the limb and ran straight for Suann.

Her eyes narrowed, and she clamped down her jaw, creating a grimace that people who knew her acknowledged meant it was time to run, but this ignorant beast kept charging at her. His leer persisted even when she planted her feet, crossed her arms in front of her head, and hurled herself straight at his midsection. At the moment of impact, she drove her knee into his groin. Her unexpected strength shocked him, and he fell on his back with a thud. Quickly she straddled his chest, pummeling him with her fists. One blow bloodied his nose, and another did the same to his lip.

He rolled around on the ground, clutching himself, and moaning as Suann stood over him, jeering insults at him and relishing her victory. Leaving him writhing on the grass, she turned to see how Robin fared with the other two.

Keenan stepped toward Robin just as Robin whirled around and laid him flat with a swift elbow to his face and a second blow to his gut. Keenan fell hard, while the man with the eye patch pulled out a jagged knife from his waistband and swung it wildly at Robin, who folded himself at the waist to avoid the blade. With his knife still held out in front of him, the man made another wide swipe at Robin's midsection. Robin grabbed his wrist with both hands and twisted the man's arm back and away. The man yelped in pain when the bone in his arm snapped. He dropped the knife while Robin continued to twist the arm, ramming his knee repeatedly into the man's face.

Just then the man with the broken nose and the throbbing man parts regained his senses enough to grab Suannoch's ankle and jerk it so she fell onto her back on the ground. Quickly he sat up and slid his hands up her legs inside her kirtle. He laughed, thinking after he punished her, she would be his to do with as he wanted. But mid-chortle, she rolled up onto her shoulders and powerfully kicked one foot into his chest and the other into his face, forcing him onto his back again.

Sitting once more on his chest, she pressed her thumbs into his eye sockets as hard as she could. He screamed in pain. She kept pressing until she felt one eyeball loosen and soften. She let up on her grip, but he kept screaming.

"Is the ride over now?" she asked grimly, her spittle flying into his face. "Are ye done with me for good this time?"

His wail of agony said that he indeed was done with her and would be done with everything for a long while.

Meanwhile, when Robin finally released his opponent, the man sucked in a ragged breath, clutched his broken arm, and staggered over to his fallen companion with the broken nose and now injured eye. Holding each other up, they stumbled out of the grove.

"Come back here, ye fools!" shouted Keenan, who saw that once more he'd been bested by the Sassenach. Slowly he came to his feet, clutching his stomach and retching down his tunic. "She is an ugly bitch! No' worth a tinker's curse!" he shouted as he, too, ran away.

Robin started after him, but Suann grabbed his arm. "Let them go. I dinna think they will bother us anymore."

"You put out his eye!" he said.

"I had to make certain that he wadna come at me again. I canna fight a bigger, stronger man twice. I had to stop him."

"Where did you learn to fight like that?"

"Thalassa taught me."

Robin smiled and shook his head. " 'What is better than wisdom? Woman. And what is better than a good woman? Nothing.' "

"Thalassa is a good woman! Yer quote is Chaucer, the *Canterbury Tales*, right?"

He nodded.

"She taught me how to protect myself against tormenters as a child, and after I grew into a woman, against any violent attacks. I have used what she taught me often."

In a voice edged with concern, he asked, "Why did I not know about these attacks on you?"

"No one dared if they saw ye around. They only found their courage if I was alone, but they soon learned." She jutted out her chin and pulled her shoulders back. "They soon learned."

Enraged that any man would molest Suann, he demanded, "What men at Makgullane attacked you? What are their names? They will be gone before nightfall and sorry for it!"

Suann smiled her answer. "I am grateful for yer protection, but Thalassa taught me well, and just like these men, they are already gone."

Robin sniffed and turned to jerk the axe out of the tree limb. "It looks like that bunch of sorners did not follow my directions to leave. I need to find out where they are camped and see how many they are, but first I will take you home, so you and Thalassa can gather your things and move into the manor house. 'Tis not safe for the two of you out here alone now."

"I am going with ye."

"Nay, 'tis too dangerous now that we know these louts are still about."

She pulled herself up to her full height, which put the top of her head at Robin's shoulder and fixed him with a sharp eye. "Ye wadna tell Thalassa to go home and hide, and ye winna tell me!"

Even though she could be aggravating, he did like that stubborn independent streak of hers. He admired her strength, both physically and in spirit. She was no typical Highland lass, and she would never allow Robin or anyone else to tell her what to do. A fundamental part of her nature was to speak up and speak out.

He said, "I can see that the only way I can keep you safe is right by my side, but there is one more thing we must do before we go."

Robin began searching the patches of dirt and fallen leaves under the bent tree limb. Soon Suann joined him until they found the halves of the shilling they had both dropped when Keenan Gray and his henchmen had appeared.

Holding up both pieces, Robin said, "Here is mine. 'Tis the one with the bent corner." He handed her the other half, but instead of taking it, she lifted his half with the bent corner out of his hand.

"Now that we have chosen each other," she said, "we maun keep each other's coin. Ye will have the one I carried, and I will have yers. Just as we always have belonged to each other, the coins will belong to us."

She kissed her half of the coin with the bent corner and slid it into the cloth pouch at her waist. Then she stood on her tiptoes to kiss the man who held the other half of the coin.

As Robin leaned into her, she whispered, "Ye can take me now."

He stopped his exploration of her with his lips and hands, even though, at this moment, his entire body wanted her desperately, painfully. The temptation to make her his own nearly overwhelmed him, but so much had happened in the last few hours. Today they had declared their true feelings for each other; that meant their relationship needed to change, too.

Robin recognized that he adjusted slowly to change while Suann accepted changes in short quick bursts. Each of them would have to give a little, and although he guessed he would be doing most of the giving, he didn't mind. She was worth it. Being longtime childhood friends was only part of their connection, and it would take a delicate balance to turn that deep, abiding friendship into their new deep, abiding commitment of love. It would not be easy.

Over twelve years, they had become as much a part of each other emotionally as two people could be, but their physical relationship would be new. Although they could build their physical lovemaking on their longtime bond of the heart, only time could smooth the transition from friends to lovers.

These new feelings of love toward Suann mixed badly with the rage he had needed to defeat the Grays, and at the same time raised old demons. His childhood had been so chaotic and uncertain that he had never been able to predict his life from one minute to the next. Every day his guts had twisted like a fish on a hook.

Then he had met Bretane, predictable Bretane. The man meant what he said, and he said what he meant, and as Robin began to trust in that security, he gradually learned to make sense of his own life. He organized his work schedule, coordinated all the chores that needed to be done by himself or by others, and he learned to keep his emotions buried below the surface. He taught himself to be even-tempered, and after a time it became second nature, until today, a day full of newness, uncertainty, anger, and love. The muscles at the back of his neck and his shoulders tensed painfully.

"We need time together first," he said.

"We have had many years together already," she said as she ran her hands up and down his chest, slipping one under his sark, letting the warmth of her hand move across him.

He held her away from him as he scanned her rich green eyes. He wanted those eyes to swallow him up, but he couldn't let that happen now. He wasn't ready, and even though she thought she wanted to make love with him, she, too, was not ready for a change of that magnitude. Things still needed to be said.

In a voice heavy with regret, he said, "But our time together has not been in the same way as you...as we both, want now. We need to get to know each other in a different way, to learn to be with each other in a different way. The time has to be right, and too much has happened today for us to understand it all. Here in the trees, after defending our lives, is not the way I want our loving to begin."

"Do ye love me, Robin?" she purred from deep in her throat.

"I love you, Suannoch."

"Then make me yers."

He groaned because he had to convince her to wait before they rushed into anything sexual. The nights of

63

only imagining Suann in his arms were not yet over.

To distract his body and Suann's persistence, he changed the subject. "We have to find Gray's camp, and if as I suspect they are becoming reivers, we need to be ready. Other reivers only occasionally venture this far north, and they respect Bretane. We have an unspoken agreement that if we do not choose sides, they will not bother us. But we have no idea what to expect from Keenan Gray. If 'tis only twelve of them like we saw three days ago, then chasing them off will not be hard, but if there are more, the estate will have to protect itself. The nearby attacks we have heard about could be the Grays testing their strength."

She withdrew her hands from his chest and stuck out her lower lip. "Robin always thinks of his duty first."

"Not always." He gave her a peck on her forehead. "I wish we had weapons beyond my knife and the one Keenan's man dropped." He withdrew his flat blade from its sheath and ran his finger along the edge. " 'Tis dull from use around the estate, and the little pointed thing you carry will not do us much good."

Pulling a small dagger from the folds of her overdress, she said, "It has been of good use more than once." She lightly jabbed the tip into his stomach, and he gently pushed her back.

"We'd best be off, so we can be back before dark," said Robin. "Tramping around these hills after sunset can be more dangerous than any one-eyed sorners!"

The many dells and valleys around the rugged hills of Makgullane were familiar to Robin and Suannoch. Some paths made for smooth walking through grass and heather while other stretches became rugged, rocky, and steep. The often-treeless Highlands offered little cover, so they stayed to the edges of the ridges as much as possible to inspect the areas below without being noticed.

Suann skipped ahead to pick wild berries for them to share. With a red stain on her lips, she said, "Do ye remember when I told ye that I wanted to be the Queen of France?"

"Aye, and I told you that the job was already taken."

"Is it still taken? I think I would like to be the Queen of France."

" 'Tis still taken. You would have to learn to speak French, you know."

"Nay, I wadna. If I were queen, I wad make everyone speak English, but not yer English—mine with the proper Scots accent." She skipped ahead again before stopping to face him. "Why is it ye ne'er learned to speak like a proper Scot? Ye have been here long enough to learn it."

He popped another berry into his mouth. "I am not born Scot. I am English. I speak like I should."

"Ye have been here in the Highlands near as long as ye lived in bloody England."

"It does not matter how long you have lived in a place. 'Tis where you are born. I was born in England, so I keep talking like someone born in England."

Suann curled her lip and looked at him askance. "I think 'tis because the lads gave ye a hard time when ye first came to Makgullane, so ye keep the English talk just to spite them."

He grinned and winked at her. "Spite is as good a reason as any."

Abruptly changing the subject, she asked, "Do ye still want to be a juggler?"

He bent down and picked up three fist-sized rocks, which he tossed in the air one at a time until he juggled all three above his head. "Do you think I could make a living at the fairs?"

"Only if I picked their pockets while ye had the stones in the air!"

"Watch this," he said. "Do you see that thistle growing up between the rocks over there? The one with the purple bloom?"

"Aye."

Pulling his arm back, he threw the stone, neatly severing the bloom and leaving the stem waving in the wind.

She started to clap but hesitated when the breeze carried a strong odor of smoke and the low murmur of a large group of people toward them. Robin let the rocks fall as they both dropped to their knees and crawled to peer over the edge of the ridge. What they saw turned their stomachs. Grays—over fifty of them camped below!

The land had turned from a well-kept grove of small apple trees into a trampled mass of weeds and mud. Many of the trees had been reduced to stumps, and Robin grimaced, appalled at the wanton destruction of this food supply. Bretane had taught him that staying fed in this beautiful but unforgiving land required hard work and constant attention, something that these worthless wanderers had no notion about. They lived only for their immediate wants and needs.

What would Bretane think if he saw this? It would break his heart. His proud spirit thrived like the heather that grew wild and tenacious, no matter how anyone tried to subdue it. He may have given up his sword, but he had traded it in for another powerful weapon, his voice for justice under the law, and he would never give up the fight.

Bretane would drive these squanderers off his precious land even if it rained pitchforks down on his head!

Over the bemired expanse of the dell stood dozens of small tents and makeshift lean-tos, each with its own cooking fire. Gathered in small groups around these low fires sat people as tattered and wretched as the land. Two women wearing the traditional scarlet skirts crawled out of a tent, followed by two men adjusting their plaids.

"Prostitutes," said Suann with a sniff.

Some distance from the other campsites was a family dressed in gray coats with red hats: lepers.

"Keenan wore a red hat," said Suann. "How could they let a leper lead them?"

"Most likely he is not cursed with the disease. He wears the hat to keep people away and make them afraid of him. They might pity him with that red birthmark on his face, but they will be wary of a leper. Look, I see Hugh." He pointed to the boy at the edge of the camp munching on a half-eaten brown-tinged apple. Robin watched him pull a worm out of the fruit, toss it to the side, and finish the apple, core and all, in one bite.

The change in the wind carried another sickening smell up the side of the hill, rising from the decaying bodies and bones of maybe a dozen cattle and goats, where the meat had been cut off and what remained left to rot. Two men wandered over near the corpses and relieved themselves in what had obviously also become the camp's pissynghole. The putrid odor permeated the entire camp like a thick fog.

"That smell is so bad I can taste it!" said Suann, covering her mouth to hide the sound of a gagging cough.

However, it was the sight of swords, axes, and knives piled up behind one of the tents that disturbed Robin the most. "They are arming themselves with weapons stolen from places around here, and I do not like the look of it. These people do not live by the same rules as the rest of us, and that makes them very dangerous."

"What are we going to do?" asked Suann.

"Prepare!"

The trek back to the estate was quicker and easier now that they had found what they were looking for.

She took his hand. "We have never held hands before."

"Aye, we have," said Robin. "Many times I pulled you across the stream or up into the loft so we could throw hay down on Callum when he mucked out the stable."

"I dinna mean like that. I mean like a man and a woman do when they are alone together. Have ye ever held hands with someone like this?"

He looked at her out of the corner of his eye. He could hear it in her voice. Her question could only lead to trouble. "Aye," he said cautiously.

"Many times?"

He answered slowly again, "Enough times."

He had thought that the subject of other women,

especially Glynnis, had been nothing more than good-natured teasing on her part, but maybe it wasn't. Now that their relationship had grown deeper, maybe other women would become a sore topic. He had never hidden from her that he spent time with other women. Maybe he should have.

Using her thumb, she rubbed the back of his hand. "Did ye like it when she did this?"

"Suann, stop it." Trying to change the subject again, he said, "Thalassa must bring as many of her herbs and medicines as she can to the manor house. If it comes to a fight with the Grays, we will need them."

"Aye, she will bring them. Did ye like it when Glynnis held yer hand? Or when she held other parts of ye?"

"I do not want to talk about Glynnis." His already overburdened nerves flared up like an itch he couldn't scratch.

"I will find out about Glynnis sometime. Ye will tell me. Ye can count on it." She dropped his hand before quickly adding, "I have something to show ye. 'Tis a secret place. 'Tis not far."

Suann led Robin over the next hill to a rising slope covered with small trees and scrub bushes. Meandering through the foliage burbled a stream over and between the rocks, creating several small cascades that emptied into a wider stream continuing down the hill and out of sight.

"This place is beautiful," said Robin.

"Aye, 'tis, but that isna what I want to show ye. Follow me."

She led him up the hill along the edge of the stream, jumping from rock to rock and pushing aside overhanging brushes and branches until she neared the top of the rise. There she pulled apart several overgrown thorny bushes, revealing a narrow entrance to a cave. She signaled for him to follow, and as soon as he stepped through the opening, the bushes sprang back, hiding them completely.

Inside, the cave enlarged almost immediately until Robin could stand upright. Suann located a lantern on the floor near the entrance, sparked the flint inside, and lit it.

"This is our secret place," she said. "Thalassa's and mine. We have been getting it ready for a long time."

The stream began inside the cave, flowing on the floor along one wall from a source at the back of the cavern. "A natural spring," he said.

"Aye," said Suann. "It starts high on the back side of the mountain. After a thousand years, the water hollowed out the cave. Even if someone found the source of the water on the other side, they wadna ken that it flowed inside the mountain to this side. No one kens about it except me and Thalassa, and now ye."

Crates and shelves, all filled with crocks and sacks of preserved foodstuffs, lined the rocky walls of the cave. Two small cots piled high with blankets and quilts sat in one corner, and firewood against the other wall. Several large buckets of charcoal were farther back in the cave.

"The smoke is pulled out the back, too, so from this side of the hill there is no hint that anyone is here."

"Someone could live here for years," said Robin, amazed at all the provisions.

Suann lit two more lanterns. " 'Tis our safe place. When we first stayed here, I was verra little. 'Twas when Hubert came. We stayed for over a month until he left."

"Who is Hubert?"

"I dinna ken, but Thalassa said he was dangerous. Now we bring fresh supplies every time we come."

"I thought I knew everything about you, but today all these secrets keep coming out. First, you already knew how to read, and now this cave. I am beginning to think I do not know you at all. Why did you not tell me about this place?"

" 'Tis a secret," she said plainly. "The only reason ye ken about it now 'tis that we might need it, ye and me. We call it *Secretum Flumine*. 'Tis Latin for Secret by the Stream."

"I know. Father Bernard made me study Latin. I hated it, but I learned it."

Suann moved very close to him before putting her hands on his waist and whispering, "Do you think this could be a secret place for us?"

He stepped into her and slid his hands up and down her arms. He wanted her so much. "Aye, a secret place." He lowered his head to kiss her.

Without moving her lips away from his, she said, "Wad Glynnis like this place?"

"I do not know, and I do not care." He deepened his kiss.

Putting her hand between his legs and rubbing what she found there, she whispered, "Does Glynnis touch ye like this?"

Robin felt his entire body stiffen, and not just because of where she held him with her fingers. His stirred-up emotional state rose to a level he hadn't experienced since his childhood.

Never knowing what to expect from his brutal father, Robin had tried in his childish way to guess how his father might react. If he could figure it out, maybe, just maybe, he could protect his brother and sister or maybe avoid a beating himself, but it proved impossible. He learned never to look his father in the eye because the man interpreted that as a threat, but at the same time looking at the ground made his father accuse him of cowardice and deserving of a beating. No decision or choice Robin ever made was the right one. On the day of the fire that killed his family, shattering everything Robin had ever known, it took every ounce of his strength just to take his next breath. Today, he felt the same way.

His mind raced out of control as masses of long-buried feelings and remembered fears flooded to the surface. He could hear the crackling fire and smell the smoldering ashes. With no way to push those memories away, he could not stay the man he had been for twelve years.

His sexual frustration broke the final straw on his already overtaxed body and mind. The last three days had been too much. First, the Grays in the yard, and Suann telling him she was marrying another. Then the three men attacked them in the grove, and along with the discovery that his heart belonged to Suann in new ways, he couldn't put it all into his formerly ordered existence. For twelve years, he had prided himself on keeping a calm grip on his life, but this day had not been calm from the moment it began.

And here stood Suann, who for as long as he had known her had refused to tolerate his moods, who demanded mutual respect, and yet today she tried to bait him into an argument about Glynnis, a woman who had never meant anything to him and never would. He needed time to rest and recover, not defend his past to the woman who held his future. Yet she continued to plague him.

"Does Glynnis ken the secrets to making ye feel like a man?" she purred.

In a sudden burst, like a river rushing down the waterfall, all restraint left him, leaving him with his heart hammering and the blood pounding in his head. Roughly, he pushed her away, and she stumbled against the cave wall. "That is enough! Stop this talk!" His face became a dark mask as he shouted, "I will not have Glynnis or any other woman thrown up at me every time you take a notion! No more!"

She righted herself and marched toward him, saying with ice in her voice, "I want to ken how it was with her." She hit him hard in the chest with both hands. "I have to ken that ye are mine and mine alone. That Glynnis is banished from yer thoughts and yer life forever! I deserve to ken, and ye will tell me! Now!" Sticking her chin out, she dared him to stay silent.

As her words goaded him beyond his limit, clouds of fury turned his eyes a murky gray.

"Is knowing what you want? Then I will show you!" He grabbed her roughly around the shoulders and kissed her hard, biting her lip and forcing her mouth open. He ravished her mouth until her lips were swollen and bruised. Grabbing at her clothes, he tore at them until her shift hung open from her shoulders. Then he pushed her to her knees and opened his trews, but just before he dropped them to the floor to expose himself to her, he saw her face looking up at him.

Her skin had turned ashen, and her eyes brimmed with tears. She was afraid, and he had never seen her like that. His strong bold Suann was afraid, and he was the one she feared.

He pulled her to her feet. Her whole body shook.

He saw the fear that as a child he had felt every day. How could he have done to her what had been done to him? How could he have become as cruel and abusive as his father? Bretane had never made him feel afraid. No matter how angry he had made Bretane, no matter what he had done or said, no matter what punishment had been meted out, Robin never felt fear. But now he had recreated the terrifying nightmares of his childhood in Suannoch. The one he loved was afraid of him, afraid of what he might do to her.

All she had wanted to know was that he loved her and no one else. Every time she had seen him with another woman, it must have been like a knife to her heart, but how could she have known how little Glynnis meant to him? They had never spoken of it, and she deserved to know how he truly felt. Today, all she had done was ask, and even though she had persisted in that often maddening way of hers, she didn't deserve his wrath or his physical abuse. No matter what, he had no right to use his strength against her! How could he have let it happen?

For the last twelve years, he had tried to wipe out any trace of brutality that his father might have left in him, but today he had failed. He took out his rage on the woman he loved. He had become the man he hated.

He dropped his hands to his side, turned his back to her, and stepped away.

Chapter Five

Ashamed, desperately ashamed.

Slowly, he closed his trews and tied them at his waist. He did not turn around. He couldn't face her. He could barely face himself.

The awareness of how he had abused the woman he loved ate at his gut until he doubled over, clutching his stomach. The dull empty ache in his heart nearly swallowed him. He deserved her hate. She would never forgive him, and if by some miracle of God, she could, he would never forgive himself.

Resting his hand against the cool damp wall of the cave, he closed his eyes and leaned his head on his extended arm. Even the simplest of thoughts wouldn't form, only raw, ugly anger, regret, and all-pervading sorrow. The long-buried places of hurt and madness in his soul had escaped, and they had raged at Suann. How could he have let it happen?

He heard her moving around behind him, and he hoped she would find a knife to plunge into his back. He hoped she would—he deserved it—but all was quiet, and she did not stab him.

He stood there for a long time before choking out, "I am sorry." The words echoed quietly against the cave walls.

She didn't answer, and her silence nearly suffocated him. "I should be flogged." After another long lapse he said, "Bretane will flog me."

"Robin," she said softly.

" 'Tis too much to ask you to forgive me, but I hope that someday…someday." He couldn't finish his thought, his hope really, that someday far in the future she might be able to forget what he had done to her. He never would.

"Robin." Her voice, although gentle, echoed painfully in his head.

"Please find something to put on and start for home. I will follow and make sure you are safe. You will not have to look at me. I will stay behind the whole way."

"Robin," she said again. "I want ye to look at me."

He lifted his head and prepared himself for her wrath. He wanted her words to maim him. He wanted her fists to beat him black and blue, although nothing she did or said would ever be as shattering as the anger he had released on her. Taking a deep breath, and swallowing the bitter lump in his throat, he turned around.

She stood just a few feet behind him. He expected to see her in the clothes he had torn off her, but instead she wore a diaphanous white chemise that revealed every curve of her body from her neck to her toes. The dark nipples of her breasts and the shadows of the hollows at her hips showed through the sheer cloth. Her lips were bruised, her honey-colored hair a tangled mess around her shoulders, but the worst was the expression on her face, an expression he had never seen on her before, fearful but still full of love. It brought tears to his eyes.

"I…am sorry—" he began.

"No more words."

"I am less than a man."

She repeated more firmly, "No more words." Stepping close, she took his hand in hers, her hand so small, her fingers long and narrow, her palm moist and warm. He had overpowered her with his size and strength when he should have protected her. He was a beast.

Gently, she pulled him toward a low stack of folded blankets and quilts on the other side of the cave. Then, lying down on top of the quilts, she tugged at his hand until he knelt on the blankets beside her.

Again, he opened his mouth to speak, but she came up on her elbows and put her finger to his lips. "No words can take back what happened. No words can take back what I said to cause it. I was wrong."

" 'Tis my fault and my burden to bear." He dropped his head. "I will regret it for as long as I live."

She came to her knees in front of him, and the light from the lantern reflected off the green of her eyes. She lifted his chin. "I said 'no words.' Shh. I mean it, Robin, no more words."

Taking his hand, she pried open his fingers and placed a gentle kiss on the palm. Her eyelashes fluttered against his skin. She then held that kiss to her cheek, letting it linger there, all the while never taking her gaze from his face. In a slow, sensual move, she moved his palm to her neck and gradually placed it softly on her shoulder.

Taking his other hand, she kissed its palm just as tenderly and completely with lips that spoke what no words could. Wrongs had been done by both, and now was the time for absolution. She pressed his hand to her cheek in a way that made his heartbeat quicken with hope, hope he didn't deserve. Dragging it to her chest, her nipple rose through the sheer cloth to meet his hand, and she pressed his fingers around her breast.

Her hands, now free, slid under his sark and pushed it over his head, and he tossed it on the floor. Then, tenderly, she kissed her own palms and with them caressed his cheeks before skimming her hands down his chest over the soft mat of hair, and then back up to his cheeks.

The sensations engulfed him as he understood that she wanted to repair the damage done. He wanted that, too, more than he wanted his next breath, so he struggled to push his guilt and regret into a small corner of his chest. The pain would never vanish completely, and he would never forget what he had done, but he hoped he could make the memory fade for her. He had used his strength against her, and he had to make her see that it would never happen again.

She kissed his cheek and locked her arms around his neck. When he dropped his hands to her waist, she moved, pulling him with her until she lay on her back on the quilts. He slid down beside her, stretching his legs along the length of her body, face to face, breath to breath. A beckoning upturn of her lips crossed her face as she pulled him in to kiss her. This time there was no anger, no frustration in his kiss. He drank in the sweetness of her lips.

Lifting his head, he softly traced his thumb around the bones of her face. Moving along her eyebrows and down her cheek and jawbone, his thumb caressed her mouth, and she closed her lips around it, sucking noiselessly.

He smoothed the hair away from her face and pressed his hand against her neck to feel her pulse, slow and steady. She wasn't afraid. Yet, still hesitant, he trailed his hands down her neck and along her body. When she put her fingers over his and caressed his hand, he knew she could forgive him. Slowly, he began to forgive himself. Together, they would find their way back. One of his hands cradled her head while the other eased off his trews so his long legs could embrace hers.

As his hands continued to roam over the sheer cloth of the gown, she raised her hips to meet him, and he lifted the material to touch her bare skin. She felt warm and flushed. He encircled each breast with his fingertips, stroking the tender flesh, and then smoothing each rib until he found her hip joints. With his palm, he held the bone and ran his thumb up and down the indentation there.

She whimpered in the most exquisite way.

His fingers slowly and gradually reached her thighs and between her legs, where he found her womanhood swollen with passion and softly wet. He touched and stroked her as she hummed acceptance deep in her throat.

Lifting onto his elbows, he moved his lips away from hers and with his kisses followed the same path down her body that his fingers had just done. He unhurriedly feasted his way down her belly with slow, soft kisses, to the place where his hand had teased and pleasured her. When his mouth surrounded and tasted her there, he relished the delightful combination of the honey color of her hair, the richness of her laughter, and the joy of her heart. Hearing her soft moan and seeing her hips move in unison with the rhythm of his tongue made this lovemaking beyond anything he had ever known. This was how their first time together was meant to be.

He suckled her delicate flesh, kissed it, and licked what made her a woman until she quivered beneath his lips. When he lifted his eyes, he found that she had slipped the gown over her head, and her naked body glistened in the dim light. Unhurriedly sliding his body up hers, he kissed every inch of her until he reached her lips again. He moved his hips between her legs.

He came into her slowly, patiently, until he felt her clench around him and pull him deeper. His movements inside her glory were even and gentle. They spoke of amends and restoration. They spoke of how he wanted to erase her memory and make a new one, one built on the truth that he had loved her for as long as he had known her, and that he would love her for as long as he drew breath and even beyond. He murmured, "My love," with each soothing thrust. He vowed that she would never again know the kind of anger he had unleashed on her. Never again would she see the worst that a man could be. Never again would he be that man.

He wanted their joining to last forever, but gradually he felt himself coming to the edge of the precipice, and with a gasping breath, he fell. Swirling and flying, then soaring, he realized that she soared with him. In unison, they rode the wind of their loving, higher and lower again in waves until together they rested back on the mountain in each other's arms.

He collapsed onto her and rolled to the side, but her body followed him, and she would not let him leave her. How long they lay in the aftermath neither of them knew, but forever would not have been long enough.

"Thalassa will be worried," whispered Robin.

"I ken," she said.

They walked back to Thalassa's cottage hand in hand as the cloud-filled night sky forced each of them to concentrate on the ground before their footsteps. When they came in sight of the cottage, Robin took Suann in his arms and said, "Will you forgive me?"

She looked up at him. "There will be many times when ye will need to ask me for forgiveness and many times that I will have to ask it of ye, but today there will be no words, except these. We have declared that we belong to each other. I have loved you always, and I always will."

"Where I have chosen, steadfast will I be."

"Never to repent in will, thought, nor deed."

They shared a deep and delicious kiss before he left her and turned down the path toward the manor house.

"Thalassa and I will be at the house tomorrow," she called after him.

He waved back to her one more time.

Robin knew this path from the cottage to the manor house like the back of his hand, so the darkness didn't worry him. What did worry him were the footfalls he heard behind and beside him, making the leaves and twigs crackle and crunch. He could see nothing in the darkness, but when he stopped walking to listen, the sounds stopped, too.

Robin debated returning to the cottage, but he couldn't risk bringing the possibility of danger to Suann and Thalassa. Scanning the thick hedgerows on either side, he saw nothing but darkness. It was only a half mile to the house, almost home. He started walking faster.

The unaccustomed sounds returned immediately. Drawing his knife from his sheath, he held it at the ready as his eyes flickered from side to side. He started to run.

Like a swarm of flies, they were on him, rushing out of the blackness, shouting as they surrounded him and pummeled him with their fists and the hard heels of their boots. A dozen or more men attacked him at once. Two of them swung thick sticks at his head, one catching his cheek on the splintered corner. He staggered back and tasted blood dripping down his face.

Robin swung his knife out into the sea of fists and feet and heard a yelp of pain every time he made contact. He swung his knife again, but this time someone sliced his arm with a dirk on the inner side of his wrist. His knife fell. A swift blow to the back of his knees with another branch buckled his legs and sent him flat on the ground. The strikes intensified, as if knowing that he was down gave his attackers courage.

Blow after blow rained on his back, his legs, and his head. He scrambled to reach out for whatever he could, and several men fell on their backs after he latched onto their ankles and pulled. The pounding against his body was relentless.

Eventually two of the assailants tugged on his arm, found his hand, and stomped on it until the bones in his hand shattered. His ribs cracked, his eyes swelled shut, and blood ran from jagged gashes on his legs, forehead, and cheeks. They rolled him onto his back, and the pummeling continued.

Suddenly the shouting stopped, and he heard a familiar voice say, "We meet again, Sassenach! This time ye winna be ordering us off yer land! And we will be leaving with something of yers."

Robin felt a tug on the top of his right ear and then a sharp sting of pain as a knife sliced through the skin. The crowd cheered as the man kicked him facedown again.

"Will they sing songs about us, lads?"

"Aye!" shouted the others.

"Who is the most feared of all the reivers? Is it Johnnie Armstrong of Gilnockie?"

"Nay! No more!"

"Is it the men of Keenan Gray?"

"Aye! Aye! Keenan Gray!"

Robin did not know how long the beating continued after that. When he started to choke on his own blood, his eyes closed, and he felt no more.

Chapter Six

Young Hugh, a boy with no name except for the one he gave himself and with no one to call him their own, shuddered as he watched the Gray men attack Robin. The men landed one blow on top of another, but Robin bore the beating and did his best to fight back. Not once did he cry out or beg for mercy, but after they kicked his legs out from under him, his chance for escape disappeared.

Hugh knew that the Grays, especially Keenan, found their courage only in numbers. Not one of them could take the beating they gave to Robin without sobbing and pleading for pity. They would cover their heads, roll up in a ball, and not even try to defend themselves the way Robin struggled to do. They would cry like little babies! Silently, he cheered every time Robin's knife found its mark or his hand jerked one of the men to the ground. The Grays were cowards and bullies, something Hugh knew all too well.

In the Grays' camp, every night when he curled up on his threadbare blanket, Hugh prayed to grow tall and strong, so he could return to Keenan, Tinker, and Torrin what they gave to him, but so far, he had remained small and thin. These men assaulted Hugh on a regular basis for no apparent reason other than they knew he couldn't fight back. The women slapped him for looking at them too long or in the wrong way, and it seemed like every look he gave them was wrong. No one existed lower in the Grays' pecking order than Hugh.

If it hadn't been for the girl, Mercy, who fed him from whatever portion she got, he would have run away. Nay, running away wouldn't solve his problems. It wouldn't get him more to eat or a warmer place to sleep. The Grays were all he knew, all he remembered knowing.

Mercy told him that he was ten years old, but he had no idea if it was true or not. He had a vague memory of a house with a lot of women who washed his face and tousled his hair, but he also had memories of men who dragged him out of that house and locked the door, leaving him to shiver in the cold and the rain until one of the women brought him back inside. Still, in these memories he always had enough to eat.

Then, for a reason Hugh never knew, everything changed, and from that day on he was always hungry. He remembered huddling in a corner behind a tavern trying to keep a rat from stealing the half-eaten meal he had dug out of the trash bin. It wouldn't be long before one of the kitchen boys came out and chased him away, so he had to eat fast.

He remembered Keenan suddenly appearing at his side in the alley, hauling him up by his neck, and dragging him over to a fishmonger's shop. There he proclaimed that this boy would work for the fishmonger for three days for no fee except food once a day in exchange for the large salmon Keenan wanted but didn't have the money to buy.

"This lad is my son, and he is a hard worker," said Keenan. "I ken he looks puny, but he is strong, and he will do what ye tell him. Right, lad?" He cuffed Hugh on the head hard enough to ring his ears.

"Aye, Da," Hugh replied, thinking he should see where this ruse went before protesting that it was all a lie. Besides, Keenan had a painful grip on his neck.

The shop owner, short and squat with a bulbous nose, protruding eyes, and smelling like the ocean, said, "If he is such a good worker, why are ye giving him up?"

"I canna feed him, but with this fish, I can feed my other five bairns if ye will feed this one. It breaks me heart to be without the lad, but I promise ye I will return to collect him in three days."

"Are ye hungry, lad?" asked the fishmonger with a voice gravelly and rough and hands to match.

"Aye," said Hugh. He would do just about anything to get something in his belly. To help confirm Keenan's story, he looked up at his captor with adoring eyes and what he supposed might be an adoring expression. He couldn't remember ever looking at anyone with tenderness before.

"What is the lad's name?"

Keenan stared blankly at the boy, so Hugh said quickly, "Hugh."

"Aye, 'tis Hugh," said Keenan as if he had known it all the time.

"All right," said the man. "Leave the lad here, and the fish is yers."

For three days, Hugh hauled and cleaned fish and ate his fill at every meal. The fishmonger treated him kindly, and Hugh began to like this place. Then Keenan made good on just about the only promise he ever kept. He came back to claim Hugh. Using the boy to get free fish had been easy enough, and he wanted to try it again, so he grabbed Hugh by the neck and dragged him away, and the dodge continued. Most of the time Hugh ate well for a few days in exchange for work, but Keenan always returned to snatch him away.

"I can use an agreeable lad," Keenan had said. "And if ye isna agreeable, I will blacken yer eyes! Understand?"

Hugh understood.

Tonight, from the hedges along the side of the road, Hugh heard Keenan shout, "We meet again, Sassenach!"

Hugh winced when Keenan grabbed Robin by the ear and sliced it off. It felt like a spider crawling up his spine and into his hair, and the tingling sensation deepened until his stomach threatened to oust its meager contents.

To take his ear? Could anything be so cruel and meaningless?

Never again would he go along with whatever Keenan said just because he was hungry and cold. Being with the Grays only to get fed and have a ragged blanket to sleep on at night would never be enough from now on.

Robin had spoken kindly to him and had fought Ronald for some of the cheese and bread and had told him that he would be safe at Makgullane. Robin didn't deserve Keenan's cruel treatment, and Hugh would do his best to make certain it never happened again.

The beating ended, and the Grays vanished into the night until the only sound Hugh heard was their fading cheering at their victory over the reeve of Makgullane. Robin lay face down in the dirt with his blood puddling around him. He didn't move.

Stepping out of the thicket, Hugh approached the still body. Squatting down he gently touched Robin's head. It felt warm, so he wasn't dead yet. The gash on his cheek looked bad, but Hugh knew enough that Robin's worst injuries would be in places that no one could see. He laid his hand on the man's back and waited to feel him take his next breath. After a long time, Robin's chest finally moved.

"Ye're hurt bad," said Hugh. "There is no' much I can do, but I will pray that ye dinna die. Even though the Lord ne'er answered my prayers afore, mayhap He will do it for ye. A good man doesna deserve to die by the hand of the likes of Keenan Gray."

Hugh crouched beside Robin, stroking his head and back to comfort him, and whenever a large glob of blood appeared at his mouth, Hugh carefully wiped it away with the edge of his tunic. Several times Robin coughed, and Hugh lifted his head to help him rid his throat and chest of the blockage.

Hugh sang to him. He hoped it would help Robin, but he mostly sang to keep his own fears at bay that whatever he did wouldn't be enough to save the first good man he had ever known. He had no idea where he had heard these songs that came from deep inside his memories, but every time he repeated a verse, he became more certain of the words.

One ditty made him laugh. It was called "When I Was Young I Had No Sense."

When I was young I had no sense,
I thought I'd go to sea,
I climbed aboard a Chinese ship
And the Chinese came to me,

They toppled me right over
And put me on to boil,
And while the pot was boiling,
They sang a Chinese song:
"Eeska munga gee I funga fe fi fo fi thumb,
Dip your nose in the butter,
Sugar my tea."

His favorite part of the song was the words in Chinese. They probably weren't real Chinese words, but Hugh liked them anyway. In an odd way, he didn't feel so afraid for himself or for Robin when he sang this bright tune.

Sometimes Robin got restless and started to twitch. Since moving around would aggravate his injuries, Hugh sang a lullaby. It seemed to calm Robin, so he would lie still again.

Baloo baleerie, Baloo baleerie,
Baloo baleerie, Baloo balee.
Gang awa' peerie faeries,
Gang awa' peerie faeries,
Gang awa' peerie faeries, Frae oor ben noo.
Doon come the bonny angels,
Doon come the bonny angels,
Doon come the bonny angels, Tae oor ben noo.
Sleep saft my baby, Sleep saft my baby,
Sleep saft my baby, In oor ben noo.

Hugh sat beside his friend and sang to him all night long.

After the sun had risen over the hills, Hugh found his way back to the Grays' camp.

"Where have ye been?" growled Keenan when he saw the boy.

"Nowhere," Hugh answered.

"It doesna look like nowhere! Ye got blood on yer tunic and yer vest. We give ye a fine vest, and ye ruin it!" He thumped Hugh on the head and turned away. Almost immediately he turned back, his eyes bulging. "Is that yer friend Robin's blood?" he asked, throwing his hand out in Hugh's direction.

Before Hugh could answer, Keenan pushed him to the ground and kicked him in the ribs. The veins on the man's neck swelled into angry blue ridges as he kicked the boy again.

Mercy ran up to Keenan and grabbed his arm, crying, "Dinna do it!"

Keenan gave her the same hard push he had given Hugh, and she landed on her back beside the boy. Pointing a sharp finger, Keenan said, "If he betrays me again, I will give him the same beating I gave that fopdoodle from Makgullane! Is that what ye want, lad?"

"Nay," said Hugh softly, hiding his own furious look by covering his face with his hands.

"That is right, cower, ye toad! Dinna let me see yer double-crossing face!"

Keenan stormed off to release some of his fury on one of the scarlet-skirted women.

Jumping up, Mercy pulled Hugh to his feet. "Ye maun get out of his sight. He willna think twice to kill ye, just like he did that Robin. He's been bragging all night about how he beat the life out of the man, and he wad do it again to anyone who dared to cross him."

Whispering in her ear, Hugh said, "Robin isna dead, at least no' yet."

Mercy's eyes widened as she looked around to see if anyone had heard them.

"They will find him, the ones at Makgullane. I saw them coming, so I ran off and came back here."

" 'Tis dangerous for ye here," said Mercy. "Keenan doesna trust ye."

"I ken, but because he doesna, he will keep me close. That way I can find out what he is going to do, and mayhap stop it."

" 'Tis verra dangerous."

"I have to try. I have to do it for Robin."

****

Shortly after sunrise, a search party from Makgullane set out to find Robin.

When he didn't appear in the kitchen to break his fast, alarm swept over the workers on the estate. Robin never deviated from his daily morning routine, up at sunrise and assigning the day's tasks to everyone eating at the kitchen table. Just as the seasons determined the patterns of work on Makgullane, Robin determined the patterns of each day. They'd come to depend on it.

He had already started preparations for the arrival of traveling teams of sheep shearers who sheared the entire flock and then moved on after a few days. Over the last week, Robin had directed Shane and his crew to gather in the sheep from the fields and house them in a covered pen built by Darby and Will to keep them dry until the shearing. Robin assigned Henry and two of the younger lads to inspect each beast for cuts, sores, and other skin issues, and the women to stitch burlap bags for the fleeces while Marta and the kitchen maids began setting aside food to feed them all. It had been the same every spring. The estate thrived because of Robin's predictable habits, and with him gone, everything came to a standstill.

A quick search of the yard revealed that Robin hadn't been delayed by checking on the horses in the stable or by getting out the tools to be sharpened in preparation for the sheep shearing, so Darby took charge and began barking orders to find their reeve.

He sent the women to search every outbuilding and structure on the estate on the chance that he had injured himself and could not call for help. George, Martin, and Ralf left to walk east toward Kirkcaldy. They spread out and called his name with orders to go three miles before heading back.

Shane, Darby, and Patrick headed west in the direction of Thalassa's cottage. She might know where he had gone. It didn't take them long to find Robin's motionless body in the brush beside the road.

"Shane, run back and bring a wagon! And some blankets!" said Darby as he and Patrick carefully rolled Robin over to examine his wounds. When Darby saw the gruesome mess, he shouted, "Hurry! The ground is soaked with his blood." Imploring he said, "Robin, dinna leave us! What have they done to ye?"

Shane soon returned with a horse and a small cart, followed by Glynnis and Maggy running behind him. The three men gently lifted Robin into the back of the cart and set his head on Glynnis's lap while she wailed, "Robin, my fine Robin! Dinna die! Please, Lord, dinna take my Robin!"

"Shut yer mouth! Yer screeching is burning me ears!" said Darby. "If the Lord is to save him, then he will do it for all of us! Slowly, Shane, as steady as ye can. He canna take any jostling. Every bump opens up his wounds."

The word spread quickly that Robin had been

found, and by the time the cart arrived back at the manor house, everyone on the estate waited anxiously in the yard.

"He's hurt bad," said Patrick to those who closed in on the cart. "Dinna bump him."

"Take him inside," said Glynnis. "He can have my room."

"Nay," said Marta, the cook, after taking one look at Robin's battered body. "Put him in Bretane's room. 'Tis bigger and has the softer bed. 'Tis what Bretane would want. Ralf, ride like the wind to Edinburgh and tell Laird Bretane what has happened. He will want to be here."

That set Glynnis to wailing again. "He canna die! He canna die!"

Once the men laid Robin on Bretane's bed, Marta began cutting off his blood-soaked clothing. "Maggy, fetch Thalassa."

"Nay!" shouted Glynnis, locking her fingers around Maggy's arm. "I will tend to him. I winna have that witch touching him!"

A quick slap across her cheek from Marta silenced her. "Thalassa is the only one who can heal this man. His hurts are too great for me or ye. If ye truly want him to live, ye will be quiet and do anything and everything Thalassa says. Maggy, why are ye still standing there? Fetch Thalassa! Make certain she kens how badly he is hurt. Move!"

Maggy bolted from the room.

Some of Robin's bloody clothing had dried and stuck to his skin. Marta soaked those spots with water and then ever so carefully pulled the cloth away. As she did, raw skin tore, bringing tears to Marta's eyes. "I am sorry, lad. So verra sorry."

She thanked God for the blessing that Robin didn't move or make a sound.

By the time Thalassa and Suannoch arrived at the bedroom door, Marta had washed as much dried blood from his face, chest, and back as she could. Many of the cuts and scrapes she uncovered were wide, deep, and still gaping open, seeping blood while throbbing purple bruises covered nearly every other inch of him, especially his face, which resembled a piece of bloated, rotten fruit.

Stepping in front of Thalassa, Glynnis pulled back her shoulders. "We are doing as much as can be done for him. Ye can go home." Her light-brown eyes narrowed, and her forehead furrowed, giving her round face a formidable aspect. Other people often acquiesced to her demands when she glared at them like this, but Thalassa was used to people trying to intimidate her, and never had they succeeded.

Even as a child, Thalassa had refused to let anyone make her feel less than she was. She knew the value of her skills, and she knew her own mind. She never had any need to raise her voice or to raise her hand because she depended on the strength of her character. This younger woman was a kitten without teeth compared to Thalassa's lionhearted spirit.

With a wordless stare, Thalassa watched Glynnis until the younger woman sulked away to lean against the wall, pursing her lips into a petulant pout.

Thalassa lifted the sheet to look over her now-naked patient. "Ye have done a good job cleaning the wounds, Marta. Help me mix the herbs to make a poultice and a tea that he will need to drink every hour.

Have ye sent for Bretane? He will want to be here afore the lad dies."

Glynnis gasped and started to cry again, but a stern look from Thalassa ended her bawling.

Slowly approaching the foot of the bed, Suannoch held her breath, terrified at what she might see. Her face paled and her hands trembled, but her fears and worries were of no importance. Robin needed her full attention. "What can I do to help?"

"Show Marta what to do with these," said Thalassa, handing her daughter the bag of herbs. "Glynnis, fetch me a dozen eggs and separate out the whites. I will need the whites to soothe his wounds after I stitch them. Darby, gather five large stones from the stream. Then heat them over the fire. Cool them by throwing the hot stones back into the stream and then bring them to me as quickly as ye can so I can soothe his bruises."

Darby dashed out of the room, but Glynnis moved much more slowly. Muttering under her breath she said, "Ye willna keep me from my Robin, ye striped-hair witch." A sharp look from Thalassa sent her scurrying.

Thalassa examined every part of Robin, starting at his head, taking note of each injury. A gaping gash ran across his cheekbone under his eye from his nose to his jawbone, and the skin around his eye had swollen into a purple blood blister.

"Suann, wash all my knives and needles with as much soap as ye can find. Dry them with a clean towel and bring them to me as quickly as ye can. I maun stitch his cheek. His beautiful face will have a scar, but it canna be helped. I also have to open the swelling around his eye before it bursts on its own. Get a leech

95

from the jar in my bag."

She brushed his hair off his face, tugging on strands that had dried and embedded in his torn ear. "What have they done to ye? What kind of a man wad steal a man's ear?"

Suann rushed over. "Why would anyone do that?" she said. " 'Tis such a senseless gesture, especially after this terrible beating."

Thalassa said, "Get me a pair of sheep shears. We maun keep his hair out of this open wound. There is naught enough skin left on the ear to stitch closed so it will have to heal open."

After Patrick came back with the shears, she trimmed and sheared off all the blood-crusted hair on that side of his head. Then she laid small pieces of cloth that had been soaked in her homemade poultice over the top of his raw ear.

For two hours, Thalassa bound the smaller gashes on his arms and legs with torn strips of cloth and then stitched the larger ones closed. She made small, neat stitches, especially across his cheek. "It will no' be a heavy scar like Bretane's, but a thin line. 'Twill fade over time, but it winna disappear. 'Tis his for the rest of his life."

"I dinna care," whispered Suann to her mother. "I only care that he lives. He will live?"

Thalassa shrugged her shoulders, and Suann swallowed the hard lump in her throat.

"Suann, the bones in his left hand maun be set," said Thalassa. "Feel the bones in yer own hand. See how they are straight like the ribs of a fan? Gently rub his hand until ye feel his bones straighten like that. It may feel like pieces of crushed stone under the skin but put them in order as best ye can. Be careful with his thumb, for without use of a thumb his hand is useless. Then we will bind the hand on a board until it heals."

"I can do that!" declared Glynnis.

"Nay," said Thalassa firmly. "Ye winna touch him with your filthy fingernails."

"What do my fingernails have to do with it?"

"The church and its physicians say that ye canna work on a wound if yer nails are dirty. Scrub them, lass. Then ye can bring me freshly washed bedding and change his bed. 'Tis already soaked with blood and sweat."

Glynnis yapped, "Let me see yer hands!"

Thalassa held out her hands, which she had washed thoroughly including under her pale fingernails before and after she stitched every wound.

Sticking out her bottom lip, Glynnis said, "Why do ye keep me from my man?"

Suann stepped beside Glynnis, her face only inches away, and yelled, "He isna yer man!"

Before she could go on, Thalassa put her arm between the two women, saying, "Yer arguing winna help him. Go, Glynnis, do as I bid ye."

After Glynnis left the room, Suann's temper still burned. "She canna claim him. He is mine!"

"If he lives, then he will tell her himself, and she will ken the truth. If he dies, it matters naught."

Tears swam yet again in Suann's eyes, but she brushed them back. All that mattered was that he live, and she would see that he did if by nothing more than the sheer power of her own will.

Robin required round-the-clock care. His dressings needed to be changed, the pus, blood, and ooze washed away, and he had to be spoon-fed every hour with teas of sorrel and marigold to keep his fever down, along with Thalassa's own mixture of herbs to prevent his wounds from festering. Twice a day, Suann bathed his deep bruises with the warmed stones from the creek, and Thalassa insisted that he be rolled from his side to his back and then to his other side at two-hour intervals to relieve the pressure on his healing skin.

Two days passed before Robin could swallow on his own, no longer needing his throat massaged to force the fluids down, but by the fifth day he still had not moved on his own or made a sound except for his ragged breathing.

"I am afeared he is injured under the skin, that his lungs have water in them, mayhap blood," said Thalassa. "We have to help him stay strong so his body can heal itself. Suann, if he starts to gag or his breath is wet and choked, put more pillows behind him so that he sits up straighter."

"Aye, I will."

"I will do it," added Glynnis. "I will be sleeping here again tonight."

Suann didn't bother to respond because she, too, would be sleeping on the floor beside the bed just as the two women had done every night, Glynnis on one side and Suannoch on the other—the difference being that Glynnis slept through all necessary dressing changes or liquid feedings. Her eyes squeezed especially tight if Robin needed his bodily eliminations tended to, but that didn't matter to Suann. He belonged to her, and she would do whatever it took to keep him alive. If she had to do this for years until he awoke and spoke her name, she would. *Where I have chosen, steadfast will I be!*

On the sixth day, his eyes opened.

Glynnis had gone to the kitchen to get something to break her fast while Suann rested her head on the bed, eyes closed. She heard a raspy sound.

It sounded like a hissing duck.

Something touched her head. She tried to brush it off, but she couldn't.

His hand! He was awake!

"Robin! Good morning!" she said with a sunny feeling she hadn't felt since they had found him.

He made another hissing duck sound.

"Are ye hungry?"

Slowly, he shook his head and made the hissing sound again. He tried to sit up, but he didn't have the strength. Falling back, he hissed again, this time urgently.

"What can I do for ye?" asked Suann, desperate to help him, but not having any idea what he wanted.

Just then the door burst open, making a thunderous *bang* when it slammed against the wall. Bretane filled the doorway. Covered with blackened road dirt, he reached up to wipe his face, and the grime smeared in streaks over his cheeks and neck. "Is he alive?" demanded the laird.

"Aye," said Suann. "He just now woke up. Has been six days."

"I got here as fast as I could once Ralf found me." He stepped close to the bed, and Robin hissed yet again.

"I dinna ken what he wants," said Suann in a frantic attempt to keep her voice steady.

"I do. Get me a bucket and then leave us."

She quickly handed Bretane the bucket she used to carry soiled rags out to be washed, but she hesitated before leaving.

"Out, lass, and hurry! He needs to piss! No matter how close to dying a man is, he deserves his dignity and his privacy."

Suann scampered into the hall, pulling the door shut behind her, but she heard the sounds of Robin emptying his bladder into the bucket, and Bretane encouraging him the whole time. " 'Tis a lot of piss, lad, but dinna worry. I will be here to help ye from now on. What has that woman done to yer hair? Half of it is gone! And she took yer ear with it!"

A few minutes later, the door to the hallway swung open, and Bretane roared, "Bring me a cot!" He handed out the urine-filled bucket. "And bring me a clean bucket!"

Within a few minutes, Patrick and Henry appeared with a cot, followed by Maggy carrying bedding. "Put it against the wall," Bretane ordered, "and tell Marta I am starving. I havena eaten for two days. I will take my meals here until the lad can walk to the kitchen on his own."

Kneeling beside the bed, he laid his massive hand on his ward's arm. "I am here," he murmured. "I rode two horses into the ground getting here as fast as I could. I thank ye for not dying before I arrived."

Robin tried to smile, but his torn lips split open and leaked blood. He quickly closed his mouth.

"Dinna talk, lad. Rest easy. I am here."

For the next week, Bretane didn't leave the bedroom, and he forbade visitors from coming farther than the doorway except Thalassa. "The lad doesna need yer bothering him. I am here!"

Marta brought all his meals to him, and he used the

same bucket that Robin did, always ordering someone to empty it immediately. "We have enough to do without putting up with the stink!"

Every day he washed Robin from head to toe with warm water and soap, carefully avoiding all his wounds. He took instruction from Thalassa on how to change the dressings and refused to let anyone else do it. When Robin grew a little stronger, Bretane supported his ward's back against his own chest as he spoon-fed him watery porridge and mashed turnips.

Robin grunted when he'd had enough, but Bretane insisted on one more bite. "Nourishment sustains ye. The more the better!"

Robin grumbled a reply before opening his mouth for the last morsel. After each feeding, he collapsed on the bed and fell into a deep sleep.

When the fever had been gone for two days, ale replaced the teas, and Bretane made sure he got his own share of the brew.

With his throat still bruised and swollen, the only words Robin had spoken since they found him were "Keenan Gray." Once Bretane heard from Glynnis and Maggy about the beggars who had visited and heard from Suann about the three men who attacked them and what she and Robin had seen at the Grays' camp, he concluded the worst.

"We must be prepared because it appears this Keenan Gray is hoping to establish his own reputation like that of Johnnie Armstrong. The fastest way to do it is to be as vicious and brutal as possible. This beating they gave Robin may be only the beginning, and we need to be on the lookout for more such crimes."

Suannoch had already taken on the task of

preparing the estate for potential trouble so Bretane could keep seeing to Robin's recovery. She wore trews cut down to fit her slender body and wrapped her head in a scarf that completely covered her hair until it looked like a cap worn by young boys. No one would take as much notice of a boy wandering the hills as they would at seeing a girl or woman alone. She walked the countryside, searching for signs of where Keenan had moved his camp from the destroyed apple orchard.

Several crofters reported the theft of their chickens, a goat, and some pigs. One farmer reported that one of his shepherds had lost part of an ear trying to prevent the theft of his sheep. Keenan seemed intent on spreading fear. As his reputation grew, so did the need for Makgullane to be ready.

On the estate, Suann attempted to prepare the workers for a possible attack from the Grays, but the farmhands and houseworkers had been raised in relative peace and had little training in combat fighting. Disputes among the clans of the Highlands had gone on for centuries, but Bretane had convinced many of them around Makgullane that negotiation settled these disagreements faster and more permanently than the sword. As such, most of the people of Makgullane had grown up in a time of peace, so convincing them to train for hand-to-hand combat proved difficult. Even though Robin's beating enraged them, they viewed it as a one-time, random act by long-gone ruffians and saw no need to listen to Suann's dire warnings.

She tried to organize the men into shifts for guard duty. She wanted to hold practice sessions with everyone using whatever tools they had in hand as weapons to defend themselves, but convincing them to go along with her plans proved impossible. No one listened to Thalassa's daughter.

"Do ye plan to put a witch's spell on them? Turn them into toads and frogs if they come near?" They laughed and pushed her away.

She tried turning to the women for support, but with Glynnis opposing her every chance she got, this, too, seemed impossible until after three days of begging and pleading, they suddenly started listening to her. The men chose straws for the hours they would walk guard duty, and both the men and women asked Suann to show them defensive techniques she had learned from Thalassa using their brooms, hoes, and farming tools.

Although relieved by their cooperation, Suann asked, "What changed yer minds?"

They simply shrugged and went about their training.

Little Fergus told her the truth. "Laird Bretane called all of them to the window outside Robin's room when ye were out and told them to listen to ye. If they didna, they would pay the price. He didna say what the price was, but no one wanted to find out."

"So, this is Bretane's doing?"

"He made them swear not to tell ye. He wanted ye to do it on yer own."

"But ye told me."

Fergus grinned and shrugged. "I am just a wee lad, so he didna make me swear."

Suann tousled his hair. "But I will make ye swear that ye winna tell Laird Bretane what ye told me. I want them all to think they are doing this because Bretane said so, not because the daughter of Thalassa did. They can save face that way. Do ye swear?"

Fergus nodded, thrilled to be included in the secret.

During the third week of Robin's recovery, Bretane began lifting him up to sit on the side of the bed for short periods several times a day. "I have seen too many men lie abed too long, and their joints ne'er work right again," he explained. Robin complained bitterly in his croaky voice about the pain, which Thalassa called a good sign. "When the patient is whining, it means the body is healing."

"The cure is worse than the beating!" protested Robin.

"Would ye prefer to be left on the road bleeding into the mud? It can be arranged to haul ye back there," said Bretane.

Sheepishly Robin said, "Nay, milaird, I will stay here and thank you for all your kindness."

"Then put yer arm around my neck. If ye are a good lad, I will have Marta make ye a tart. Would ye like a tart?"

"Aye, sir, I would."

"So would I. Marta, make us two tarts!" he called. "One spoonful for Robin, and I will have the rest!"

During that same third week, Bretane ordered books be brought down from his library, and he read to Robin hour after hour until his voice became as hoarse as his patient's. Suann crouched in the hallway out of sight to hear the tales of *The Iliad* and *The Odyssey* by Homer. She had heard the stories before, but she enjoyed them even more because Bretane read them with all the expression and dramatics of an actor at the fair. He bellowed at the exciting parts and murmured at the quiet ones. He changed his voice for each character, and his wail of the Sirens as they tempted Odysseus was bone chilling.

Every night, she waited until she heard Bretane's window-rattling snore before crawling into the room and kneeling beside Robin's bed. Gently, she kissed his cheek before curling up under the bed to sleep until the sun peeked over the windowsill and shone in her eyes. Then she slipped out the door, so no one discovered she was breaking Bretane's rule about visitors.

During the fourth week when she kissed Robin's cheek, she heard him whisper, "Again."

"Robin!" she whispered back as she touched his now healed lips with her own.

He moved his mouth against hers and lifted his good hand to the back of her head. Grasping her head scarf, he tossed it on the floor and ran his fingers through her hair. "Again," he said, and she obliged.

"Would ye like me to leave ye two alone?" asked a deep voice from the cot.

Both Robin and Suannoch turned toward Bretane.

"Well, I winna! He is still too ill to wrestle with ye. Robin, close yer eyes! Suann, get under the bed and get some sleep."

Suann and Robin smiled at each other and then, after one more kiss, did as they were ordered.

"And, Suann, tomorrow night bring a blanket. Ye have spent too many nights on the cold floor. Do ye hear me?"

"Aye, Laird," said Suann.

Robin's hand fell over the side, and Suann held it until morning when she slid out from under the bed and left.

The next morning Robin demanded a looking glass and a razor be brought to him. "I cannot stand this beard any longer!" He scratched his chin with both hands. "Bretane, will you shave me?"

Bretane said, "Are ye certain ye want to be clean shaven? Ye look like a brawny Scot with the hair on yer face."

"Bretane," said Robin, "I have been clean shaven for as long as I have been in Scotland, and I will be clean shaven for the rest of my life, which, God willing, will be in Scotland."

Robin's first look in the mirror startled him. Could this face looking back at him be his? He had lost considerable weight, and even the beard couldn't hide his sunken cheeks and eye sockets or the green and yellow bruises.

"What have you done to my hair? 'Tis gone on one side, and..." His voice changed from surprise to alarm. "And my ear! What did he do to me?" Very cautiously he touched the jagged edge of his ear. "He sliced it off!"

"It couldna be stitched closed so yer hair had to be cut away," said Bretane. " 'Twill grow back soon enough."

"I look like a half-sheared black sheep!"

"Aye, but 'tis the rest of us ye should pity. We are the ones who have to look at ye!"

Robin tossed back the sheet to examine the rest of his body. His numerous bruises had faded to the same greenish hue as the ones on his face, and most of his cuts and gashes had scabbed over. Last, he gently rubbed his finger over the cut across his cheekbone.

"Ye will wear the scar proudly," announced Bretane. " 'Tis a sign that ye are stronger than whoever wanted to do ye harm. Besides, no one liked looking at yer pretty face. Ye scared the wee bairns!"

Robin laughed, but then grabbed his stomach against the pain that laughter sent through his ribs. "Bretane, please, the razor."

As more days passed in Robin's slow but steady recovery, Bretane made it his mission to find Keenan and see that he suffered for beating Robin nearly to death. Not wanting Robin to overhear, he talked to Henry and Patrick in the hallway in as soft tones as his booming voice allowed.

"No man treats one of mine so sorely without paying the price. Have ye seen any sign of him and his bunch of thieves lately?"

Henry and Patrick told him how they had gone to the site of Keenan's camp only to find it deserted. They told Bretane how the land had been ruined and was now a mass of tree stumps, mud, decaying animal carcasses, and human waste.

Bretane stuck out his chin at this abuse of God's creation. "The Highlands are a gift from our Lord, and 'tis ours to care for. It will take years for this land to be of any use again. Henry, 'tis yer task to restore that land. Make yer plans, what ye think it will cost, and how many men it will take. When Robin is well, show him yer ideas, and if he approves, ye will get it done. *A tuigsinn?* Understand?"

"Aye, Laird!" said Henry.

"Patrick, did ye see Keenan when he came to the house? Will ye ken him on sight?"

"Aye, Laird! He is an ugly *bassa*! He has a red stain covering half his face."

Bretane laughed. "Then he will no' be hard to find. Tell me when and where ye spot him."

Henry interrupted with, "Ye ken that Robin will no' seek revenge himself. He will fight to protect Makgullane, but if he alone is insulted, he will walk away. I have seen it happen. When I wad give the man a punch in the jaw, Robin wadna."

"Do ye think Robin is afeared?" asked Bretane with a harsh glare.

Henry took a step back. "Nay, Laird!" he said. "It takes more mettle to stay silent than to swing a fist."

"Robin is a man of courage and restraint. I, on the other hand, am no' bound by such good manners. I will find Keenan and make him regret the day his *màthair* bore him! Patrick, can ye find him?"

"Aye, Laird!" said Patrick.

Chapter Seven

A few days later, Patrick came to the doorway of Robin's sickroom and knocked softly on the doorjamb. "Laird, I need to talk to ye. Can I come in?"

"Nay," said Bretane, standing from his chair at the desk. "Robin is asleep. The pain in his leg kept him up last night. Thalassa gave him something, and he is finally asleep. Can it wait?"

"Nay, Laird, 'tis verra important."

"All right," grumbled Bretane. "We can talk in the hall, but be quiet. If ye wake him, I will…"

He did not finish his threat. Bretane never finished his threat. He left the punishment to the wrongdoer's imagination, but Patrick knew that whatever it was, he wouldn't like it. Some of the other lads on the estate thought their laird might be a threatening wind and nothing more, but none were willing to risk it. The scar on his face proved that he had fought fiercely in battle, and they feared he might just be prepared to be that fierce again.

"I have found Keenan and some of the Grays," Patrick whispered.

Bretane grabbed his shoulder. "Where, lad? Tell me!"

" 'Tis near to the edge of yer land to the south. It doesna look like he has set up a permanent camp there. More like he wants to stay on the move. They have slept in a couple of places, but didna stay in any of them more than a day or two."

"How do ye ken where he is now?"

"I saw him face to face. We passed them on the road. I turned back later to follow. It wasna yet noon, but they stopped and set up their tents and fires. 'Tis no more than an hour ride from here."

"How many Grays do ye think there are?"

"I counted twenty-two men and ten or twelve women. They had a few bairns with them. Suann said she saw more when she and Robin found their first camp, so there maun be deserters."

Bretane paced the hallway, his hands clasped behind his back. "Keenan is a fool who canna lead men and only another fool wad stay with him. Any man with half a mind wadna trust him for verra long."

He stopped pacing in front of Patrick. "We're no' enough men at Makgullane to attack and conquer the bunch, but I intend to teach Keenan a lesson he willna forget for what he did to Robin."

"We stand with ye, Laird!"

"First, send Ralf into Kirkcaldy again to ask Sheriff Duncan to come see for himself. Mayhap the sheriff can arrest them. I dinna think so, but if trouble comes, we can at least say we tried to do it lawfully. 'Twill be our defense." He chuckled, knowing that what he intended to do had no defense. "Then ready four mounts. Tell Shane and Darby they are coming with us."

"What about Robin? Who will tend him?"

"I will get Marta to sit with him." He paused. "We will hope that he sleeps through until next morn, but send for Fergus just in case. He can help Robin if he has to piss. Robin would ne'er let Marta do it."

"Aye, Laird!"

"I will get all of us weapons. Now be off!"

As Patrick ran off, Bretane peeked in to make certain that Robin still slept, and then he headed to the gathering room at the front of the manor house. On three of the stone walls in the room hung his collection of swords, dirks, and axes that had served him so well in his younger days. He had battled alongside his own clansmen and those of other clans to keep the English out of Scotland, but all he ever gained was the scar along his eye and cheek and the loss of his entire family.

At the age of twelve, he saw his father, Cameron, beheaded by English troops who had called his father out in exchange for the life of his oldest son, Allister, whom they held captive. The soldiers had promised to release eighteen-year-old Allister, but instead when he attempted to stop his father's execution, they cut off his leg and left him to die in the sun.

After seven years of almost continuous fighting, Bretane had come home to heal his wounded face, only to find the land scorched and his mother and two sisters dead of starvation. Then and there he vowed never to take a wife until Scotland was free from the violence and chaos he had lived with his entire life. He continued to fight next to cousin after cousin, comrade after comrade, until they all perished in battle, all except Bretane who came home to claim what remained of Makgullane. He was thirty-two years old, but with the body and the soul of a man much older.

After seeing the last of his kin die in a raid on English soil, he found Robin by the side of the road. Carrying the boy home became Bretane's way of making peace within himself and with a world that had taken so much from him. For the boy's sake, he gave up the sword and began working to settle differences through peaceful and lawful diplomacy. His voice in Edinburgh represented the Highlands in Parliament, and he vowed to do whatever he could to prevent more violence and death and ensure that Robin never again experienced the kind of cruelty that had marked both their childhoods.

However, Keenan Gray did not deserve peaceful negotiation. The man had nearly killed his Robin, and the man would suffer for it!

As the four men from Makgullane approached Gray's encampment, they immediately noticed how quickly the squatters had spoiled the land. Already, they had tramped paths between their dirty and torn tents. The area they used as their pissynghole smelled foul, and they made no attempt to cover it over. It appalled Bretane how apathetic the Grays acted toward their living spaces, appalled him how they abused his Highlands. Aye, his Highlands, and no one had the right to ruin the land he loved!

"Patrick, which one is Keenan Gray?" asked Bretane.

"The man pacing in front of the green tent." Patrick pointed. "Over there, in the red hat, but I saw his face and he is no' a leper."

"Show yer weapons, but keep them down at yer side," said Bretane to his men before he shouted, "Keenan Gray! We are here!" His voice carried across the glen and echoed against the hill beyond. All heads turned in his direction, and an eerie quiet fell over the camp.

Keenan straightened up to see who called him out. He quickly assessed that the Grays outnumbered the intruders, but would the men still with him be able to defeat even these few strangers? Hunger and frustration ran high because of their meager success in collecting the riches he had promised them.

None of his followers knew anything about survival in a rural area. He recruited them from the streets of cities and towns where the hogs had already been butchered, and often already cooked, before they were stolen and eaten, where they could get out of the rain in an alley, an inn, or a tavern instead of shivering in the flimsy tents they had now. It also terrified most of them to sleep in the complete darkness and silence of the Highland sky, enough so that the strongest of Gray's followers abandoned his cause to go back to the city, leaving only the weakest still believing in Keenan's promises of a wealthy future.

"Come closer," shouted Keenan to the men on horseback, "so I can see ye."

"Nay," said Bretane. "We want to talk to ye. Come closer to us." In a low rumble, he added, "If ye dare." The implied cowardice of that phrase often encouraged the enemy to make rash mistakes in anger.

Keenan ducked into his tent and stepped back into the open with his sword in his hand. "Follow me, lads," he said to the ones nearest. "We will see what these lubberworts want."

At first, none of the others made a move. "They want to talk to ye, no' us," said one.

"They are armed," added a second man.

"They look ready for a fight," said another.

Keenan faced his men and shook his fist. "They are

farmers, no' soldiers! Their swords are just for show. They said they want to talk, and talking is all they will do! Follow me!" When no one moved, he hissed out the words, "Move with me, or I will run ye through meself!" Waving his sword in their direction, he added, "No food for cowards who dinna follow me now!"

Seven of the hungriest Grays reluctantly picked up their dirks and trudged behind Keenan until they stood about ten yards away from their visitors.

"What do ye want to talk about?" asked Keenan.

Bretane, Shane, and Patrick dismounted and dropped the reins, knowing that their well-trained horses would stay in place until the men mounted again. Darby had been told to stay on his mount until Bretane signaled him.

Bretane said, "Do ye ken how my man got beaten to a bloody pulp more than a fortnight ago? Do ye ken who might have done the monstrous deed?"

"We have heard naught about a man being trounced, have we, lads?"

"Nay," they said in unison, but their barely controlled laughter gave them away. Two had the good sense to hide their faces, but the others just opened their mouths and let out loud guffaws.

"They sliced off his ear," said Bretane. His voice stayed steady but threatening. "Mayhap ye ken the gutless louts who wad waylay a man alone and then take a trophy like his ear. Mayhap some of ye wad like to try yer hand when the numbers are evened up, mayhap us four against, let me see, how many of ye are there?" He pointed at each man as if counting. "I see that there are no real men among ye. This will no' be a fair fight. There are four of us and none of ye."

The laughter stopped.

Bretane swung his sword at Keenan, lopping off his red hat. On that signal, Patrick and Shane charged at the others, who turned and ran as fast as they could back toward the tents. Patrick stabbed two of them on their backsides with his dirk. He only pierced the skin, but it would still make sitting uncomfortable for a long while. Shane lifted one up by his tunic and sliced the garment apart while the now naked man kept running. Darby kicked his horse into a gallop to trample through the tents, collapsing each one and poking his sword at anyone who came too close.

Bretane did not intend to be so lenient with Keenan, whom he now held in place with the point of his sword at the man's neck.

"Now we can talk privately," Bretane said with a stony expression. "Ye are naught but a sharg, the runt of the litter, a weakling afeared to stand alone and face what he has coming."

Keenan gasped for air as he dropped his sword. "Ye wadna kill an unarmed man."

"Aye, but I wad," snarled Bretane. He drew the blade across Keenan's neck, leaving a shallow yet bleeding cut in his skin.

Keenan swallowed his scream.

"Now hold out yer arm," said Bretane. When Keenan hesitated, he repeated louder, "Hold out yer arm!" When Keenan obeyed, Bretane left another cut on his forearm that would eventually heal but would always be a reminder of Bretane's strength.

"Lift yer tunic!" demanded Bretane. This time Keenan complied, only to feel the sword slice another painful but superficial cut across his belly. This time he screamed.

"My name is Bretane of Makgullane. If ye ever do harm to any of mine again, I will follow ye to the ends of the earth and my next cuts will be deeper…and deadly. I want ye all off my land by nightfall! Do ye hear?"

As Keenan turned to run, Bretane swatted him on his backside with the flat side of his sword. Keenan yelped and kept running.

Hugh watched all of this from a safe distance, not because he feared Bretane's revenge, but because he didn't want to hide his wide grin.

****

Everyone knew about Robin's first trip out of his sickroom to eat in the kitchen, and they gathered around the massive table to wait for him. When he hobbled in, leaning heavily on the cane Bretane had carved for him, the crowd cheered.

He smiled and waved them silent. "Have you never seen a three-legged man before?" Laughter and hearty words of greeting sounded as he sat heavily in a chair at the end of the table.

Marta set a heaping bowl of warmed oatbread covered with melted cheese in front of him. "I am sorry 'tis no' heartier, but Thalassa ordered simple food for three more days to see how yer stomach handles it."

" 'Tis just fine," said Robin as the first spoonful touched his lips. "I am tired of porridge and mashed turnips. 'Tis delicious. So, what has been going on since Bretane and Thalassa locked me in the bedroom for no reason whatsoever?"

"Darby's been doing a fine job managing the estate in yer stead," said Patrick, clapping Darby on the back.

"All the sheep got sheared and the fleeces sold for a tidy profit, thanks to him working us nearly to death. It did make him mighty grumpy, though, and we will all be happier when ye're back in charge!"

"No one will be happier than me!" said Darby with a grin. He waved his hand around the room. "These are a lazy bunch of slackers who dinna hop fast enough to do my bidding!" The crowd booed with the same lightheartedness until Darby said seriously, "Robin, will Laird Bretane let me visit ye to tell ye what has been going on while ye have been sick? I need to ken what ye think we should do. 'Tis a big job, and I could use yer help."

Before Robin could answer, Bretane entered the kitchen and ordered, "Back to work, all of ye! Let the lad eat his meal in peace. Marta, where is my food?"

"Right here, Laird." She set a bowl of oatbread and cheese in front of him.

"What is this? 'Tis not a fit meal for a man!"

Marta grinned along with everyone still standing around the table. "Thalassa says ye're to eat what Robin eats so he doesna get jealous. She says ye are to set the example."

Bretane scowled and growled under his breath to Robin, "Lad, ye're trouble. Ye always have been." He put a hearty spoonful into his mouth. "Now back to work, all of ye!"

Robin motioned for Darby to come closer. "Come this afternoon. I will make sure Bretane lets you in."

Darby nodded and left with the others, all except Marta and Glynnis who set to washing the pots and getting the food ready for the next meal. No one noticed Suann crouching in the corner by the door.

"So, lad," asked Bretane when he finished his bowl, "is yer stomach taking to this wretched meal?"

Marta shook her spoon at him.

"Aye," Robin said.

"I have something to say," interrupted Glynnis.

"Nay, ye dinna!" snapped Marta. "Fetch me more water to heat over the fire."

"No' until I talk to Laird Bretane and Robin!"

Both Robin and Bretane put down their spoons and looked at Glynnis.

Bretane had dealt with many complaints from Glynnis before, and he didn't look forward to this one. "Well, what is it?" he asked.

Glynnis's face blushed a bright red. "I…dinna think ye will like my news, but it maun be told and it maun be made right. Laird Bretane, ye maun make it right," she began.

Neither Bretane nor Robin responded.

Marta stood beside Glynnis and took her by the arm. "Ye shouldna be doing this. 'Tis no' right."

"They will find out soon enough," said Glynnis, shaking off Marta's grip. " 'Twill be now." She sucked in a deep breath and said all in one gasp, "I am bairned. I have missed my curse for two months." She took a quick breath, and added, "The *athair* is Robin."

"Nay!" exclaimed Robin.

"Aye, 'tis ye. Ye maun make it right. Ye maun marry me."

Robin put his head in his hands, and when he straightened up again, he saw Suannoch standing in the corner, her hands balled into tight fists. She stared at him for a brief moment before darting out the door and away from the kitchen.

"Suann!" he called. He tried to stand and go after her, but the sudden exertion proved too much for his still-weakened body, and his legs buckled beneath him. "Suann!"

"Let her go," said Bretane. Putting his arms around his ward, he all but carried Robin back to his bed.

Glynnis followed them the whole way down the hall, demanding to know what they intended to do about her situation. "Ye canna leave me to have a bairn alone. 'Tis Robin's duty to wed and give the bairn his name! Dinna walk away from me!"

Once he set Robin on the bed, Bretane turned his fury on the girl. "Get out! We winna forget what ye have told us, as much as we wad like to! Go away! Robin and I will talk about it. Now leave!"

She cowered at his voice and dipped her head, but she lingered in the doorway. "Ye can send me away now, but after Robin and I are wed, I will no' be yer servant. And ye will no' send me away again! Do ye hear me? Ne'er again!"

Bretane stamped his foot, and Glynnis darted out of sight.

"It cannot be true!" said Robin, his hand holding his now-throbbing head. "I have not been with her since…I cannot remember how long ago. I have lost all track of time in here. Please, God, it cannot be true."

"No decision will be made until ye are better, but if what she says is true, then ye willna have much choice. We canna let her shame Makgullane."

Robin turned his face away from Bretane and let out his breath slowly. "There is something else I have to tell you," he said in his low still raspy voice. "Before the attack on the road…Suannoch and I…we declared our love and…pledged ourselves to each other. We…we made love." He turned back to his guardian, his face twisted with grief. "Suann and I are pledged, and nothing will keep us apart! Please, Bretane, you must see that I cannot, I will not, marry Glynnis!"

"I had hoped ye and Suann wad see for yerselves that yer friendship had grown into something more, but this news from Glynnis changes everything. Ye dinna have a choice now. As much as ye, and I, wish it to be different, ye dinna have a choice. If there is a bairn."

Without waiting for Robin to speak, Bretane sat down in the rocking chair by the window and opened the book on the nearby table. "We will see how Homer finishes his tale." He began to read aloud.

Robin closed his eyes and leaned back on the pillow. "Please, send for Suann. I have to talk to her."

"Later. For now, rest. Let yer heart and hers settle down."

For the next few days, Robin did anything but settle down. He took his daily walk through the halls and even briefly in the yard, all the while begging Bretane to find Suann and bring her to him, but Bretane remained insistent. "Ye both need more time. I will speak to Glynnis and bring ye the news, but that is all I will do."

Chaotic thoughts raced through Robin's mind, but overriding them all was his need to talk to Suann. Together, they could sort this out. She'd always been able to make him see the right of things, to help him come to grips with his emotions, and to ease his troubled feelings. With her on his side, he could deal with whatever difficulties arose.

But the bairn Glynnis carried destroyed everything.

He and Suann had pledged themselves to each other, and now they would forever be apart, separated by a woman he couldn't love and by an innocent child who needed him. Still, he had to see Suann. He had to make her understand that he would never love, truly love, anyone but her for the rest of his life.

Suann did not sleep under Robin's bed that night, and when Robin awoke he found his half of their coin on the floor where her head should have been. He now had a broken coin to match his broken heart.

Bretane helped him get dressed that morning, handing him a rough woven work shirt, a plaid, and socks. Before Robin could protest and demand trews, Bretane said, "Lad, if I am the one dressing ye, then I am the one who decides what ye will wear. 'Tis time ye wore clothes fitting for the Scot that ye are."

Robin looked at him askance.

"Then the Scot ye have become!"

Robin fingered the plaid. The plaid represented more than just clothing to him. Wearing it meant that he would be leaving behind everything English. He could easily renounce his poverty-stricken childhood, but it also meant he would be leaving his mother and younger siblings. He didn't know if he could do that. Then he remembered he could keep them close with the embossed metal token in his pouch.

He said, "If I am to put this on, you will have to show me how to do it."

Bretane patiently taught Robin how to fold and gather the yards of material and secure the plaid around his waist. With Robin finally dressed, Bretane handed Robin his cane and grinned, saying, "Yer meal is in the kitchen, me fine-looking Highlander, so off we go, lad."

"I feel dizzy," said Robin, dropping quickly onto the bed, "and my leg hurts. Could you bring my food in here? Just for this morning?"

Bretane curled his lip. "Ye wadna be thinking of running off, wad ye?"

"Nay, Laird," said Robin. "I would not get very far, not with the way this leg is aching." He rubbed his right calf vigorously.

"All right, just for today. Ye make yer way to the desk, and I will bring yer food. Ye can eat there."

No sooner had Bretane disappeared down the hall than Robin hobbled in the opposite direction to the back door of the manor house. He turned and started making his way behind the house when suddenly Bretane appeared at the opposite corner with his arms crossed on his chest. "Ye maun think me doitit, lad. I will carry ye back into bed if I have to."

"I am begging you! I have to talk to Suannoch. I cannot let this stay between us any longer! I have to tell her—"

"And what will ye tell her? That ye left a bairn in another woman? That she maun learn to live without ye? Do ye think she will be happy about it?"

"Nay, but I have to see her!"

Bretane took Robin by the shoulders. "She is gone, lad."

"What do you mean? Where?" asked Robin, his heart pounding both from the exertion and from the news that she had left Makgullane.

"Thalassa winna tell me. She said 'twas a secret place."

Robin hung his head. "I know the place, but I cannot get there by myself, at least not yet. Take me back to your room. She will be safe until I am well enough to go to her."

Robin worked relentlessly to get his strength back. He ate whatever Marta offered and demanded more. He doubled the times and the distances he walked, and when Bretane found him exhausted and forced him to bed, Robin pulled himself up to a sitting position in as many varied ways as he could think of. If he could not walk to her, he would crawl! Every night he looked under the bed, hoping to find Suann, but she did not come.

One week later, two letters arrived for Bretane. One had been written perhaps weeks ago, and the other more recently. News traveled slowly across the rugged hills of the Highlands.

He conveyed the contents of the first letter with enthusiasm to a gathering of the people of Makgullane. "Our sixteen-year-old King James V has been delivered from captivity and assumed control of the monarchy of Scotland under his own hand! The family Douglas that held him captive for all these years has been exiled and all their lands confiscated."

"How did he escape?" shouted someone.

" 'Tis no' entirely clear, but after two attempts to free him that ended disastrously, it appears he simply rode away with two servants. Some of his guards, the twenty footmen who daily scoured the park for two miles around every time the king went outside, are suspected of being complicit, but now that the Douglases are banished, they will be free from retribution."

"Now we have a real king!"

Bretane continued. "The young king appears to be

more than ready to take command of his government and is already issuing edicts to control the unrest, especially in the Border Marches. However, it will take time for him to hold complete power. He maun learn how to run a kingdom and learn who he can trust for good advice and counsel. All indications are that he is determined to do so."

"Long live the king!"

He shared the second missive privately with Robin in his room. "Lad, ye maun hear this news so ye can be prepared."

Robin let out his breath slowly, dreading that this news could only make his problems worse. "Tell me."

"Angus Gladstone has written that he will be arriving within the month to claim Suannoch as his bride. He has waited long enough. He will be traveling with his uncle, and they will be returning to Stirling after he and Suann are wed."

Robin choked back the lump in his throat. "Does Suann know?"

"I have told Thalassa, who I am certain will tell Suannoch. Lad, ye maun face the fact that when ye and Glynnis wed, Suann will be free to take Angus as her guidman as arranged over two months ago. Angus postponed his coming because ye were hurt, but he canna wait any longer."

Robin stayed silent for a long time. How had his life gotten so out of control? Since coming to Scotland, it had been orderly, and except for the occasional misadventure, he could predict exactly what he would be doing every single day. His life had gone just as he planned it ever since he reached manhood. It had gone just as he needed it to be.

But after he and Suann had opened their true hearts to each other, his life had scattered into a thousand pieces. When they argued over Glynnis, he reacted in the cave in a way he could never have imagined he would, but she had forgiven him, and he thought they would live in the sunshine together for the rest of their lives. Then he had been beaten near to death by worthless strangers, and now Glynnis carried his child.

Nothing would ever change that his heart belonged to Suann wholly and completely. She lived in his soul. His actions toward Glynnis, however, which he previously thought had little or no consequence, had dug his grave and covered it over, and his guilt stood on it like a lonely tombstone.

Suannoch would marry the man from Stirling, and Robin would never see her again. He didn't know how he would cope with that, but somehow he would find a way to move through his days while staying devoted to Suann until the moment he stood at Heaven's door.

Late one evening, he said to Bretane, "I must find Suann. I am going to her tomorrow, and you will not stop me."

Her soft voice came from the doorway. "No need to find me. I am here."

Chapter Eight

Robin got to his feet as best he could and started to limp over to her, but Suann put up her hand to stop him before he had taken two steps.

She cocked her head with interest. "Ye're wearing a plaid. Bretane must be pleased." Her expression immediately turned sour. "I am here to tell ye that the man from Stirling is coming, and unless he is a wart-covered toad with wings, I will be his wife. I will leave Makgullane with him."

He had never seen her looking so beautiful and so sad at the same time. "Please, Suann, we have to talk."

"Nay, we dinna. Ye want to tell me how sorry ye are, but it wad do no good. We both regret many things, I as much as ye. What I regret most is that Glynnis will be yer choice."

"She is not my choice!" Robin nearly shouted. Why couldn't she see his agony? He no more wanted Glynnis than he wanted to be beaten again by Keenan Gray. Suann had his heart, and he carried her coin as a sign of his devotion to her and only her!

"But ye did choose to bed her, and now she will have ye as her guidman. But dinna worry about me, Robin, I winna be alone."

"Please listen, Suann. I love you! Here, take back your coin so I will know that you still love me." He took the half coin from the nearby table and held it up.

"Nay, I canna carry yer coin. Ye may say the words, and ye may feel it in yer heart, but it canna be. Love for us is over. It has to be. Yer first duty is to her bairn. Ye are his *athair.* We will both live with that, ye here at Makgullane and me in Stirling."

"This is not how I want it!" pleaded Robin.

A tear dripped down her cheek. "I tried to find some peace at the secret cave, but I couldna. If I wasna crying, I paced the floor. I couldna sleep through my nightmares, nightmares of ye, Robin, of ye dying in my arms. I couldna bear it!" Her last words came out in a wet, choking sob. "My heart can only heal if I am far away. Good-bye, Robin."

"Suann!" called Robin. "Come back!" He took a couple of steps toward the door, but soon realized that he could not run after her. He hadn't the strength in his legs.

He slumped on the bed. His actions had crushed their love. His behavior toward Glynnis had been at the very least selfish and at the worst reckless. He had tried to drown his loneliness and frustration in her bed with no thought that she might think it meant something more or that he might have to pay a price. He had used Glynnis as a substitute for the woman he really wanted. He'd been a fool in so many ways! Now he had to live with the aftermath. Suann would disappear from his life, and Glynnis would be in it whether he liked it or not, and he had to decide how he could live with both.

Being forced to abide by other people's decisions frustrated him beyond bearing. Keenan Gray decided to beat him. Glynnis declared she carried his child, followed by Bretane telling him that he had no choice but to marry her. Finally, Suann decided to abandon him and marry another. Somehow, some way, he had to regain control of his life. The choices had to be his!

The beating, his painful recovery, and the loss of the woman he loved had thrown him back into the relentless confusion that had been his childhood. He had never fully regained his composure after the turmoil of the day when he and Suann had professed their love or from the vicious attack by the Grays that had forced his mind to shut down so his body could heal. But no more. He resolved to take back his life.

Stretching out on the pillows, he arranged his thoughts and organized his future. What did he want? What did he need?

When he had made his decisions, he said to Bretane, "Send for Glynnis."

Glynnis appeared in the doorway while Robin stood beside the bed, his face grim.

"Robin, I have ne'er seen you in a plaid. Ye look wonderful!" she said. "We have so much to talk about."

She started toward him, but he put up his hand to stop her just as Suann had done to him. Then, straightening his shoulders, he looked her directly in the eye. "Hear what I have to say, Glynnis. Bretane is here to witness my words so there is no misunderstanding."

Bretane stayed seated at the desk with his back to the couple.

"I will marry you," said Robin.

Glynnis clapped her hands. "Robin, I will make ye so happy."

"But it will be in name only. We will not live together or in any other way be husband and wife."

"But Robin," she begged.

"Do not speak. You and the child will have my

name and my protection, but that is all of mine you will have. I will raise the child as a good father should, but I will not be a husband to you. I will have a house built for you and the child, but I will never visit there except to fetch the child. It will be no secret that we married only for the sake of the child."

"Robin, ye dinna mean that. Ye love me!"

"I do not love you. I will call the priest when it is time for us to wed. Now leave me, and do not come back." He immediately turned his back on her.

She wailed and sobbed. "Ye dinna mean it! Ye canna do this to me!"

Walking over to her, Bretane put his hands on her shoulders. "Robin has said his piece, and ye have heard it. Now 'tis time for ye to leave."

"How can he be so cruel?" she cried, peering around Bretane as he held her firm. "He has used me for his own pleasure, and he has left me with a bairn. How can he forsake me? I winna let him. He is mine. Do ye hear me? Mine!" She pounded her fists on Bretane's chest.

"Ye have to go, Glynnis. Ye have what ye want. Ye will be wed. The bairn winna be a bastard, and ye winna be a shamed woman. 'Tis the best it will be."

"Please, Robin, ye are shaming me. Everyone will ken. Ye love me. I ken that ye do! Ye laid with me over and over."

He could not look at her. His voice turned ice cold. "Aye, I did but not for love. I am sorry for that. 'Tis my fault for not being more careful about how I spilled my seed, and I will endure the result. You will be wed."

"Ye canna treat me like this. I hate ye! I hate ye!"

Slowly, Bretane turned her around and forced her

out the door. She screamed all the way back to the kitchen, "I hate ye!" After turning the sobbing girl over to Marta, Bretane returned to the bedroom.

"Ye were verra hard on her, and she didna deserve it," Bretane said. "She may not be a woman ye can care for, but she didna plant the bairn herself. Ye did."

In a voice as forlorn as the last fallen leaf of autumn, Robin said, "Are you ashamed of me? For what I have done?"

"Nay, lad, no' ashamed. I am worried and concerned."

"I am sorry," said Robin. "There is naught else I can say except that I am sorry."

"She will behave better when she sees that this is the only way," said Bretane, placing his hand on his ward's own hand. "None of this will be pleasant, but ye are doing what maun be done. A man is free to bed a woman, but he isna free to give her a bairn because the bairn doesna have a choice. Ye have made choices for Glynnis and for the bairn, and now ye maun live with both. Ye understand that, do ye, lad?"

"I will do right by the child and wed Glynnis because it is the only thing I can do. Do you understand that?"

Bretane nodded.

****

It took two weeks for Keenan to live down the shame of being cut and humiliated by Bretane, but through his usual bullying and cajoling, he convinced the remaining fifteen men and five women that they still had the right and the strength to take whatever they wanted.

"Good riddance!" he said of the ones who had

deserted his cause. "They are without a vision for what can be ours! Ye saw that this laird didna kill me. He only threatened, and a hollow threat at that. I am no worse for his visit!"

He lifted his tunic, exposing a still raw cut that pained him greatly every time he moved, but he gritted his teeth and spoke loudly. "See, he could have gutted me, but he didna. Naught but talk. A jessie, a coward, and a milksop. No' a man of action. But we will take action."

"He will kill us!" shouted a man.

"No' if we are smart. I have a plan to claim what we are due, what we deserve. The rich have kept us low so they can look down on us from their lofty nests, nests that could be ours. We will have ours. Are ye ready to live like the high and mighty?"

His followers did not respond as enthusiastically as he hoped, but it still gave him enough cheek to plot how to teach Bretane a lesson without risking another visit from the man.

Hugh sat at a distance from the group and listened intently to every word Keenan said. If he wanted to foil any attempts by Keenan to hurt Robin again, he had to be focused and careful. He must not forget any details of the plan so he could do whatever he had to do to make certain that Keenan would fail.

Clouds covered the moon on the first night the Grays visited Makgullane with mischief on their minds. These thieves and beggars had been taught all their lives how to get in and out of places without being caught. That skill kept them alive and out of prison, so it turned out to be laughably easy to get around the inexperienced men patrolling Makgullane.

They chose a flock of Makgullane sheep grazing on a hill to the east as their first target. As usual several of the lame-brained animals had wandered out of sight of the young shepherd watching the flock. The boy dozed peacefully since only an occasional wolf who howled a warning first ever passed by, not men creeping silently.

It took but a minute to hoist a sheep over the shoulder of a man and carry it off after a quick tying of a rag around the snout stopped any fearful bleating. Seven sheep went missing that night. Hugh pulled dark-blue threads from the lining of his vest and tied them around a low bush near where the sheep had been taken, hoping someone would notice and understand what his message meant.

Two nights later, the men sneaked into the Makgullane barn, stable, and shed to steal hoes, shovels, and scythes. Ronald earned himself a hard cuff on the head from Tinker when two of the hoes he carried off clanked together. Again, Hugh tugged off threads and tied them to the hooks where the tools had been.

Another night, the Grays liberated several chickens from the coop along with any eggs still in the nests. Hugh's vest now split open in several places along the seams where he had ripped out threads, so he used his knife to cut small pieces off the hem to leave in the chicken nests.

The next time the Grays raided, they didn't take anything. They left something instead. In several visible places around the outbuildings, the men lifted their plaids and deposited what they could in foul-smelling piles.

Hugh did not leave any blue material that night. It disgusted him too much.

Chapter Nine

During the weeks before Angus Gladstone and his uncle came to claim Suann, Robin strived to get his life back in order. Even though he didn't have full use of his broken fingers and he continued to limp, he returned to his duties as reeve of the estate. First, he reviewed with Darby all the things the young man had accomplished in his absence, and, after listening to Darby's report, Robin decided that things had gone well, very well. He also decided that Darby had earned a promotion from laborer to assistant reeve, which pleased Darby to no end.

Robin also moved back into his own room in the corner of the storage barn. When he turned eighteen years old, he had decided a man needed to have his own place, a private place that belonged to him alone. So, he set to work and built a twelve-by sixteen-foot room into the south corner of the barn.

After framing in the necessary two walls into the corner of the barn and setting in a door, Robin held his first gathering in his new room. In exchange for food, drink, and good company, he invited everyone on the estate to take turns tramping around on his dirt floor until it was hard and firm. Marta fed everyone who arrived to stomp through the space in circles while talking and singing. It took three days and a nearly constant flow of people, but finally the floor was ready, and a good time had been had by all.

Since he would continue to take all his meals in the manor house, he needed only a stone slab large enough to hold a small fire for heating the room in the coldest months. He also cut two openings into the outer wall to let in more light, which were easy enough to cover with woolen blankets if need be to keep out the wind. He furnished his new room with a cot, a table, and a chair, all of which he built himself. It was small and sparse, but it was his!

Now eager to get back to the familiar space, he opened the door to discover that his room had been thoroughly cleaned and redecorated. A full-sized bed and new bedding, including an intricately designed and colorful quilt, had replaced the cot. New more colorful blankets hung at his windows, and a woven rug replaced the rush mats in front of the bed and table.

A large lantern hung from the ceiling with two other smaller ones placed on shelves against the walls. He would no longer need to squint to read or do his figures by his one small light.

His jaw fell open at what he saw in the middle of the room. His handmade table had been moved to the back wall to accommodate a large desk, the one from Bretane's upstairs study. "Darby, really?" he gasped. Bretane's most prized possession was now his!

He rubbed his hand along the smooth edge, remembering how he had leaned against it for his punishment when he was fourteen, and he opened a drawer, remembering how Bretane had sat beside him and patiently taught him how to keep the records for Makgullane.

"Who did this?" he asked Darby, who had a big

grin on his face.

"I have no idea. Mayhap 'twas the fairies." The grin never left.

"Fairies! Well, you tell the fairies that I said, 'Thank you very much.' "

"Do ye like it?"

"I do. Now tell me how you have prepared for any mischief Keenan Gray and his gang might bring to us."

Darby filled him in on all the plans that the men with Suann's guidance had made, and Robin again approved.

The next day in the middle of the afternoon, Robin sat at his desk going over accounts when young Fergus burst in. "Ye maun come, sir! He has been hurt!" the boy cried in his high-pitched voice.

"Who has been hurt?"

"The man on the road. His name is Jamie. He is bloodied, and they took his cloak and his boots! I canna carry him. Ye maun come!"

Robin quickly closed his books and pushed back his chair to follow the boy. "Where exactly did you find this man?" he asked as they trotted down the road leading away from Makgullane.

"On the road, in the bushes. Just sitting there verra quiet. I asked his name and if he needed help, and he said, 'Aye.' I said I wad get ye."

"You did the right thing, Fergus."

"He is over there." The boy pointed to a tall hedge of thorny bushes where, right in the middle, waited a young man with flaming red hair, a narrow face, and blue eyes. Just as Fergus had said, he just sat there, not moving or making a sound. Dressed only in a long thin undershirt and barefoot, he looked to be not yet twenty and he seemed helpless to escape his predicament.

"Let me help you, Jamie," said Robin, taking the young man by the arm and lifting him out of the bushes. Fergus tugged at Jamie's shirt until the thorns holding the material loosened and set him free.

"Ye are most kind," replied Jamie in a delicate accent indicating an educated, upper-class upbringing. "I seem to have had some trouble."

"What happened?"

"Robbers attacked me, a most raggedy bunch of thieves, although two of them wore elegant silk coats. They jumped out of the bushes and dragged me off my horse. They didna ask for my coin, just pulled me to the ground."

"Did one of them have a red stain on his face?" asked Robin.

"Aye, he did. Do ye ken these men?"

"I am afraid I do."

Jamie shook his head and kept talking. "They stripped off my cloak and overshirt and fought over who would pull my boots right off my feet. Then the one with the red stain stomped on my ankle for no purpose. I didna fight them. I wad gladly give up my clothes and my horse to avoid a beating. Such things can be quite easily replaced. One kept shouting, 'Remember Gray Kee! Remember Gray Kee!' "

"I think you mean Keenan Gray. He is the leader, and he is cruel just for the pleasure of it."

The boy's eyes widened with alarm. "One of them grabbed me by the ear and waved his knife in front of my face. Then the lad came by, shouting and carrying on, so the man let me go and pushed me into the bushes. Ye rescued me, lad," he said to Fergus.

Robin brushed back the hair on both sides of the young man's head. "Fergus, you came just in time. Jamie's ear is unharmed."

"Oh my!" exclaimed Jamie, covering his ear with his hand. "Why wad he want to slice my ear?"

"We have had a great deal of trouble with the Grays around here lately. They are trying to establish themselves as a new gang of Border reivers in this eastern edge of the Highlands. Keenan Gray's trademark is taking the ears of anyone who opposes him." Robin scraped back his hair to expose his own torn ear.

Jamie gulped. " 'Tis a horrible thing! I am doubly thankful to ye, lad."

Fergus's smile showed the nub of one of his four missing front teeth that had started to grow back in.

Robin said, "Makgullane is not far from here. I can take you back to my room and get you some help. Would that be all right?"

"Aye, it wad." Jamie leaned heavily on Robin, limping from what appeared to be a badly sprained, if not broken, ankle. "I thank ye for yer help, but I am curious as to why an Englishman is in this lonely part of the Highlands. Yer accent is English, is it no'?"

Robin nodded, but Fergus answered the question with his usual enthusiasm. "Robin has been here all me life, and we dinna care that he is a Sassenach. He lets me work in the stables. I earn a penny every day!"

"A whole penny? Are ye a good worker?"

"I am! If I am no' then Robin will be angry." He added very seriously, "And ye dinna want Robin to be angry!"

"I will remember that," said Jamie with a wink at

the man who practically carried him. "I can be verra good when I want to be."

After reaching Robin's room in the back of the barn, Robin helped Jamie to the bed and said, "Fergus, go fetch Thalassa. Tell her that a man is hurt."

But as Fergus opened the door to leave, there stood Thalassa. "Hallo, Fergus. Is Robin about? I want to check on him."

"Aye, he is!" said Fergus. "I found a man on the road. He is hurt, so me and Robin brought him back here!"

"Did ye now?" Thalassa quickly crossed the room. With no word of greeting or introduction, she ran her fingers over Jamie's swollen ankle. "How did this happen, lad?"

He sucked in his breath when she touched a tender spot. "Robbers did the deed."

Thalassa said, "No doubt the Grays. The same ones who nearly beat Robin to death well over a month ago. Ye are lucky they only stomped yer ankle. What about yer ear?"

"I still have my ear," said Jamie. "I see ye survived their beating, Robin. Did they give ye the scar on yer face, as well?"

Robin ran his finger along the line on his cheek. "The missing ear and this scar are the least of what they gave me, but I can live with both. Thanks to Thalassa, I am well in every way that matters. Still a little stiff, but overall none the worse for wear."

"Are there many of these bandits in this part of Scotland?"

"Aye," said Robin. "There has been no strong king to keep them restricted for years. The March Wardens do their best, but they cannot be everywhere. The Border reivers like Johnnie Armstrong or Adam Scott, the one they call 'The King of Thieves,' do most of their mischief south of Edinburgh. Not much trouble around here until now, but the news is that King James has taken back his throne. Mayhap he will do something about it."

"Mayhap he will," said Jamie. "These men are a threat to his crown. 'Twill take a strong hand. I hope he will be up to it. Are ye a physician?" he asked Thalassa.

"She is better than any physician I have met," said Robin. "You can trust her."

Jamie nodded. "So, do ye think 'tis broken? 'Tis verra painful."

After declaring it only badly sprained, Thalassa placed a poultice over the ankle and wrapped it tightly with strips of torn cloth. "Ye will need to stay off it for a few days. Robin, are ye willing to keep him here?"

"Aye," said Robin. "I can pull out my old cot and sleep on it. You can share in my food. Marta always sends too much. Jamie, you are welcome here until you are ready to leave."

"I am most grateful," said Jamie. "Most grateful." He made a slight bow from his sitting position.

Jamie proved to be just the distraction Robin needed. Caring for the young man gave him something else to think about besides the heartache of losing Suann, which would certainly last for the rest of his life. Robin nursed Jamie by helping him wash, bringing him food, and changing his dressing at Thalassa's instruction. Since Jamie had no interest in leaving Robin's room, and because it took all of Robin's still weakened energy to complete his chores around the estate and then do things for his guest, Robin never thought to bring people in to meet him. Every night, he collapsed on his cot in a thankfully dreamless sleep.

The workings of the estate fascinated Jamie. Obviously he had not had any experience on an operational farm, so the very basics of growing crops and taking care of animals needed to be explained to him. Intrigued by the variety of seeds Robin showed him, Jamie sorted them into various groups, such as ones that grew into trees or bushes, ones that grew under the ground, and ones that became flowers. He challenged himself to recognize each seed by name and when it needed to be planted and harvested. He asked about the growing times of the crops and how much a bushel would bring at the market, often hobbling over to the window to observe the hogs and chickens in the yard. He made Robin explain exactly what happened before an animal got to his table as food, even though he cringed at the parts that involved killing and then dressing them.

" 'Tis most cruel to eat them," he exclaimed, "although they do taste bloody good!"

But how Robin kept the accounts interested him the most. He wanted to learn how to do orderly and balanced bookkeeping and insisted that Robin show him which column each tally should go in. He studied the pages of the ledger, absorbing everything he could about how to prepare a budget and how to manage expenses and income. Some days when Robin came in from working he found Jamie sitting on the bed with the records all around him, studying them page by page.

"I will put them back in the right order," Jamie assured him, and much to Robin's relief, he always did.

Hoping to keep Jamie out of his paperwork, Robin asked, "May I bring you a book to read when I am gone? Laird Bretane has a large collection."

"I wad like that. History particularly interests me, military history if ye have it, but anything will be fine. I havena had much opportunity to read verra many books. Do ye have any poetry?"

Robin delivered six books the next day, including two recently published books of poetry entitled *The Ploughman's Tale* and *The Palice of Honour*. Within two days, Jamie had read them all and asked for more. Robin gladly obliged.

Fergus appeared every day after working in the stable to spend time with his man, as he called Jamie.

Jamie enjoyed having a playmate as much as Fergus did. Fergus taught Jamie the game of hazard using the dice he always carried in his pouch. He explained the rules slowly and carefully, as Jamie had no experience playing games of chance, which Fergus found very strange. He'd been playing games like this for as long as he could remember.

" 'Tis verra easy to learn," Fergus said. "I will be the first caster, and I will throw the dice. That number is me main, so then ye will bet on how ye think I will do on the next roll. Then I throw again. If I roll my main, I win and nick all bets. But if I roll a two or a three, then I lose, and I maun match yer bet. If any other number comes up, then that is my chance, and I get to roll again. If I roll the chance, then I win; but if me main comes up again, I lose. Do ye understand?"

"I think so," said Jamie. "What will we bet with? I have no coin. As a matter of fact, I have ne'er had any coin. If I lose, I canna pay ye back."

"We can play with rocks. The older lads play for coin, but my *màthair* wad thrash me silly if she thought I risked my money. 'Tis too hard earned."

Jamie proved a quick learner, and after a week, he had a much larger collection of stones than Fergus.

Jamie then taught Fergus another game, called hundreds, that did not involve any wagering. He said he had always played it with numbers that players kept in their heads, never with dice, but the dice worked very well for the game. Each player took turns tossing the dice and adding the results of the spots. The first one to one hundred won the game. At first Fergus balked at all the numbers, but when Jamie explained that Fergus could use this technique to add up the pennies he earned, he became much more eager to play. He soon could add the numbers faster in his head than Jamie did, or at least that is what Jamie led him to believe.

Fergus also delighted in telling his new friend some of the jokes he heard from the older workers. "Here is one Darby told me." While telling the tale, he acted it out, much to Jamie's delight.

"A king went to ride off on a quest," said Fergus as he galloped around the room. "Before he leaves, he locks up the queen with a chastity belt and calls in his best knight and hands him the key."

Putting his hands on his hips and standing with his legs apart, Fergus said in the deepest voice he could muster, "He says to the knight, 'Here is the key to my queen's honor. Should I fall in battle, 'tis for ye to release her from her belt so she might marry again.' "

Galloping around the room again, he said, "Then he leaves on his quest. At the top of a hill, he is surprised to see the knight riding after him as fast as he can. The knight shouts, 'My lord, my lord, wait! Ye have given me the wrong key!' "

Jamie laughed until Fergus scrunched up his face and said, "I dinna understand. Why didna the king give the knight the right key?"

That made Jamie laugh even harder. " 'Tis a verra bawdy joke, and 'tis a thing ye will ken when ye're older!"

Jamie, a thin lad, fattened up on Marta's food, or, as he called it, plain cooking. " 'Tis no' so sweet and soft as what they usually give me. It gives a person something to chew on, and I find that I prefer ale over wine. Could ye have Marta write down her recipes?"

Robin chuckled. Apparently this young man, although not seeming to be a good student himself, had been raised by educated people and had no notion that the majority in Scotland went unschooled.

"Marta does not read or write. She does it all from memory or by tasting. Before you leave, I will have her make a bag of food to carry with you. But first we have to find you some new clothes and some new boots. You may think that clothes are easy to replace where you came from, but 'tis not so around here. People wear their clothes for a long time and have no second set to spare. I am also certain that my old boots will be far too big for you. There is a cobbler in Kirkcaldy, but it would take weeks to get a pair made, and their price would be dear."

"I have no coin," said Jamie, holding out his rocky winnings. "Do ye think he will take rocks for boots?"

"You have rocks in your head if you think he would! You will have to live in that old nightshirt of mine for a while longer."

Ten days after Jamie's arrival, Thalassa declared him fit to continue his travels if he promised to use Robin's old cane whenever he walked, but the question of new clothes and boots still remained.

That night Suann appeared at Robin's door with a bundle of clothes in her arms. For an instant, Robin's heart skipped a beat until he realized she hadn't come to see him.

"Thalassa made these for Jamie," she said. "She didna take his measures, but she thinks they will be close enough for him to wear." Suann brought a work shirt, a gray plaid, heavy socks, and a long black wool cloak with a hood.

"Where did she get all this cloth?" asked Robin.

"She has many surprising things."

Jamie thanked her heartily. "Tell Thalassa that I will be forever grateful. I will repay her when I can."

"No payment necessary," said Suann. She turned sharply and left the room.

The next day Fergus solved the problem of the boots. "Here, Jamie," he said as he proudly handed his man a worn, but still usable, pair of brown boots with fur lining. "These belonged to my da, but he doesna need them."

"And why is that?" asked Jamie as he slid the boots over his stockings. "Did the cobbler make him a new pair?"

"He is dead and buried on the hill."

Jamie stopped tugging on his boots and reached over to put his hand on the boy's head. "I am verra sorry that yer *athair* is dead. My *athair* has been dead a long time. I ne'er kenned him, but I still miss him."

"Dinna worry. Robin takes verra good care of me."

Robin smiled for the first time in a long time at Fergus's praise.

The next day Jamie put on his new clothes and boots, slung Marta's food bag over his shoulder, picked up Robin's old cane, now his, and bid farewell to Robin, Fergus, and Thalassa.

"Good-bye, my friends," Jamie said. "I will ne'er forget ye, and I will repay yer kindness someday."

Wrapping his arms around Jamie's waist, Fergus said, "Be safe. Dinna get yerself robbed again. I may no' be there to find ye another time." He then stepped back and took Robin's hand. Again, Robin smiled.

"I promise to do my best," answered Jamie, and he started down the road away from Makgullane.

As Jamie walked out of sight, Thalassa said, "Ye ken who he is, dinna ye?"

"A poor bedraggled boy?" said Robin.

"Right now he looks poor and bedraggled, but that is His Royal Majesty, King James V of Scotland."

"Nay!" protested Robin. "He ne'er said a word about being a king or even acted like one. A king would not be traveling by himself, out here among the people, without all his household entourage."

"This one wad," said Thalassa, turning and walking back to her cottage.

"I played hazard with a king!" said Fergus. "Wait until I tell Shane and Darby!"

"Best not to," said Robin. "No one will believe that the skinny boy who ne'er left my room is our king. I am not sure I do. Besides, he's gone now and 'tis better to let him go in peace, whoever he is."

Chapter Ten

Two days after Jamie left, Robin stood again on the road leading to Makgullane, this time waiting for the man from Stirling and his uncle. Late in the afternoon, two riders came into sight. Robin waved them down.

The younger of the two men sat on a black horse with a white blaze pulling a small open wagon carrying several boxes and two leather satchels. The man, lean with a receding hairline of brown hair, had eyes of the same lackluster shade. His thin lips and smile exposed crooked but white teeth. "We are expected at Makgullane," the young man said with a tremble in his voice. "If we dinna arrive soon, someone will look for us. Let us go, or there will be trouble for ye." Straightening himself up as much as he could, he said, "Stand aside."

"I do not intend to rob you," Robin said quickly to ease the man's fears. "I am here from Makgullane to greet you, if you are Angus Gladstone."

"That I am, and this is my uncle Hubert Duffy." Angus continued to prattle on, seemingly more out of concern for his safety than good manners. "He isna my uncle by blood, but we are family just the same. He helped raise me, and he is here to look out for my interests. We have come for my betrothed, Soo-ann-ick. And who might ye be?"

"I am Robin, the estate reeve, and her name is

Suannoch. If you intend to marry her, you should at least know her name."

"I do apologize, but she and I have no' met. We will get acquainted before we wed. I have heard many fine things about her. Do ye ken her well?"

Know her well? Robin thought. I know her better than anyone! And why does the name Hubert Duffy strike me as so familiar?

"Aye, I know her," said Robin.

The uncle, astride a chestnut mare, sat much taller in the saddle than his nephew. He had a square face with a broad chin covered with a well-trimmed silvery-gray beard. His large round eyes shone a deep green, although one eyelid drooped, almost closing that eye. He wore his hair, the same silver gray as his beard, pulled back and tied in a queue down his back.

Duffy leaned over his saddle to get a better look at Robin. "Yer accent is English," he said in a velvety voice. His tone didn't seem accusatory, but more reflective of his curiosity at finding an Englishman in this part the Highlands. "Why does Laird Bretane employ an Englishman as his reeve?"

"I am Bretane's ward. He raised me, and he entrusts me with running the estate when he is away in Edinburgh on government business."

"Ye remember, Uncle," said Angus. "I met Laird Bretane in Edinburgh. We struck up a conversation, and he spoke so highly of an unwed woman on his estate." Turning back to Robin, he said, "So ye are the one who became ill, the one who delayed our coming here to collect my bride for nearly two months."

Aye, became ill against my will. But Robin said, "Aye, but I am well now. I wanted to meet you and see who intended to take Suannoch away from Makgullane. We will miss her very much, and we wish her to be happy and well cared for in her new home. You will see to that, will you not? None of us would like to see her unhappy."

Duffy's velvet voice turned harsh. "Who are you to question us about our intentions?"

Before Robin could respond, Gladstone turned toward his uncle and said, "Uncle, we have had a long journey on rough roads, and we are both verra tired. I am certain this man would only want the best for any woman on the estate." To Robin he added, "I assure you I will take good care of her. Is the main house of Makgullane ahead?"

Robin gave both men a long appraising look before saying, "Aye, about a half a mile." He smacked the horse's rump and sent the horse carrying the future husband of his beloved on its way.

After Robin walked back to the manor house, he saw the two men from the road being welcomed by Bretane and the rest of the household. Robin couldn't bring himself to watch Suann meet her new husband, so he made his way back to his room to go over the accounts for the estate, although he doubted he would be able to keep his mind on them for very long.

"Welcome to Makgullane!" said Bretane in his hearty voice. "Angus, how was yer journey?"

Angus stretched out his hand toward Bretane who guided him down from the saddle. Chuckling as he rubbed his backside, he said, "We made it with only slight injury. 'Tis good to see ye again, Bretane. I would like ye to meet my uncle who accompanied me from Stirling, and I am so glad he came. He fostered me like his own son after my da died, and his advice always guides me well." He extended his hand to the man still seated on his horse. "Let me help you, Uncle."

The older man acknowledged his nephew's assistance and with great effort, lowered himself to the ground and bowed slightly to the welcoming crowd. "These Highlands are most beautiful," he said to Bretane. "I think even this horse enjoyed the scenery. What a privilege it maun be to live here." He smiled and extended his hand to his host.

Bretane took his hand. "We wadna live anywhere else! The Highlands get into yer soul. I will take ye to yer rooms so ye can freshen up. Then ye can meet Suannoch and her mother. They live only a short way from here. Ralf, take care of the horses. They have brought our friends a long way and deserve a good rubdown and a bag of oats. Angus and Hubert, follow me."

As the three men walked through the parting crowd of servants and workers toward the manor house, Glynnis stepped out of the line and touched Angus Gladstone on the arm. She curtsied. "I am verra glad to see ye here."

"Are ye Suannoch?" asked Angus.

"Oh, nay, milord," she said, looking at him from under her eyelashes. "I am Glynnis. If there is anything ye need, ask me. I will help ye any way I can." She quickly added, "We are all glad that ye are here for Suannoch."

Marta and Darby rolled their eyes.

Angus took Glynnis's hand in his and pressed his other hand, with its well-manicured nails, on top of hers. "I am pleased to meet ye, Glynnis. If Suannoch is as lovely as ye, then I will be verra pleased."

Glynnis ducked her head, smiled, and curtsied again but did not withdraw her hand.

"This way, Angus, Hubert," said Bretane. "Our cook has some refreshment prepared for ye."

Angus let go of Glynnis's hand but turned his head to keep his eyes on her as he followed Bretane into the house, nearly stumbling over the door sill as he did.

After both Angus and Hubert had rested for an hour and then enjoyed tea and shortbread in the kitchen, Bretane said, "We should go see Suannoch. Ye maun be eager to meet her and to ken her. I am certain that ye will find her to be a fine young woman. She lives a short walk from here."

Hubert slowly pushed himself to his feet. "I find I am more tired than I expected. May I meet yer betrothed later, Angus? I wad like to rest. We can talk at our meal, and ye can tell me all about her."

" 'Tis fine, Uncle. Bretane, can we be on our way? I would verra much like to meet Suann."

"How do ye ken her short name?" asked Bretane after they started down the dusty path toward Thalassa's cottage.

"A man greeted us on the road. He told me how to properly say her name. He had a scar on his cheek, and verra short hair on one side of his head."

"Ye met Robin. I trust he wasna rude to ye."

"Most polite, although the look of him did frighten us a bit at first."

"Some thieves attacked and beat him verra badly, and his hair had to be cut away from his slashed ear."

Angus's eyes opened wide. "Why would they cut his ear? Are we in danger from these ruffians?"

"Nay," said Bretane, putting his hand on the younger man's shoulder to reassure him. "We have no' seen or heard of them since then. They have moved on."

Bretane knew that to be a lie. Apparently, his visit to the Gray camp had not intimidated Keenan enough to leave the Highlands, because the Grays had left clear signs of their continuing presence several times over the past week. A number of sheep had gone missing along with one hog. Nine chickens had disappeared from the coops with scraps of dark-blue cloth left behind in their empty nests. Blue threads had replaced missing tools. Leaving the cloth and the threads made no sense, but two days later, the message from the Grays became very clear. Human waste had been found near the outbuildings. It would only be a matter of time before Keenan showed up demanding payment to leave Makgullane alone. If Bretane paid, then Keenan Gray would require the same from other nearby estates, and his vicious cycle of threats and cruelty would continue. Gray had to be stopped, but short of murdering the man, Bretane didn't know how it could be done. The March Wardens wouldn't even investigate, let alone attempt to apprehend Gray, until some real damage had been done. Then it would be too late.

Bretane changed the subject. "Ye should ken that Robin and Suann are…" He hesitated whether to tell Angus the depth of their relationship. He decided against it. "They have been friends since they were young, and Robin will only want the best for her."

"He made that verra clear."

"See, up ahead is Suann and Thalassa's cottage. Are ye nervous?"

"Aye, I hope she likes me. I am no' buirdly like the other Highlanders we have met." Angus's rounded shoulders, the result of long hours at a loom and at ledger books, might not impress Suann, but he hoped she would appreciate his agile mind, even temper, and strong work ethic.

"Suannoch wants a kind, caring man. Ye are such a man."

As soon as Angus and Bretane stepped within the low stone wall around the cottage yard, Suann opened the door to the house. "Please, come in," she called to them.

The tidy main room smelled sweetly of the many small bunches of herbs hanging from the rafters, some medicinal, some for seasoning. Windows on three sides let in streams of light, illuminating a large table with benches on both sides. Two padded chairs had been placed on either side of one of the windows, and the kitchen space stretched across the entire back wall. Along that wall sat two rings of stones spaced about three feet apart, with a tiered metal ring in the middle of each designed to hold pots of varying sizes above the fire laid under it. When building the house, Thalassa had insisted on placing a square opening in the wall near the ceiling to pull out the smoke, which nearly eliminated the smoky smell within the house except on the coldest months when the hole was covered. An archway to the left led into the only other room, a bedroom with two neatly made beds and a small table between them.

" 'Tis a verra nice place, well designed," said Angus. "I am Angus Gladstone, milady. I am happy to meet ye." He held out the package from under his arm to Thalassa. "I brought some of my best cloth for ye. I hope ye like it."

Thalassa tore away the paper wrapping and unfolded six ells of soft, dark-green wool fabric and six more ells of an even finer cloth dyed a rich shade of yellow.

"I employed several of the best spinners in the area to prepare the threads for weaving," said Angus, "and dyers to make certain the color is smooth and even. I insisted that my gifts for ye be of the highest quality."

Thalassa had never held such excellently made material, and she recognized how much care had gone into preparing these pieces. "These are most beautiful," she said. "Yer gifts are appreciated." She extended her hand toward him, and he took it, kissing the back of it lightly.

"And ye maun be Suannoch," Angus said, turning toward her. "Did I pronounce it correctly? A man I met on the road told me how to say it."

Suann asked, "A man on the road?"

Bretane said, "Robin welcomed our visitors."

For a moment, the thought of Robin sent sensations of remembered loving through Suannoch, but she forced her longing away. A new future lay ahead for her, and she had to seek it out. "We have more than one visitor?" she asked.

"Aye, my uncle came with me," said Angus. "He is also interested in meeting ye."

Suann's eyes darted over to her mother, who gave a single nod.

"Angus, wad ye like to go for a walk?" Suann asked. " 'Twill be proper if we stay within sight of the cottage."

"That wad be fine," answered Angus as he swept his hand toward the door. "After ye. Lead the way."

Once the pair had gone, Bretane said, "So, Thalassa, do ye think he will do as a guidman for Suann?"

"He is no' an ugly man, though small and somewhat delicate, and he has verra fine manners. Suann will have to decide if she will live with him. What else do ye ken about him?"

"Angus has been without his *athair* since a young age. The man died when a horse threw him. The uncle who came with him today is a good friend of the family who helped raise him. Angus's *màthair* died a year ago."

Thalassa pulled a face. "He wants someone to cook and clean for him now that his *màthair* is gone?"

"Nay, his *màthair* had been ill and bedridden for many years. Angus took care of her while running his cloth business, verra successfully I might add. He has the resources to hire a maid, but now he is ready for a companion, ready for a true wife."

"I hope my dochter is ready for a true guidman." Thalassa paused before adding, "One who isna Robin. Her heart is broken, ye ken, but she is learning to accept what has to be. I hope it winna take her too long."

Bretane sighed, knowing that this marriage would be difficult for Thalassa as well as for Suann and Robin. "Ye will miss her verra much."

"Aye, I will, but I have been alone before. She will write, and I will visit."

Suann and Angus returned to the cottage a short while later. They walked very close to each other and talked quietly until they reached the door.

"I will call on ye tomorrow morn, if that will please ye," he said.

" 'Twill be fine," answered Suann. "Thank ye for walking with me."

"My pleasure. Bretane, I will be able to find my way here by myself tomorrow."

After the men left, Thalassa stirred the pot of stew on the fire as she asked her daughter, "Do ye think ye will be pleased with him?"

"He is pleasant and kind. It will have to be enough."

Thalassa closed her eyes and hoped that kindness truly would be enough for her strong-willed child.

Back at the manor house, Angus said to Bretane, " 'Tis a lovely day. Do ye mind if I look around myself? I winna go too far."

"Look wherever ye please," said Bretane. "I will see if yer uncle wishes a game of chess."

Angus nodded and made his way around to the side of the house, where he had seen Glynnis taking down the clean sheets she had draped over the clothesline to dry.

"Glynnis, is it?" he asked when he came close enough for her to hear him.

"Aye," she said. "How did ye like Suann?"

"She is pleasant enough, but she is thin and boney. I prefer a woman to be fine and nicely plump as ye. A round face like yers is most pleasing to me."

Glynnis looked at him steadily for a moment before taking down the last sheet, folding it, and putting it on top of the others in the basket. "Wad ye like to see more of Makgullane? I can show ye, if ye dinna mind."

"I wad enjoy that verra much."

Over the course of the next week, Angus visited with Suann every morning and walked with Glynnis every afternoon.

Chapter Eleven

Angus and his uncle had been at Makgullane for a fortnight, when Robin heard a knock at the door to his room. When he opened it, it startled him to see Suann standing there. She wore a red kirtle under a tan overdress, and no shoes. He had not expected to see her again.

"I wad like to talk to ye," she said. "Is it all right if I come in?"

"Aye, aye." Robin held the door open and ushered her in with his hand. " 'Tis good to see you!" he said a little too enthusiastically. "Come in!"

He had wanted nothing more than to be this close to her again, and his heart nearly pounded out of his chest. Had she changed her mind? Would she stay? Did he dare hope?

"The room is changed for the better," she said, looking around. "The quilt looks like Mae Towdy's work, and this is Bretane's precious desk. It maun be hard for him to give it up."

"He wanted me to have it. It makes things a little crowded in here, but 'tis easier to work on than the old table. Now I have a separate place to eat." They both looked over at the napkin still covering the plate on the table.

"Sometimes I am not hungry," he said.

"I ne'er kenned ye to no' be hungry."

A few moments of stillness settled over them before Suann said, "I came to say good-bye."

Robin swallowed hard, realizing that having Suann love him again had only been a fantasy, a daydream. Even though his hopes were now crushed, he refused to let it turn him into a ghost of a man. It would be difficult, but he needed to be strong enough to let her go without losing his soul.

"Be happy," he whispered.

Suann took a long deep breath before speaking. "I have spent time with Angus, and he is a good man. I will go with him to Stirling, but I couldna leave without…The last time we spoke, we didna have a proper parting, but we have been friends for too long to no'…say the proper words."

A dull, empty ache swallowed his heart. "We have been more than friends," he said.

"I ken, but I couldna leave without…" The tears she promised herself not to shed tonight came anyway. "Robin, you brought me so much joy, and now all I have to give in return are tears." She clutched her stomach, choking on her sobs.

Robin dashed to her side and put his arms around her. "Don't cry," he said as he rocked her back and forth.

"I have to leave ye!" she sobbed in gasping breaths. " 'Tis the last thing I ever thought I wad do!"

She looked up at him, and as her tears fell, both their hearts melted. He brushed her wet cheeks with his palm and as his thumb touched her lips, all that had gone on between them since that morning in the kitchen vanished.

Robin picked her up and carried her to the bed

against the back wall, sitting her on his lap. They explored each other's lips and necks almost furiously, and soon they fell back on the quilt, legs and arms wrapped together, their body heat mingling and burning.

Between kisses Robin said in a barely audible whisper, "Suann, do you know what will happen if we do not stop right now?"

"Aye," she said without hesitation. Pressing her lips against his, she moved her tongue across his mouth and teeth. "I told myself I wad come here to talk to ye for the last time, but I kenned in my heart that words wadna be enough. I ne'er want to forget that ye love me."

Robin answered her with his hands, urgently removing her clothes and then his own until nothing separated them. Their kisses said what their voices of regret could not. Never again would they murmur secrets that only the two of them shared. Never again would the words of their poem be spoken—*Where I have chosen, steadfast will I be*—because they would be apart forever. Even as their bodies ached to leave a touch, a caress, something, anything to remember, they could not bring back the life they had dreamed of having together. This night would be all they had left.

There had already been too many words between them. Now there would be none, only feverish lovemaking. They had begun, truly begun, their lives together, and now they would leave each other the same way, together, as one.

She closed her eyes as he claimed her tender breasts and quivering thighs.

She had to remember this!

His eyes stayed open, so he could see her loving him. He had to remember this!

Frantic to be as one body, they feasted on each other until they could wait no more. Both of them found release almost as soon as he plunged into her. In the aftermath, as it had the first time they kissed in the trees, their hearts beat in unison.

Their true farewell came the second time they made love. This time they took their time touching, tasting, and savoring each other, treasuring the act of love. She covered him with her body and moved against his stomach and legs to give to him as much as he gave to her. She skimmed her hands over him, trying to memorize the warmth of his skin and the softness of his hair. He savored her long, delicious kisses. They tried to inhale every scent and feel every sensation, every touch, every kiss, and to implant memories in their minds that would comfort them for the rest of their lives. This moment would be their last together.

When they could no longer wait, their joining became the expression of their lifelong devotion, one that had grown from enduring friendship to enduring passion.

Later Suann stood in the doorway holding Robin's hand for the last time. Her thumb rubbed gently over his fingers. "*Beannachd leat, mo ghaol*," she said. "Good-bye, my love."

"Suannoch," he murmured. He could not bring himself to say good-bye.

Just as the door started to close behind her, he said, "Wait." Opening the right-hand drawer of the desk, he took out half of their split shilling, the piece with the bent corner. "This is for you."

She took it in her hand and said, "Mine forever."
The door closed quietly, leaving them both alone.

Chapter Twelve

The night of Suannoch and Angus's betrothal banquet came all too soon for Robin.

Marta, basking in her glory, prepared a meal fit for a king! What an opportunity to cook elegant dishes instead of food just meant to fill a belly enough to accomplish a day's work! At last, she had a chance to make some of her mother's renowned recipes, and everyone could hardly wait to see what she would have on the menu.

She set the table in the gathering room with the best plates and dishes from the cupboards, including a half-dozen pewter cups and a very special silver saltcellar handed down from Bretane's mother. Before each place at the table she placed a large embroidered white cloth. The cloth served as a napkin since only the rudest of guests would consider licking their fingers, and Marta would never let anyone in her house be accused of such crudeness. She made certain to have enough clean cloths for each guest after each course.

Marta also made certain that her dishes looked as elegant in their presentation as they tasted. Her onions, chives, radishes, carrots, turnips, and cabbage had first been seasoned with herbs and flowers such as violets and cowslips, and then carved and formed into decorative shapes. Marta learned this skill from her mother, and she lovingly passed it on to the younger lasses.

The menu included broth with almonds, legs of mutton with lemons, and game pie stuffed with oranges, stewed capons, roasted deer, and hog's liver. Some of these foodstuffs could not be found in Marta's pantry, but she had Bretane's permission to locate and purchase whatever she needed. Ralf and Patrick had returned from each of their food-searching journeys with as much as their cart could carry.

Soups, pottage, roasted meats of lamb, pork, pigeons, and partridges warmed in the kitchen, waiting their turn, along with Bretane's favorite, haggis. Marta protested she would only serve haggis, made from chopped liver, heart, and lungs of a sheep, then mixed with beef or mutton suet and oatmeal, seasoned with onion, cayenne pepper, and other spices, and packed into a sheep's stomach to be boiled, to the common folks, but Bretane insisted it be on the menu. "Everyone loves haggis!" he declared. Marta groaned, but did as her laird wanted.

First, the soups would be served, followed by a variety of breads, then the meat dishes, and after that cherries and raspberries, baked or covered in sauce. These fruits complemented the vegetables. The next and final offering would be several kinds of cheese to close off and seal the stomach, as per the custom. Marta expected everyone to leave the table with bellies so full that they ached. In fact, she would be insulted if they didn't!

Bretane opened his wine cellar, overjoyed to have an occasion that called for his finest bottles, which he proudly displayed on the sideboard. With Marta's help, he planned a different wine or ale to complement each food course.

Angus and Hubert were the first to arrive for the betrothal celebration in the gathering room that afternoon, followed by Bretane and an obviously reluctant Robin. Bretane had insisted his ward and reeve attend, even though Robin tried to beg off, saying he didn't think he could abide in the same room with the man taking Suann away from Makgullane. He also did not want to see Glynnis who would be one of the serving maids.

"Ye can hold yer temper and yer tongue for one meal!" Bretane had bellowed at Robin's complaints. "Damn yer good manners, and stuff yer mouth with food if ye feel the need to speak! And ye will wear a plaid!"

Robin, who had worn a plaid ever since he recovered from Keenan's beating, wrinkled his nose in frustration at Bretane's lack of recognition of his new acceptance of the Scottish style of dress, but so be it. What he wore didn't matter. He had no choice but to come to the meal and face the inescapable truth that Suann now belonged to another.

The four men stood around the table, three engaged in conversation and drinking wine while Robin sulked near the doorway. All the men wore their breacans, a plaid without the over-the-shoulder sash. Angus and Hubert wore red with a sett of crisscrossing broad blue and narrow yellow threads while their bright white shirts, made of the finest linen, signified their sophisticated lifestyle in the city. Bretane and Robin wore breacans of sea green with a sett of narrow red and yellow strands, and shirts made out of the more common countryside materials of flax and linen, thus proudly displaying their Highland heritage.

The men had been waiting for about thirty minutes when Maggy dashed into the room and announced breathlessly, "Thalassa and Suannoch have arrived."

Quickly putting down their cups, the men stood ready to greet the guests of honor.

Suann entered first, in her gown with a dark-blue bodice, sleeves, and front skirt panel over an orange underskirt. She had piled her hair up on her head and covered it with a flowing golden silk headscarf and then a braid of white blossoms. Curtsying, she said, "Greetings."

Thalassa came in directly behind her, dressed in a forest-green gown fitted to her neck with long white sleeves cuffed at her wrists, and a lustrous gold chain with thick links around her waist. She had pulled her black-and-white-striped hair back off her face and held it in place with a jewel-studded, stiff headband.

Thalassa's eyes quickly sought out Bretane and then Angus, nodding to each in turn. She acknowledged Robin to the left in the same manner. Next, she saw Hubert Duffy, and immediately the color drained from her face, her violet eyes blazing with fury and fear.

"Ye!" she shouted, shaking her finger at him. "There will be no wedding! Ne'er! She will ne'er be yers!"

Grabbing her daughter roughly by the arm, Thalassa shoved a bewildered Suannoch out of the room. She stumbled at the door, but her mother's long strides kept her moving. Bretane started to go after them, but Hubert stopped him. "Let them go," he said firmly.

"What just happened?" asked Bretane, blinking in

astonishment. "I thought the match pleased Thalassa. What could have happened between yesterday and today?"

An equally baffled Angus said, "Our conversations this week have been most pleasant. Neither of us said anything untoward or even the least bit upsetting."

Robin bolted straight up from the wall with his face in a stony expression. "What did she mean?" he growled. "Why did she run at the sight of you, Hubert?"

Collapsing into the nearest chair, Hubert folded his hands on the table. His usually ruddy complexion turned grayish. "If only I had seen her before today, I could have warned ye," he said. "We spent so much time away from the estate visiting Bretane's friends and neighbors, and the rest of time I stayed in my room, too tired to go with ye to see yer betrothed. If I had seen her or her *màthair*, I wad have told ye the truth! Angus, I am afraid I have led ye into a disaster of my doing."

"What are ye talking about, Uncle?" said Angus. "How can ye be responsible for this?"

Hubert looked away before saying, " 'Tis a tale that maun be told. I am verra sorry that it has to be now." He sighed and began. "I came to Makgullane nearly twenty years ago, searching. Bretane, this was before ye came home to stay for good, so ye didna meet me. I only spoke to yer servants, and they couldna give me any hope that I wad find what I sought, so I left and ne'er spoke of it to anyone again."

"What could ye possibly have been looking for?" asked an incredulous Angus.

After a long, unsettling pause, Hubert said, "My daughter."

The air in the room fairly shuddered until Robin

spoke up. "What are you saying? Do you mean that Suannoch is your daughter?"

" 'Tis with deep regret that I didna tell ye why I came to Makgullane before. I wad ken her *màthair* anywhere with that thick black hair and those violet eyes. Thalassa is the woman I kenned many years ago, and Suannoch is the child I came looking for."

Robin's voice grew husky as the implications of Hubert's words sank in. "Did you desert Thalassa, leaving her alone to have her baby?" He knew all too well the choices a man had to make for the sake of a child.

"Nay, she deserted me."

Suddenly, Robin remembered why the name Hubert sounded familiar when he met the man on the road. At the *Secretum Flumine*, the secret place by the stream, Suann had said that she and Thalassa hid there years ago because of someone dangerous named Hubert, but Suann didn't know why. Robin was determined to find out now.

"Tell us what happened!" he demanded.

"Angus, I ne'er wanted to tell ye this," said Hubert with a desolate look on his face. "I didna want ye to think less of me. She broke my heart, and 'tis the reason I ne'er took a wife. I couldna get the pain out of my heart."

Robin slammed his hands on the table. "Tell us about Suannoch!"

"I need wine."

Bretane poured him a cup, which Hubert downed in one long gulp. He folded and unfolded his hands as he spoke.

"I first saw Thalassa at the fair. She told fortunes

and sold potions from a tent on the edge of the fair, and she had the most beautiful face I had ever seen. O, those rich lilac eyes, a color I had ne'er seen before or ever imagined that eyes could be. I fell into those eyes at first glance, and my heart soon followed. I loved her completely and fully. She smiled at me and asked if I wanted to hear what the future held. When she took my hand, I felt a slow warm feeling flow through me, and I kenned that she possessed me as completely and fully as a man can be. Do ye understand? Please, Angus, say that ye understand!"

Angus placed a comforting hand on Hubert's shoulder. "Go on, Uncle."

Robin knew how it felt to belong wholly to a woman, but now Suann would never be his because of Glynnis and the baby. Still, he would give up everything, even his own life, for her, and he wondered what Hubert had given up for Thalassa.

Hubert went on. "As tall and well-formed as a woman could be with her firm round breasts, curved hips, and long graceful legs. Little did I ken that she had been created for that verra purpose, to entice a man like me. Unmarried and naïve about the ways of women, I didna realize how she hypnotized me, but later, she used her magical charms to make me risk it all for her."

"Thalassa is not a witch!" said Robin. "And you had better not let Suann or me hear you say that again!"

Hubert blanched at Robin's anger. "She had her ways, and I could not resist. I followed the fair to every town it went that summer, and I spoke to her whenever I could. She read my fortune a dozen times, all the while smiling and speaking kindly to me, inviting me like a spider into her web."

Robin scowled. "Thalassa can be formidable, but she is not deceitful."

"Mayhap she has fooled ye the way she fooled me."

Robin tightened his jaw and didn't speak. Defending Thalassa would only prolong this man's story, and Robin needed to hear it all.

"One night, she walked away from the tents into a lonely place hidden by trees and rocks. She called to me in a voice like a Siren, and I followed her." His voice became husky and his eyes took on a wounded look.

"Alone and deep in the woods, she turned and took my hand. She leaned close and whispered, 'I have things to show ye, things that only I can show ye.' She moved my hand to her breast and stepped even closer until I could feel her breath on my neck. Then…I am ashamed to tell ye the rest." He dropped his head to his chest.

"Uncle, go on," said Angus. "We ken this is difficult, but we maun hear it all if we are to understand what happened here tonight."

After a moment, Hubert continued. "She touched my man parts, stroking and caressing me until I thought I would explode. Then she lifted her skirts, lifted my plaid, and pulled me into her. She felt warm and wet, and I had ne'er kenned such wonder afore. She moved her hips over me in a rhythm that made me feel amazingly alive. I could not escape until she let me go, spent and exhausted."

Bretane cleared his throat and poured Hubert another cup of wine. Then he took one for himself and offered the bottle to Angus, who declined, and to

Robin, who put the bottle to his lips and emptied it.

"I tried to stay away from her, but her hold on me remained too great. She had swallowed my heart, and I belonged to her. The next night I heard her tell the man and woman she lived with to go and enjoy a drink at the tavern, that she would be fine alone. As soon as they had gone out of sight, she waved to me. I kenned I should walk away, but I couldna. She possessed me.

"This time we didna leave her tent. When I stepped under the flap, she had pulled her skirts up and bent over the bed, baring her arse to me. 'Touch me,' she said in a voice like honey. 'Touch me here,' and she placed her hand on her own backside. 'Am I no' pleasing to ye?' she said. Aye, she pleased me like no one I had ever kenned. I came closer, and she grabbed on to my plaid and pulled me into her, this time from behind. I tried to stop this ungodly act, but she wadna let me. She held me inside her until I finished, again spent and drained. I ran out of the tent, and I ne'er saw her again."

Robin felt nothing but pity for this man and nothing but anger at the tale he told. It could not be true! Every word of his tale had to be a lie. "What made you come here twenty years ago?" he asked.

"Two years later, I found the same tent at another fair. I asked about her, but no one kenned where she had gone. Then the man who showed the trained bear on a chain said that he had heard from his sister in the Highlands of a woman with dark hair and violet eyes who had a child. That child could be mine, so I went searching for her."

Hubert reached for Angus and pleaded with him. "Angus, ye ken how I always wanted a child. I have always felt incomplete without a son or daughter of my own. 'Tis why I am dedicated to you, Angus. Ye are no' my flesh and blood, but still my son in every other way. I ne'er wished for yer da's death, but I thanked Heaven when yer *màthair* asked me to take his place, and I have been a good *athair* to ye. Have I no'? When Thalassa came into this room tonight with a daughter, I kenned I had finally found her and the child. I will ne'er forget those violet eyes."

"But how can ye be certain that Suann is yer child?" asked Bretane.

"She is the image of my mother, a delicate woman with yellow hair."

"And she has yer green eyes," added Angus.

Chapter Thirteen

When Robin could no longer stand this pitiable old man's sniveling or his shameful tale, he stormed out. He had questions, but none of them would be answered by staying here and listening to Hubert cry and beg for forgiveness.

Angus, Bretane, and Hubert sat silently at the table.

"Where is he going?" asked Hubert after he finally lifted his head.

"Most likely to see Suannoch," said Bretane, pacing along the wall. "They have a special friendship, and he will want to talk to her."

"Special friendship," echoed Angus. "What do ye mean by that?"

"They have known each other since childhood. Both verra lonely as children, they became friends. They may seem a strange pair, with her being a lass and him a lad, and with their four-year age difference, but I ne'er kenned two better friends than Suann and Robin."

Angus gave his host a look of uneasy puzzlement. "Is there more to it than friendship? Has he claimed her as his?"

Bretane sighed, knowing that Robin wanted to claim Suann, and in a very real way already had, but because Glynnis carried Robin's child, it would never be. It broke Bretane's heart that the young man he loved like a son would be trapped in a marriage with a woman like Glynnis, but Glynnis could not raise that child alone. A man of Robin's ethical character would never allow it, nor would Suannoch, which is why she had chosen to leave Makgullane with Angus.

"Nay, he hasna claimed her nor she him," said Bretane. "They share a friendship, naught else that wad concern ye."

Turning away from the other two men, Angus heaved a long, heavy sigh and returned to face them, putting his hand on his uncle's shoulder. "There is something I maun tell ye, Laird Bretane." He swallowed hard. "I came here prepared to honor our betrothal. Suann is a fine woman, but…I dinna love her as a guidman should. I had hoped that we wad grow to care for each other, but, Uncle Hubert, after yer telling that ye are Suann's *athair*, we canna wed, not now, not ever."

"Angus, please reconsider," said Hubert. "I am so verra sorry." The lines on his face etched into his skin even deeper than before. "I ne'er had the intention to turn ye from Suann. I couldna tell ye my horrible tale afore, nor tell ye that I had been here. Mayhap if I had seen Suannoch or Thalassa afore tonight, I could have spared ye this." He gave Angus a look of silent appeal.

"But, Uncle, there is something else," said Angus.

Hubert went on in a lifeless monotone as if he hadn't heard his nephew. "I will do what I can to make Thalassa see that I have forgiven her. I winna come between ye and Suann. I have ne'er been *athair* to her, and I dinna expect she will accept me now. Yer happiness is all that matters to me. Please believe me!"

The tears in his uncle's eyes tore at Angus. He had loved this man as a father for many years. "But there is something else I maun tell ye." He hesitated, wringing his hands. "Mayhap 'twill ease yer mind." After clearing his throat several times, he said, "I love another. 'Tis a woman from Makgullane."

Bretane bristled. "Who wad betray Suann?"

"She is no' to blame. I found her. I courted her. I have been with her every day since we first came here. Now I ken I canna leave her. Mine was an obligation to Suann, but with this woman, 'tis more. We are well suited, and we are in love. 'Twill be a good marriage." He stiffened his back and jutted out his chin to emphasize his words. " 'Tis what I want. 'Tis what both of us want."

"Who?" said Bretane, dragging out his words. "Tell me who dared interfere with a betrothal!"

"I winna let ye punish her," said Angus. "I will take her away afore ye do her harm."

"Do others around here ken?"

Angus nodded. "I wad think so. We didna hide, but we didna want to upset Suann, so we kept to ourselves."

"So, I am the only *amadan dall*? The only blind fool? Tell me who she is!"

After a long minute he spoke. " 'Tis Glynnis. I love her, and she loves me. She is the one I will wed."

Bretane sat down hard in the nearest chair. "Glynnis, Glynnis," he repeated softly. "Has she agreed to marry ye? Do ye ken she is bairned?"

****

Every day Keenan waited for some retaliation from Bretane for his forays onto Makgullane land, but none came. He concluded that the laird held so much contempt for the Grays that he couldn't be bothered by things as trivial as the loss of a few sheep, some tools, and a few stolen chickens. It hadn't even offended the man when they left their waste!

Keenan could not tolerate these insults! How dare the big man with long graying hair not think enough of Keenan to strike back? The Grays deserved notice, and they would not be ignored!

The grumbling among his remaining followers increased daily, and he had to show them a victory or even the most dim-witted would leave him. Every night Keenan preached on their success with each theft. He convinced them that no response from Laird Bretane meant the Grays had won over a man too cowardly to come looking for the culprits. Keenan also bragged that since they had not seen hide nor hair of Robin, they had finished him off. Now word would soon spread of their viciousness and all the people on the surrounding estates would fear for their lives and submit to the will of the Grays! He asked the woman, Kathleen, to come up with a song celebrating these glorious victories, which she did, and Keenan led the singing every night.

The Grays' sense of entitlement and their bravado increased with each of Keenan's triumphant speeches. With their cheers, they vowed to rid Makgullane of all its tenants and claim the house and the land for themselves. At last they would no longer be homeless vagabonds but landowners, and from there they would take whatever they wanted. No one would dare oppose them!

Keenan shouted, "Do ye think that Johnnie Armstrong and his men look like filthy beggars when they go about their business? Nay, every one of them is clean and sweet smelling!"

So, they set to making their rags look the best they

could. Everyone washed their tunics in the stream, scrubbed their hair and beards, and banished as many fleas and lice as possible. In exchange for helping the men look presentable, Keenan promised every woman yards and yards of rich cloth and a chest of jewels to adorn their fancy new gowns. Very soon the victory would be theirs!

****

Bretane, Hubert, and Angus paced in silence while the betrothal food went cold and uneaten, until fifteen men led by Keenan Gray shattered the silence by riding or walking into the yard surrounding the manor house at Makgullane. Every one of the intruders triumphantly entered the yard, convinced they had come to claim all their leader had promised them.

Astride his horse, the one he had stolen from the red-haired boy on the road, Keenan called out, "The Grays are here! Meet the new owners of this fine piece of land!" And reminiscent of Bretane's taunt, he added, "Come out if ye dare!"

On his signal, the others clanged their weapons together and sent up a loud roar.

Bretane moved to the window to see who made the racket, and as soon as he recognized Keenan Gray, he went into action. "All of ye, take a weapon and be prepared to take on these beggars!"

Angus's voice rose to a near screeching pitch and his whole body shook. "I dinna ken how to fight! I have only held a sword to have my portrait painted. I ne'er used it against a man!"

"Ye winna have to use it!" said Bretane as he handed the smaller man a claymore and a Templar short sword. Angus could barely lift either of them.

"What do I do with these?" he protested.

"Just try to look menacing. Hubert, take these two." When no one took the swords, Bretane asked, "Where is yer uncle?"

Angus shrugged and called out, "Uncle Hubert! He's gone!"

The commotion outside also brought everyone from the kitchen into the gathering room. "How can we help?" asked Patrick.

Bretane gave Patrick, Shane, Henry, and Ralf a sword or a dirk from the wall. The men would make a good showing for themselves after Suann's training.

"We can help," said Marta. "The lasses are no' afeared!"

"Pick up whatever you can get yer hands on," said Bretane. "There is safety in numbers. All of ye, protect each other. These Grays winna give ye much of a fight, but dinna take chances. All we want to do is scare them off. They are no' worth losing an arm or dying for."

Everyone around the table nodded.

"Now, take a big breath so yer lungs are full and follow me, shouting as loud as ye can!"

Bretane led the charge into the yard.

****

Robin's anger burned in his chest as he ran down the path to Thalassa's cottage. Let Bretane deal with the story that the old man told. Let Angus sit there and choke on his betrothal dinner, knowing this cockup belonged to his uncle. Robin would hear the truth from the only one who could tell him the truth! Thalassa!

Standing just outside the low stone wall surrounding the yard, he waited until Suann caught a glimpse of him through the window. She came outside.

178

Sitting on each side of the wall, they faced each other.

"I am glad ye came. I need someone, I need ye," said Suann, her eyes dark with worry. "Thalassa winna tell me anything. I dinna ken what is wrong, but she is packing supplies, so we can go to *Secretum Flumine*." She flapped her apron in frustration. "She winna tell me why! I have ne'er seen her so upset. Do ye ken what is wrong?"

Robin wanted to spit at Hubert for his lies, but Suann needed him to be calm and supportive. "Aye, I do," he said slowly. "The old man says that you are his daughter."

Suann gasped. "How can that be? Thalassa said that she found me in a burned-out croft with no one about, but she heard my cries. She said that God sent her to me, and every day she is grateful that He did. I am her blessing, so what the man says canna be true!"

"It cannot be the way Hubert tells it. I would like to hear what Thalassa has to say. Do you think she will come out and talk to me?"

"I dinna ken."

"Aye, she will," came Thalassa's deep voice as she appeared out of the lengthening shadows of the afternoon sun. "Suannoch, ye're no safe from that man!"

"Who is he?" she asked in fearful voice.

"The uncle of Angus Gladstone is Hubert Duffy."

Suann suddenly remembered their time in hiding. "The same Hubert from all those years ago?"

"Aye."

Suann's features fell. "He says he is my *athair*. Is it true?"

Thalassa nodded very slowly.

Taking her mother's hands, Suann cried, "Why did ye lie to me all these years? Ye maun tell me! I have to ken!"

Thalassa sat down on the wall while Suann squatted on the ground at her feet. "Tell me, *a'mhàthair*," she said gently.

Thalassa began in a voice so hesitant, Robin barely recognized it as belonging to the commanding Thalassa he knew.

"I couldna tell ye the real story. Ye were a bairn and too wee to understand, and I ne'er wanted ye to be ashamed of how ye came to be. I wanted ye to be able to tell the story of yer life with pride."

"I have always been proud of ye and my life. Please, tell me the truth now."

Thalassa began to speak in a distant, almost wooden voice, her eyes haunted with inner pain. "I dinna remember my parents or what happened to them. I have been alone since a verra young age. To survive, I learned how to earn a few pennies by telling people what they wanted to hear. People began to call me clear-eyed, and when a man and woman, Peter and Abbie, heard of my skill, they took me off the streets and cared for me. I began traveling with them from town fair to town fair. As my reputation as a young *amasan*, a teller of fortunes, grew we made a verra good living. They also taught me how to make tinctures and salves, which I helped sell to cure whatever ailed the customer. Peter and Abbie took the best care of me they could, and I was happy.

"When I was sixteen, Hubert appeared at my tent to have his fortune read." She paused to choke back a hitch in her voice. "He had a large, strong hand, a man over eighteen hands tall in his youth, but the lines on his palm foretold a bleak future of betrayal and sadness. I tried to ease his concern, but he became verra angry at my testimony and called me a liar and a clootie."

"Ye're no clootie!" said Suann.

Robin took Suann's hand in his and stroked it very gently.

Thalassa stared off in the distance, only nodding to acknowledge her daughter's defensive outburst. She continued. "Peter grabbed him by the collar and led him away, but the next day he came back. He apologized verra sincerely, and Abbie made me forgive him because as a customer, he had coin as good as anyone's. He came to the tent over and over, and I read his fortune every day, sometimes several times a day. I made certain that the fortune pleased him, and he followed us from town to town. I made the mistake of thinking he meant no harm."

Robin could not see Thalassa's face clearly in the growing darkness, but the expression in her voice told him how this memory disturbed her.

"One day, I had no' seen him all day, and I thought he had given up and gone home at last. I walked along a nearby wood in the evening to get away from the stuffiness of the tent when he suddenly appeared at my side. I started to call out, but he put his hand over my mouth and dragged me deep into the trees. I struggled against him, but I could no' get free of his strong hold on me.

"He growled something in my ear, but I could no' understand his words. Then he reached under my skirt and grabbed between my legs. I tried to pull away, but he backed me against a tree, lifted his plaid, and entered me, hard and fast. His grunting didna last long after I reached up and tore at his eyelid with my fingernail. That is why it droops. When I started to scream, he slammed his fist into my head, and I lost my senses. When I awoke, he was gone, but my legs and my face dripped with his seed."

"Oh, *a'mhàthair*, I canna believe he wad come here after doing such a thing to ye!"

Thalassa put her hands on Suann's face. "He is the reason I have taught ye to defend yerself. I ne'er want what happened to me to happen to ye."

"I love ye, *a'mhàthair*," Suann said.

Thalassa touched Suann's cheek and went on with her story. "I washed up in the stream as best I could, but I told no one. Who wad believe me? I should ne'er have gone off alone."

"You are not to blame!" said Robin. "The blame is his and no one else's!" Robin cringed to think that he had once used his strength against Suann, but he took responsibility for his actions, and Hubert did not.

"That was no' the last I saw of him," said Thalassa. "Two days later, Peter and Abbie had gone to the tavern, leaving me alone for the night. I slept on the cot in the back of the tent. This time I didna see or hear him until he pulled me to my feet and bent me face down over the bed, pulled up my nightshirt, and raped me again."

Suann gasped.

"When he finished, he jerked me up and slapped me across the face and said, 'Dinna call me to ye again, ye clootie! If ye do, I will have ye hanged as a witch!' Ye can see where his ring cut my chin." She pointed to the small scar along her jawline.

Suann laid her head on Thalassa's lap. "Ye're no witch," she muttered. "No' a witch."

"I kenned that as long as I stayed with the fair, he could always find me, and I wadna be able to stop him from hurting me again, so I grabbed food and a few blankets and ran off alone. I walked for miles, no' kenning where I went, ne'er stopping but to tell a few fortunes and offer what herbs I had in my pockets to anyone who would feed me. Then I realized I carried ye."

Raising her head, Suann asked, "Bairned with me?"

"Aye, lass, with ye. But I couldna stop running. I ne'er kenned when he might find me. After months of wandering, I gave birth to ye, Suannoch, in a small copse of trees by the side of the road."

"Oh, ye gave birth alone with no one to help ye." Her emerald eyes filled with tears.

"Dinna cry, wee one. As I held ye, this wet, crying bairn, I kenned that God had given me a great gift. I had been entrusted with raising a child into a woman. I wadna trade ye for anything in the world. I wad go through it all over again if I kenned that I wad have ye. Ye are my reason for living."

"Oh, *a'mhàthair!*" said Suann, wiping her own tears.

"How did you end up here at Makgullane?" asked Robin.

"In the same way ye did, lad. Bretane came by on his horse and saw me at the side of the road holding my child and feeding her from my breast. He offered me shelter at Makgullane. He said I only had to come to the manor house, only a mile away, where the babe and I

183

would be fed and cared for. I didna ken if I could trust any man until he returned with a cart to carry us. Mayhap 'twas his kind voice or mayhap the scar that cut across his face, but coming with him blessed my life, and I have done everything I can to bless his. Now do ye ken why ye maun hide from the man who came with Angus? He only wants what he thinks has been stolen from him, his bairn."

From the shadows, a voice hissed out the words, "Ye didna tell the truth about me!"

All three of them jumped to their feet.

Hubert Duffy stood not six feet away.

Robin moved between the women and Hubert. "What do you want?" he demanded.

"I want what is mine," said Hubert as he pointed a shaking finger at Suann. "Ye are a comely lass. I wad have named ye Myrtle if I had raised ye, but instead I find ye here in this wretched cottage and with this two-faced woman."

Suann stepped around Robin, who pushed her behind him again while she sputtered, "Ye winna harm me *màthair* again. I winna let ye!"

"Neither of us will let you," said Robin.

Hubert flailed his arms as he screamed, "Thalassa enticed me as only a true witch could! She is from Satan, and she has ruined ye, but come with me and I will put ye on the righteous road. Ye are like her, one who could call a man to her like the Sirens called Odysseus. 'Tis me duty as yer *athair* to set ye on a godly path."

Again, Suann leaped out in front of Robin, who wrapped both his arms around her to keep her near him while she kicked and shouted, "Ne'er will I go with ye!

Ne'er!"

"I have papers that I have carried for twenty years, papers saying ye belong to me. As a man, I have the rights to me bairns. For twenty years, I searched for ye. 'Twas by luck I came back to Makgullane with Angus and found ye where I couldna find ye all those years ago. Ye canna stop me for taking what is mine!"

"You will not be taking anyone anywhere," said Robin in a voice thick with determination.

"Do ye think ye can stop me? Do ye think Bretane can stop me?" A vein on his forehead pulsed wildly. "Right now, Bretane has his hands full with an attack from those reivers ye have been talking about. I escaped in the chaos. Myrtle, ye will come with me now!"

Reaching under his cloak, Hubert pulled out a long sleek dirk that gleamed in the fading sunlight. In one quick motion, he stepped over the low stone wall and pressed the tip hard into Robin's side. "Ye will come with me or he dies!"

Robin did not hesitate. Pushing Suann to the ground beside him, he lunged toward Hubert, fully expecting to feel the pain of the dirk entering his body. Prepared for that, it stunned him when Hubert fell soundlessly into his arms. Robin held him up as the man's red, sticky blood spurted over his arms and chest.

In that instant, Robin saw a knife jutting out of Hubert's neck. Thalassa grasped the handle of the knife, pushed it in deeper, and then jerked it up and across Hubert's throat. Hubert's head fell back. Pulling out the knife, she said, "He winna harm either of us again."

The old man's blood continued to pump out until Robin dropped his body to the ground.

Chapter Fourteen

Robin moved into action. "Thalassa, Suann, get in the house and bolt the door. I have to go and help Bretane." When neither woman moved, he shouted, "Get in the house! We will take care of this man's body later! Move! I cannot be in two places at once, and Bretane needs me!"

Before any of them could take a step, another familiar voice with its own vicious tinge came out of the glow of the setting sun. "Bretane doesna need yer help anymore," snarled the man with the red-stained cheek as he stepped over the wall, followed by what remained of his gang. "None of ye showed the Grays the respect we deserve, so as a warning to other men who may think to be brave, we have taken Makgullane as our own."

Still soaked in Hubert's blood, Robin turned to face his enemy, spewing out the words. "What have you done?"

"Do ye think an old man and a couple of bumpkins with rakes could stop us? They are lying quiet on the ground, verra quiet! And yer precious Makgullane is ours! I left a few there to take what they could carry out of the house."

Robin swept his eyes over the men in the yard, assessing their strength, as they gave a howling victory cheer.

If Keenan had truly murdered Bretane, Robin would see that Keenan soon followed, and he would take as many of the others with him as he could!

One, two, three…he counted twelve men plus Keenan, all of them armed, and him without even his knife. Thalassa and Suannoch knew how to defend themselves, but could they defeat armed men? This fight would not be easy, but he would protect both women unto his death. He said a prayer that Suann and Thalassa would survive.

Pulling back the hair that had grown over his right ear, Robin asked, "What is that pinned to your cap, Keenan?"

"So ye recognize the best part of yer ear, do ye? 'Tis my prize," replied Keenan with his customary sneer. "I collect the ears of any who oppose me. I see that ye are still alive. Last time we saw ye, we intended to leave ye dead. Naught speaks louder of fear than a dead man, but we will make certain we finish the task today! Are ye ready, lads?"

With a Celtic shout, the mass of Grays, all armed with stolen swords and knives, swarmed across the yard.

Two of them charged at Robin, but he made quick work of them by grabbing their wrists and twisting their arms back so their weapons pointed at their own bellies. Being so inept at hand-to-hand combat, their feet kept moving forward until their own weapons ran them through. They fell and bled out on the ground. Another jumped up and put his arm around Robin's neck in a choke hold until Robin reached back between his own legs, grabbed the man's groin, and squeezed. Then with a quick push of his hips, Robin twisted out of the hold.

The man collapsed, and Robin's hard stomp to the chest, and the resulting broken sternum, made short work of him.

Another man, seeing his comrades defeated so quickly, stood frozen nearby, and when Robin took a menacing step toward him, he bolted and disappeared into the trees, followed by two others who had witnessed their comrades' defeat.

Thalassa shouted a stream of words that terrified the attackers, who believed she spouted curses and spells. Robin almost laughed aloud when he realized that she had only strung together a stream of nonsensical words in Latin. Two more of the Grays ran back into the woods with pleas for God to save their souls from the witch's curses.

One man who had not yet given up the cause came up behind Thalassa and wrapped his cloth belt around her neck, thinking, as only a woman, she would be easy to conquer. He learned otherwise when she immediately twisted to the side, loosening the cloth on her throat until she turned toward him and rammed her fist into his chin. He stumbled back, and she finished him off with a fist to the face that shoved his nose bone into his brain.

At the same time, one of the few remaining men raced toward Suann, grabbed her from behind, and forced her arms against her body. In a move that Thalassa had taught her, she spread her legs wide, put her weight on her left leg and jerked her right foot up and back to stomp on the man's foot. He squealed, released her arms, and hopped around for a bit before she grabbed his hair and pulled his face repeatedly into her knee. He fell and writhed on the ground until, still screaming in pain, one of the already retreating men hoisted him up, and together they hobbled out of the yard.

Once again Keenan had no one but cowards to back up his claims of grandeur. They would never make the feared reivers he wanted or needed to accomplish his dream of becoming the most feared man in Scotland. They abandoned him at the first sign of trouble, and he now had to take his only chance to conquer his enemy. Stepping up behind Suannoch, he grabbed her by the hair, jerked her backward into his arms, and put a knife to her throat.

"Sassenach, she dies unless ye surrender!" he shouted.

The fighting in the yard came to a stop. Now only two of the Grays still stood plus Keenan. They each took a step back, relieved that the fight was over. With the girl under Keenan's knife, Robin would have no choice but to surrender quickly.

"Stay back, Sassenach!" said Keenan. "One step closer and I will slit her throat."

"What are your terms?" asked Robin, putting his hands on his knees, breathing hard.

"My terms?" Keenan laughed. "My terms are complete surrender!"

Robin straightened up. "You have my word."

"What I want is for ye to stand still while one of my men run ye through! Do ye agree, Sassenach?"

"Agreed, but first she goes free."

"Tinker, Ronald, stand ready to slice his gut!" ordered Keenan.

Tinker picked up his sword and held it out, only to watch it shake in his hand. Ronald didn't move a muscle except for his eyes that twitched and blinked rapidly.

"Nay, Robin!" cried Suann. She strained to wrench herself out of Keenan's grasp, but he stiffened the knife against her throat. A drop of blood appeared on her neck.

"Crumble left," said Robin. "On my word."

"What gibberish is this?" asked Keenan. "Crumble left?"

As children, Robin and Suann had often played a game they called Shortbread Crumble that Bretane used to teach them fighting techniques in a battle. He taught them to look out for each other as well as for attackers to increase their chances for survival. As a team, Robin and Suann shouted to each other "crumble left" or "crumble right" to avoid the rocks or sticks thrown at them by Bretane. Without even seeing which direction Bretane threw the stone, the intended victim would dodge or crumple to the ground in whatever direction the other called out.

Robin didn't need to tell her what he intended, confident that on his word she would fall to the left and duck her head.

Robin got down on his knees.

"Kneeling before me?" said Keenan with a harsh chuckle. "Just where a Sassenach should be, on his knees."

While Keenan enjoyed his taunts, he didn't notice the way Robin knelt behind Hubert's fallen body. Slowly Robin felt around with his hands on the ground until he found a fist-sized rock. Rubbing his fingers over the jagged edges, he drew it into his grasp.

"Do I have your vow that you will release the

girl?" Robin asked Keenan.

Keenan spit out a glob from between the gap in his teeth. "I make no vows to a Sassenach. Ye will have to see what I do." Then he laughed. "Oh, I forgot. Ye winna see anything. Ye will be dead!"

At that Robin shouted, "Crumble left!" and, as Suann fell to the left, Robin raised his arm in one even motion and sent the rock careening across the yard. He threw it with such force that he fell forward over Hubert's body, calling out as his face hit the ground, "Suann! Suann! Are you all right?"

She knelt beside him before he heard her say, "Aye, Robin! Aye!" Quickly tucking her under his chest for protection, he scanned the yard. It was empty of enemies except for the six bodies, four fallen Grays, Keenan, and Hubert.

With Suann still wrapped in his arms, he rolled over onto his back and pulled her across his chest. No words needed to be said. They had survived and nothing else mattered. In fact, nothing else had ever mattered to Suannoch and Robin. For as long as they had known each other, they had completed each other's world, now and always.

Thalassa walked over to Keenan's body. "He has a hole in the middle of his forehead. Ye shattered his skull."

Setting Suann on her feet but not letting go of her hand, Robin said, "Get your bag, Thalassa. We have to get to Bretane and the others!"

He started running, but Suann pulled him back. "What about Hubert? How can we explain how he died? Thalassa could be hanged for murder!"

"Hubert died in the Grays' attack," Robin said in a

voice of steady assurance.

"But, nay, he—"

Robin stopped her. "Aye, he did. He died in the attack when one of these dead men slit his throat. We do not know which one did the deed, but one of them killed him."

Suann narrowed her eyes and then looked at her mother as Robin's meaning sank in. "Aye, he died at another's hand, one of these Gray's reivers. Is that no' right, Thalassa?"

Thalassa closed her eyes and then opened them before nodding and saying, "Aye, he is dead, so it doesna matter to him who ended his life. Ye go ahead. I will follow with my supplies. Now, hurry, Bretane needs ye."

She disappeared into the cottage while Robin and Suann ran hand in hand down the path, not knowing what they would find at the end of it.

Chapter Fifteen

A blazing bonfire in the center of the empty Makgullane yard threw sparks into the air as its flames cast odd flickering shapes.

Suann and Robin stopped at the end of the path, still hand in hand, and listened for any sound beyond the crackling fire, for any indications of another living human being. Only silence. Was it true that they might be the only ones left alive at Makgullane?

"Oh, my Lord!" Suann prayed breathlessly. "Where is everyone? Keenan said they had taken the house. Hubert talked about chaos."

Robin spotted a survivor first, sitting cross-legged on the ground beside the fire. "Look!"

"What is he doing?"

There sat Hugh tossing handfuls of dirt into the air.

"Hugh, are you all right?" called out Robin.

Jumping to his feet, Hugh grinned mightily. "Ye didna die! The Lord answered my prayers!" He ran to Robin and threw his arms around the man's waist.

"Hugh, where is everyone?"

Releasing Robin, the boy said, "I tried to stop them, but they wadna listen! I tried to warn ye."

"What are you talking about? Where is Bretane?" Robin asked with a chill running down his back.

"I tried! I really tried. I wanted to help ye!" Tears came to the boy's molasses-shaded eyes.

Robin, fearing that the man for whom he would sacrifice his own life had died, barked out, "Tell me now! Where is Bretane?"

"I wanted to send a note that they had plans to steal from ye, but I canna read or write. I left pieces of cloth whenever they stole something. I tore them off my vest. See?" He held out the jagged edges of his blue vest with the gold braid. "So ye wad ken they came from me. I am sorry! Ye helped me, and I couldna help ye!"

Except for the fire, it could have been just another evening in the Highlands. Except that it wasn't.

Robin's breath came raw in his throat. "You can help me now! Where is Bretane? Where are the others?"

Hugh pointed to the manor house. "They are all inside."

Suann latched on to Robin's arm, not knowing if she could stay standing. At the cottage, during the fight, she had not felt this terror because she had been determined to survive. There she knew what she had to do. Here at the house, she feared for the lives of other people she cared about—a much greater agony.

"Are they dead?" she asked barely above a whisper. "Please tell us. Are they dead?"

Robin shook the boy by the shoulders. "Where are the bodies? Where are the dead and injured? What happened here? Tell me!"

Hugh told his tale with all the relish of a victorious fighter, relaying every incident with determination and valor as if he had done the fighting himself.

"Yer Bretane is a fierce warrior! He came out roaring like a lion, waving his mighty sword, and he took Keenan by the leg and pulled him right off his horse. Keenan landed hard on his back and screamed for the others to help him. Yer laird held off three at once. No' much of a fight. One swing of his sword and Jack and Weems ran down that path like the Virgin Mary herself chased after them. What a sight to see!"

If the lad didn't hurry up and tell his story, Robin might burst apart just like the burning logs on the fire. "What about the others?"

"Paddy came up behind yer laird, about to stab him in the back when one of yer men smacked him in the head with a shovel. Paddy fell like a sack of potatoes! Two of yers that came to our camp with yer laird a fortnight ago started charging at some of them, and they ran away just like they did afore! And ye shoulda seen yer women! Keenan had one of yer lads down and started to take his ear when a lass swung a frying pan at his back and another clawed at him with the hoe. He cried like a babe and took off, ne'er to be seen again!"

Hugh shot his hand into the air in victory and kept talking, all the while beaming with delight. "A little man stood behind yer laird with two swords in his hands, but he couldna lift them, so he just dragged them on the ground and swung them out at the feet of anyone who came close. He couldna fight them, but he screamed like a banshee the whole time, and that kept most everybody away from him."

Robin didn't think he could stand any more of the boy's prattling. "Was anyone from Makgullane hurt? Is Bretane all right?"

"Nay, Robin," said the boy. "Mayhap a few scratches, but no real hurt." Hugh pointed down the path toward the cottage. "The Grays went that way, and they didna come back. They ran so fast they left their ponies behind. Bretane told Ralf to put them in the stable and give them some oats. He said, 'Ye canna punish a horse for his rider's folly.' "

Robin took in a breath of utter relief. "No serious injuries?"

"The one called Shane tripped over one of the little man's swords and bloodied his nose. He wailed like the little man had cut off his arm! Bretane said to light the fire so if the devils came back, they could be seen well enough in the dark to chase them away again. 'Tis a mighty fine fire!"

Suann asked, "Why are ye out here all alone?"

The boy's enthusiasm vanished. "They all went inside to get something to eat. They didna say I could come, so I sat here."

Robin's relief quickly became regret. He now had to tell the boy a story with an entirely different ending, a less victorious one for the Grays. He had to tell Hugh about the bloodshed at the cottage and tell him that the men Hugh had lived with had either died or run off for good. Robin, unsure of how the boy would react to losing the only family he had ever known, put his hand on Hugh's shoulder and kneaded it gently.

With a wounded look on his face, Robin began. "The rest of the Grays will not be coming back. They found us and tried to kill me and Suann, but we fought them. This is hard to hear, but they are all dead or they ran away." He paused before adding, "Keenan is dead."

"Serves him right!" said Hugh, raising his fist in the air again. "He treated me like something he had to scrape off his boot, and what he did to ye…I didna like it!"

"You are a fine lad," Robin said.

Suann asked, "Do ye ken where the Gray women will go now with no men to keep them?"

Hugh shrugged. "They came with Keenan because he promised them a better life, but he lied. Naught much to eat and we had to sleep in the rain. They will go back where they came from, some to Stirling and some to Edinburgh. All the women make their living on their backs, so I am no' worried for them. The only one I care about is Mercy, but she is a smart lass, and she will make her way."

Hugh then hung his head and pushed his toe around in the dirt. "Robin, ye said if I needed ye, I could come here and ye wad help me. If ye dinna think me an enemy because of my time with the Grays, will ye help me now?"

Robin tipped Hugh's head up to look into the boy's round eyes. "We are friends, you and I, and friends always help each other. You are safe here."

Hugh grinned from ear to ear.

Suddenly, Robin had a crushing need to see Bretane with his own eyes. Grabbing Suann's hand and motioning to Hugh, he said, "Come with me!"

As soon as the three of them entered the house, they heard noises coming from the kitchen. They raced down the hallway past the gathering room and skidded to a stop at the kitchen doorway where a wonderful sight awaited them!

Surrounding the large oaken table sat Bretane with all the servants and workers of Makgullane. The bowls of food that had been intended for the betrothal banquet spread from one end of the table to the other, with everyone enjoying a celebration of another sort entirely.

As soon as Bretane spotted the newly arrived trio,

he held out his arms. Everyone stopped eating when he called out, "Here ye are! We have a tale of victory to tell ye! Those renegades who beat ye, they winna be coming around here again!"

As Robin neared the table, Bretane caught sight of the blood covering his shirt. "Ye're wounded, lad!" Grabbing Robin's shirt, he tried to pull it off. "Tell me where ye're hurt! Show me!"

"I am fine," said Robin, pushing Bretane's hands away.

Suann put her hand on Bretane's waving arms to stop him from ripping Robin's shirt. "He is no' hurt. We are all fine. The blood is someone else's." 'Twas not the right time to tell him whose.

"Did ye have a fight?" asked Bretane.

Robin nodded. "With the Grays."

Bretane's face fell. "Lad, we thought they ran back to where they had come from, ne'er to return. Lad, if we had kenned they had found ye…" His face paled.

Robin clasped his guardian's arms. "Aye, Keenan and the rest attacked us at the cottage after they left here. 'Twas a hard fight, but it ended with Keenan and four others dead. You did not know."

"I am sorry, lad. I wadna leave ye alone to fight them. I should have followed those mumblecrusts! I ken better than to let the enemy leave still able to fight! Forgive me, lad. If the worst had happened to ye…or Suann…" His voice trailed off as he swallowed the lump in his throat along with the knowledge that his mistake could have cost Robin his life.

Robin kept his eyes fixed on his beloved Bretane's. "There is no blame or regret. All who matter are alive and well."

"Then whose blood is on yer shirt?" asked Bretane.

Angus interrupted before Robin could answer. "We canna find Uncle Hubert. Is he with ye?" The dark shadows around his eyes underscored the lingering fear. Angus and Glynnis stood side by side against the back wall.

Neither Robin nor Suann answered.

"Where is my uncle?" demanded Angus, his demeanor quickly changing from timid to resolute. "We couldna find Hubert. We heard the reivers shouting in the yard. When 'twas all over, we couldna find Hubert. Have ye seen him? Is that his blood?"

Robin's jaw stiffened, and his arm muscles tightened. He could not show any sympathy toward the kin of that vile Hubert Duffy. He needed a calmer head to prevail, so Suann stepped in front of him.

"I am sorry to tell ye that the blood is yer uncle Hubert's," she said. "He came to Thalassa's cottage to talk to me. Ye ken why, and then the Grays attacked us, and…one of the Grays slit his throat."

Angus let out a cry and buried his face in Glynnis's bosom. As tears poured down his cheeks, she patted his back and offered comforting sounds while he choked on gurgling sobs. Wiping tears from her own eyes and nose with one hand, she kept her other arm tightly around the little man as she rested her head on the top of his.

Robin muttered under his breath, "A waste of tears for that yaldson."

Standing on her toes, and whispering in his ear, Suann said, "Angus doesna ken Hubert as such. Only we do. We winna mourn, but we will honor the grief of others who do."

Robin nodded his acceptance of her rebuke.

"Do ye no' grieve for him?" shouted Angus, lifting his head. "Yer own *athair*?"

"The loss isna mine. I kenned him no'," answered Suann in her same calm voice.

"Where is Thalassa?" asked Bretane. "Is she all right?"

"She is coming with her medicines. We thought some of ye here wad be injured…or dead."

Hugh spoke up. "I told ye that Laird Bretane made them run away. They are all bobolynes and cowards!"

"And who are ye?" asked Bretane, seeing Hugh for the first time.

Hugh's eagerness vanished. Ducking behind Robin, he buried his face in Robin's shirt.

"He is Hugh," said Robin, pulling the child forward. "He lived with the Grays, but now he is one of us. He tried to warn us about their attack, but we did not figure it out soon enough."

"Yer vest has blood on it," said Bretane. "Did ye get hurt in the fight?"

"Nay, this blood is Robin's."

"Mine? How did that happen?" asked Robin.

"I sat with ye on the road when Keenan took yer ear. I sang to ye. Do ye remember?"

Robin smiled. "So that is how that melody got in my head." He hummed a few bars of the tune.

"Aye, 'tis the song with the Chinese words!"

Bretane put his hands on his hips and looked at Hugh sternly. "I am thinking that ye're the lad who left the scraps of blue cloth in the chicken nests and the string on the tool hooks. That ye tore them off yer vest."

Hugh nodded warily.

"A clever plan." He stroked his beard and said, "I have been looking for a young chiel who can use his head." Flipping his hand toward Robin, he said, "This one thinks he kens everything. He tells me that I dinna have anything left to teach him, but I could show a *glic*, clever lad like ye a thing or two. I think that ye will learn faster than he ever did." He winked at Robin. "Come here, lad. Have something to eat…now that ye're one of us. Robin, come eat and tell us what happened at the cottage."

Just then, Thalassa appeared in the doorway. She had changed her dress after burning the one with Hubert's blood on it. "Is anyone here needing me attention?"

"Ye can look at my ear," said Henry. "Keenan tried to take it!"

"And me nose!" said Shane.

Thalassa examined Henry's ear and announced that 'twas only a nick. Then she dabbed a cloth at Shane's nose to wipe off a few drops of blood. "Both are barely wounds, but ye both will have a tale to tell yer grandbairns of how ye almost lost yer ear and yer nose. They will be proud of their fighting men."

She placed her bag on the floor and joined the others around the table, listening quietly while Robin and Suann relayed the details of the fighting at the cottage, leaving out any reference to Hubert's behavior or his death.

"I found the other half of my ear," said Robin with a laugh. "Keenan pinned it to his cap. He said I could take the piece back, but I didn't want it. I think this half an ear makes me even more handsome!" In a grand gesture, he lifted his hair to display the torn ear.

Everyone loudly agreed that his looks had been greatly improved by Keenan's knife.

Bretane sent four of the men out with a cart to gather and then bury the dead Grays on a lonely piece of land tucked between the hills on the far side of the estate. "Do no' mark their graves. They have no one to mourn them. Angus, what do ye want done with Hubert's body? We can bury him close to the demesne if ye wish. Or we can wrap the body for ye to take home."

Angus paused before pulling himself up to his full height, which came only slightly higher than Glynnis's shoulder. "I want to carry my uncle back to Stirling to bury in our family plot, but, first…Suann and me canna be mairrit."

Suann took Robin's hand and pressed herself against him. "What do ye mean we canna be mairrit?" She tried to disguise the optimism in her voice at the possibility of a broken betrothal, but a sideways glance from Bretane told her she hadn't been successful.

"Suannoch, ye're a fine woman," said Angus, "but ye ken that we are no' suited for each other. I have found another, and we will be wed."

Robin noticed for the first time how closely Angus and Glynnis held each other. He raised one questioning eyebrow. "Glynnis?"

Angus cleared his throat. "Aye, 'twill be Glynnis. We are in love. She will be my wife and I her guidman."

A dumbfounded Robin broke the quiet in the room with, "What about the child? My child?"

Putting his arm around her, Angus pulled Glynnis

even closer. "Tell them, my love. 'Twill be all right. I am with ye. They canna stop us from being wed."

Glynnis nodded. "I had no' had me curse for two months, and I thought I was bairned," she began, chewing on her lip. "I truly did, but the night ye sent me away, my curse came." Her eyes pleaded for understanding. "That night I kenned I didna carry your bairn, but I was afeared to say anything. Ye frightened me, Robin."

Robin continued staring at her.

"Angus is so kind and gentle, I could tell him the truth. He loves me, and I him. Ye didna want me as a wife, Robin, but I will be one to Angus. 'Tis for the best that there is no bairn."

People looked at each other with stunned expressions until Angus said, "I will take her to Stirling, and we will wed there. Suannoch, I am sorry, but ye ken 'tis for the best. Bretane, if there is a penalty for a broken betrothal, I will pay it. Glynnis doesna have a dowry, but it matters no'. I want her as my wife." He got up on his toes and kissed her lightly on the forehead.

At once, his tone turned harsh as he addressed Robin. "I can see ye're relieved that ye winna be required to be her guidman. I will make her happy, and ye winna be burdened with a bairn ye dinna want. Glynnis and I will have our own bairns, and they will be loved. Ye winna mistreat her anymore."

Robin tensed at the slander, even though every word of it held true, but again Suann offered calming words. "I feel the same way as ye do, Angus. We're no' suited, but I am glad that ye and Glynnis have found each other. We are happy for ye both and wish ye the best. Isna that true, Robin?"

"Aye," said Robin with his lips barely open. "I am happy for you."

Breaking the tension, Bretane began a cheer that all the others joined in. As the raucous congratulations continued, Bretane stepped close to Robin and said, "Get that scowl off yer face, lad! How much of a doitit are ye? Has it no' occurred to ye that both ye and Suann are now free of betrothals to others? Ye are free for each other!"

Chapter Sixteen

It took all the restraint he could muster not to pick Suann up, swing her around, and kiss her deeply and completely. But their celebration would have to wait. Congratulations were in order for Angus and Glynnis, and this had to be their moment.

The celebration continued until Bretane pounded his hand on the table to get everyone's attention. "Marta's feast willna go to waste. She has prepared enough for all of us here. Fill yer plates and find a place in the kitchen or in the dining hall. Eat until every morsel is gone! My wine is also for everyone to enjoy."

As the crowd pressed close to the table to take their food, Bretane led the bereaved Angus to one side and spoke quietly. "Lad, yer uncle is dead, and we will mourn properly as soon as his body is returned here. Until then, please, honor yer bride-to-be with this fine food. For tonight, find the joy in what will come in the future. We will respect yer grieving tomorrow. Can ye do it?"

Angus nodded slowly, took Glynnis's hand, and led her to the table. The others parted and made way for the now guests of honor.

At nearly midnight, the four men returned from burying the five bodies of Gray's reivers. Their cart now carried only the body of Hubert Duffy wrapped tightly in a blanket. As they approached, Angus ran to the cart, reaching out toward his uncle. "I have to see him!" he cried.

Before he could pull away the blanket, Bretane flung his arms around the smaller man and held him back. "Ye will want to remember him as the man who loved ye and taught ye well. 'Twill be no good to look on him now."

Sobbing, Angus collapsed into Bretane's arms. The others expressed their condolences, everyone except Robin, Suann, and Thalassa, who stood quietly in the background. They knew Hubert's true character and his cruel acts, but it would serve no purpose to tarnish his memory for his nephew who had loved him all his life. After Angus and Glynnis went back to Stirling, there would be plenty of time to tell Bretane the truth, and after that, there would be no need to think of Hubert ever again.

"Come with me," Robin said to Suann. Taking her hand, they slipped away from the commotion in the kitchen and out the back door, where he pulled her against him.

"Hubert became your father in a violent way," said Robin. "Does that trouble you?"

In a steady voice, Suann answered, "It does trouble me that Thalassa suffered, but he meant nothing to me. I became the woman I am the moment she birthed me, and what came before that doesna change who I am. I belong to Thalassa, and now that I am grown, I have chosen to belong to ye, and ye to me. That is enough. That is more than enough."

He leaned in to kiss her. She felt warm against his chest, her lips so sweet and soft pressed next to his. All his life, he had never truly felt like he belonged to anyone. Although he owed his life to Bretane, and Bretane claimed him as completely as a father would a son, Robin's gut still told him every day that his roots had not begun in Scotland, that he had come late and would never be one of them. Almost but not quite. This rift set him apart from everyone he knew except Suann. His life became whole the day he met her on the stairs, when she took his hand. Forever his true self would not exist without her. He belonged in her arms.

"Marry me," he whispered.

"I will," she said without hesitation.

"I mean, marry me tonight."

Her soft lips widened into a smile. "Aye, tonight."

"We will find Father Bernard."

"I maun tell Thalassa so she can be with us."

"Nay, tonight 'twill be only the two of us. After Angus and Glynnis are gone, we can have the wedding you planned with the embroidered dress and the flowers in your hair, and everyone will be invited. But tonight, our vows will belong only to us."

She nodded and whistled the greeting that belonged to them.

He returned it.

Hand in hand, they hurried to the Makgullane chapel located about a mile south of the yard surrounding the manor house. The chapel, built over a hundred years ago by the first Laird of Makgullane, had been constructed of stones and rocks dug from the ground to clear the fields for crops. The rugged rock building had wide arched wooden doors at one end and two sets of tall narrow windows on each side. Inside, a large stone altar sat on a raised platform at the far end where it could be seen by everyone standing on the floor during a service. Father Bernard lived in a small room at the back of the chapel beside the two-door oaken confessional.

A sliver of moon lit the way as Robin and Suann entered the church. As the significance of their plans sank in, they walked slowly toward the altar, holding hands, each rubbing their thumb against the back of the other's. Robin knocked on Father Bernard's door, and before long a bedraggled priest in his nightclothes, carrying a lit candle, opened the door and gawked at them.

"What is the matter?" he asked. "Did someone die?"

At fourteen, and Father Bernard's student, Robin had thought the priest already terribly old, but the man had aged considerably since that time. His gray hair now grew in small tufts across the top of his balding head and out of his ears, and his eyes had turned a milky brown with obvious cataracts. The older man squinted at them and said gruffly, "Well, what is it? Some people sleep at night!"

"We want to be married," said Robin.

"All right, come back in the morning." The priest started to close the door, but Robin put his hand against it, holding it open. "We want to be married now, right now. It will not take long to say the words."

Suann said, "Please, Father. 'Tis important to us that we be mairrit tonight. In a week or so, we will come back and be mairrit with everyone here to see it, but tonight it is only us. Please."

Father Bernard looked at them through narrowed eyes. "Why am I not surprised that ye're here asking me for a favor in the middle of the night? Ye are Robin, the lad who killed the horse in my classroom."

"Aye," said Robin, ducking his head. "I am very sorry for that. I did not know any better then, and Bretane punished me for it, and if you remember I became a better student after that."

"Oh, I remember." He looked at Suann. "Are ye the dochter of Thalassa?"

"Aye, I am."

"She has ne'er come into this church, nor ye with her. Am I to think that ye are a godly lass when yer *màthair* is no'?"

Suann's anger lit. Robin put his arm around her, but it didn't pacify her. Nothing ever would when it came to insulting her mother. "My *màthair* is a good and fine woman! She doesna come to this chapel because ye ne'er made her welcome. It doesna mean that she isna good in the eyes of God!" She paused, but her angry tone didn't abate. "Will ye wed me to this man? Tonight!"

A smirk crossed the priest's craggy face. "I have heard of Thalassa's healing, and I have heard how her dochter is strong-willed and ne'er hesitant to speak her mind. Believe me, lass, ye will need all the strength ye can muster if ye intend to marry this one! A thorn in my side for many years, but so be it. Let me get my book of prayers and my stole. Wait in front of the altar." He closed the door.

When he returned, he had a white pastoral stole draped around his neck over his nightclothes, and he carried a small book along with a three-candle brass candelabra.

"Where are yer witnesses?" When he saw none, he said, "God cares only that ye take the vows to each other, but to make it legal for the world, ye maun be mairrit in front of witnesses."

He started back to his room when a head popped up from behind the altar. "We can watch ye wed," he said. "Wake up, Tinker! We've been invited to a wedding!"

The men behind the altar stood up, and immediately Robin recognized them as two of Keenan's Grays who had run off after the fight at the cottage. He put his hand on his dagger and took a step toward them.

"Stand down, Robin," said Ronald quickly. "We are no' part of the Grays now. Keenan led us astray, but we have given up that life. Keenan wanted ye dead, no' us. Tonight, we needed a dry place to sleep afore we are on our way south. We mean ye no harm. Truly we dinna. See?" He spread open his cloak. "We are unarmed. We wad see ye wed in the hope we can earn forgiveness for the wrongs we did. Father, will ye ask the Lord to forgive us?"

"We will confess our sins," said Tinker. "We've been saying our Hail Marys for two days now. I swear we have!"

"No need to swear," said Father Bernard. "I will hear yer confession after this ceremony." He sighed. "As long as I am up, I might as well keep doing God's work." Turning to Robin, he said, "Do ye have a ring?"

"Nay," said Suann, realizing that they had not thought through all they would need tonight. "Can we still be mairrit?"

Heaving another deep sigh, Father Bernard held out his right hand. On his smallest finger, he wore a silver ring with a small red stone in the center. "Take it," he said. "It belonged to me *màthair* until the day she died when I was nine years old. I took it from her, so I could remember her, but I am an old man who winna have long to wait afore I see her again, so ye take it."

When Robin hesitated, the priest said, "I dinna give it because I have a kind heart toward ye. I give it for her sake. Lass, wag yer hand in his face so the ring will remind him that he is pledged to take good care of ye. 'Twill be a pledge before God and canna be broken without the consequences of eternal damnation. Trust me, a lad like him will need a reminder."

"I will not forget," said Robin as he slid the ring off Father Bernard's finger.

"I winna let him forget," said Suann, her eyes crinkling with a smile.

Father Bernard sighed heavily yet again and began. "Take her hands. Robin, are ye here in pledge of yer troth of yer own free will and choice?"

"I am," replied Robin as a surge of warmth flowed from her hands through his.

"Suann, are ye here in pledge of yer troth of yer own free will and choice?"

Tears of joy slid down her cheeks as she dipped her head and, still holding his hands, wiped her nose on her sleeve. "I am," she answered with a smile that lit the night.

"Inasmuch as this man and woman have pledged their troth to be married this day—I mean, night—we call upon Heaven to bless this union. Give her the ring," said the priest.

"Before that, may I speak?" asked Suann.

Father Bernard nodded.

"Robin, I have planned these words to say to ye for many years." She took a long deep breath. "I promise that I give ye my heart for all time, from the rising of the sun to the setting of the stars. I will love and honor ye through all the time that may come with the prayer that when we are reborn at Heaven's door, we will meet and love each other again and remember how we loved while we lived."

Robin kissed her on the forehead.

"No kiss yet, lad," said Father Bernard sternly.

Robin ignored him. "I have not planned my words, but they come from my heart. You are my sun each morning and the brightest star each night. I vow on my life that I will let no evil befall you anywhere on this earth as long as I live. And if God denies me entry to paradise for any sin I have done, I will burn down Heaven's door to find you. I promise."

Father Bernard rolled his eyes and muttered, "Burn down Heaven's door? I believe he will!"

As Robin slipped the ring onto Suann's finger, Tinker said, "What beautiful words! Ronald, are ye no' glad we came in here?"

The thin pale man coughed heavily before saying, "I am glad."

Father Bernard concluded the ceremony with "Ye are fully wed. Now ye may kiss the bride. I will have yer marriage written in my book to make it official. Wait here."

Robin's lips never left Suann's the whole time until Father Bernard returned, except for brief moments to take a breath and begin his kiss again. When the older man stood before the altar, he carried a large cloth bound book. "I have already written yer names and the date here." He pointed to the last line on a page far back in the book. "Come here, lads, and make yer marks," he said to Ronald and Tinker. "I will show ye where."

After the witnessing, he said, "Here, 'tis done, now be off. When ye wed again, it will be during the day or ye will have to find a priest who suffers with sleeplessness. It will no' be me in the night again! Now, ye two men, come forward for yer confessions."

Back at Robin's room, the sun made its way overhead, but the newly married couple had no intention of leaving each other's side. They had passed the night in enthusiastic and devoted lovemaking and were not ready for it to end.

"Naught will come between us again," whispered Robin as he brushed Suann's golden tresses away from her face.

"For now, our marriage will be a secret only the two of us share," said Suann. With a push, she rolled him over onto his back and climbed on top of him. His hands encircled her waist.

"You are most beautiful," he said from deep in his throat.

"And I am most talented," she said. "Be still while I show ye." Leaning over, she put a deep lingering kiss on his lips before unhurriedly moving her mouth and her suckling down his neck to his collarbone. He moaned and put his hands on either side of her face, trying to pull her up to him again, but she resisted. "I asked ye to be still. Will ye defy yer lawful wife on her first request?"

Grinning, Robin said, "I will not, but know that the next request will be mine."

" 'Twill be my pleasure. Now for yers." Her

journey of kisses moved delightfully from side to side on his shoulders. When her mouth centered on his chest, she closed her teeth on some of his chest hair, and with a wink, she tugged.

"Ow! You want to play?" He started to tickle her waist. Jerking upright, she stood up and buried her feet in the bunched-up quilt on either side of him. Putting her hands on her hips, she pinched her eyes together. "I dinna have to continue if ye insist on doing that!"

"Oh, please, fair maiden," he begged, "do not leave me unsatisfied. I will be a good lad."

She sat down on his chest. "We will soon see just how good ye are." She continued her exploration of his face, neck, and shoulders with her hands and mouth. "Ye bring me such joy," she whispered.

At last, joy! thought Robin. The first time they made love in the cave had been all about forgiveness, and the last time here in this room it had been to say good-bye. But tonight, joy would be the only thing on their minds. He had everything he wanted. He had a family with Bretane and Suannoch and a home at Makgullane. His work as the reeve gave him goals and a purpose. And with Suannoch now as his wife, he had everything, and everything would be his for all time.

She slid down to sit on his thighs, where she grasped his erection. "Ahh," he said.

"If ye say another word or ye are no' still, I will stop. Do ye want me to stop?"

He shook his head and swallowed hard. He struggled to meet her demand that he not move or make a sound, but then nothing had ever been easy about Suann. Every day since he had known her, she had challenged him, and now every day for the rest of his life he would be there to meet all her challenges. When it became his turn in this bed, he already knew what he would do to her. Only he would allow her to cry and scream her pleasure, which would serve to encourage him to make it last longer.

She stroked him so slowly, but he did not make a sound or move a muscle. When she picked up speed, he clutched the quilt in tightly fisted fingers while biting his lip to keep silent. An instant later, she ran her tongue along the length of him, and he had never known such agony or such ecstasy.

When he could bear it no longer, he said, "Please! Release me!"

"I do," she said as she straddled him and sheathed him with her warm, wet womanly core. He grasped her hips, saying, "Aye, aye!"

Moving up, down, and around, she pushed him closer to the edge of his endurance.

"A little longer," she breathed. "A little longer." Arching her back, she kept enveloping him and then withdrawing over and over, until she said, "Now, my love, now!"

His body raced out of his control. He could not stop the explosion of his passion into her, growling a primeval cry as he did. At the same time, she experienced her own shattering peak.

Spent, she collapsed on the bed beside him. "I have mairrit a verra good lad," she said. "Verra good."

Between his gasping breaths, he said, "Now we will see if you are a good lass." He leaned over her to kiss her when he felt a breeze on his bare arse. Turning his head, he glanced toward the door, and there stood Fergus. Quickly, Robin tugged the quilt over himself and dropped his legs over the edge of the bed while Suann covered herself with the blanket and curled up behind him.

"What are ye doing still abed?" said Fergus. "The sun has been up for hours!"

"What do you want, Fergus?" asked Robin, trying his best to keep his voice even.

"I have a thing of some importance to ask ye. Do ye want me to bring ye yer plaid so ye can get dressed?"

"Nay, Fergus. What do you want?"

"Ye ken Hugh?"

Robin nodded.

"He is one of us now. Laird Bretane said so."

"I know," said Robin feeling his patience about to leave him entirely.

"Me *màthair* says that he can live with us in our croft. Is that all right with ye?"

Robin gritted his teeth and nodded.

"The thing of importance is that she canna feed him. We have a place for him to sleep, but no food. Do ye see how important it is that I speak to ye?"

"I do," said Robin, giving Fergus a scorching look. "What do you want from me?"

Just then, Hugh entered and stood behind Fergus. His eyes widened. While Fergus might not understand what Robin and Suann had been doing in the bed besides sleeping, Hugh did. He had been raised by prostitutes, and he knew full well what went on in a bed with rumpled sheets and a naked man. He also spied Suann peeking out from behind Robin.

Fergus spied her, too. "Suann, are ye staying with Robin like my man Jamie did? Are ye hurt?"

Robin pressed his palms into the bed. "What do you want?" he barked.

Hugh tugged on Fergus's tunic, saying, "We should go, Fergus. We can talk to Robin later."

"Nay," said Fergus, puffing out his chest. " 'Tis now! Robin, I have done good work in the stable with Ralf, but Bretane took in three horses from the Grays and now 'tis too much work for just Ralf and me. We need a helper. Ye could pay Hugh, then my *màthair* could feed him."

As eager as he was to get back to Suann, Robin realized the significance of this request to Fergus and Hugh. "Hugh, do you want to work in the stable with the horses?" asked Robin.

The boy hesitated before saying, "If ye will let me stay, I will work wherever ye want me. I am a good worker, and I will do whatever ye say."

"But is working in the stable what you want to do?"

Hugh hesitated again. "If I had me choice, I want to learn to make things grow. But I like horses, too. Fergus says 'tis good work."

Robin scratched his chin. "I think Darby could find a place for you working in the garden or the fields. I will talk to him."

"Thank ye! Thank ye!" said Hugh. "Let's go, Fergus."

"Not yet," said the smaller boy. "There is the matter of what ye will pay him. He is bigger than me, so I think he should earn two pennies a day." He crossed his arms in front of his chest. "Do ye no' think two pennies a day is a fair wage for Hugh?"

Suann gave Robin a shove in his back and said, "I

think two pennies a day is fair for each lad. I wad pay it in order to keep such good workers at Makgullane. I wad hate to see them go off and search for work elsewhere."

With a sigh at being outnumbered, Robin said, "Hugh, I will make the same bargain I made with Fergus. If you are a good worker, I will pay you two pennies a day. But if you do not work hard, or you are late, or if you disobey Darby, then I will give you a thrashing you will not forget."

Hugh stiffened.

Robin went on, "Fergus, because you have shown yourself to be a good worker and champion for your friend, you will also earn two pennies a day. Now unless you want to be a boy who will also earn a thrashing, you had better leave right this minute and let me get back to my work!"

"What work are ye doing in bed?"

With wide eyes and a big grin, Hugh grabbed Fergus by the tunic and dragged him out the door, closing it firmly behind them.

"Now, where am I?" asked Robin. "Oh, I remember. I want to see if you are a good lass!"

With a giggle, she rolled on her back and pulled her guidman to her.

Chapter Seventeen

Three days later, Angus and Glynnis rode back to Stirling with Hubert Duffy's body in the cart that now also carried his wedding clothes and Glynnis's meager belongings. Robin and Suann did not see them off.

Robin and Suann declared those same three days the best they had ever known. They spent their days together working or just talking and enjoying each other's company, something they had missed in recent years. They spent their nights in each other's arms.

Late on the third day, twenty armed guards from the army of King James V rode into the yard, wearing tunics and hose in the king's colors of blue, red, and gold under their chest plates of light armor. Dirks hung from each man's waist belt while across their backs they carried swords in leather sheaths. Everyone working around the house and barn stopped to watch this impressive sight of soldiers riding in formation into the yard.

All the guards stayed in their saddles when the captain, a well-muscled man with rugged facial features and a trimmed black beard, ordered everyone in the yard to stand in place.

"Ye, there," he said pointing at Maggy, "find Laird Bretane and send him to me. Tell him that I am on the king's business and be quick about it."

Maggy gave a hasty curtsy before dashing into the

manor house and returning with Bretane and Robin right behind her. Bretane walked up to the captain.

"We welcome the men of King James! What can we do for ye?" he asked.

This time the king's man dismounted, forcing Bretane to take a step back to avoid the captain's boot swinging over the front of the saddle. Robin went on alert at this obvious show of disrespect.

Speaking with authority, the captain said, "We are bound from King James to find and arrest any reivers in this area before moving south to search for other outlaws. Our king has it on good authority that this estate has seen Gray's reivers. Yer cooperation is demanded by the king. What information can ye give us?"

Fergus ran over to Robin, pulling on his shirt until he could whisper in his ear. "Hugh is afeared they have come for him. He is hiding behind the house."

"Hugh has nothing to fear. He is safe here."

"Is King James my man called Jamie?"

"I think so," answered Robin.

"Do they ken that Jamie stayed here? That my man is the king?"

"Hush now. Listen to what they have to say."

The captain rested his hands on his hips while nodding as Bretane told him about some of the things Keenan and his Grays had done in the area. "The worst happened when they beat my ward nearly to death." He pointed in Robin's direction. "He stands there today by the grace of God."

Robin gave a curt nod of acknowledgment as he watched three of the soldiers dismount and walk toward the stable. He did not try to stop them.

Bretane said, "We are more than glad that our King James is taking charge of the lawless in this area. The Grays terrorized several estates around here, causing injury and worse."

The captain raised one eyebrow in a questioning slant. "What is worse?"

"Attempted murder. Keenan Gray tried to claim Makgullane as his own. They attacked this house three days ago intending to kill us all, but we easily dispatched them. My men and my women fought well against them. They proved themselves more cowards than thieves." He hooted with laughter. "Keenan Gray had dreams of greatness and nothing to back it up!"

The captain took one step closer to Bretane until they stood only inches apart. "Who did they murder?"

"They wanted to murder all of us, but they fled with their tails between their legs when they saw we wadna surrender so easily."

"Did they steal anything?"

"Nay, we wadna let them."

The captain sniffed haughtily. "Did ye follow them and retaliate?"

"Nay, we were done with them and they with us." Bretane laughed again. "No' much of a fight."

"Then explain how 'no' much of a fight' ended in murder." He did not wait for the answer. "We found five unmarked graves on yer property, fresh graves. Are they yer people buried there, and if not, then who? In that isolated place where no one could find them?"

Bretane answered directly. "The bodies belong to the Grays who died. We didna want them to rot."

The captain signaled with his hand to the rest of his guard, who dismounted in unison and moved to form a circle around Bretane, swords drawn. "Ye said that they ran off. Are ye changing yer words to say that they ran off except for the five ye killed?"

Before Bretane could answer, the captain said, "We spoke to several women on the road and later to two men who claimed to be beggars looking for work. They said that three nights ago ye attacked them without cause, Laird of Makgullane, that ye led a dozen men into their camp. No hue and cry preceded the attack as is required by March law to legally retrieve stolen goods, and ye held no burning turf on a spear to announce yer purpose. They said that ye didna like having lawful beggars on yer land, so ye chased them off, killing some of them and taking their horses. We found them on foot and running for their lives. They also said that ye kidnapped one of their children, a lad called Hugh."

Fergus clapped his hands over his mouth to keep from crying out.

"That is a lie," protested Robin. "Hugh came here of his own accord."

Bretane hesitated. Five were dead by Robin's hand, and he also had to keep Suannoch and Thalassa out of this, especially any mention of Hubert Duffy's death. The truth was complicated, and the beggars' lies had made everything much easier for the captain. No need to listen to the knotty story of the truth. All he and his soldiers wanted was to arrest the culprit and be on their way, and arresting Bretane would quicken their departure.

Just then two soldiers exited the stable leading a chestnut stallion. "Sir, this horse belongs to the king. His saddle is here, and this blanket on its back carries the royal emblem. 'Tis the king's mount.'"

Robin spoke up, but he already knew that anything he said would only make things worse. Who would believe that the lad he knew as Jamie was really King James V? That the king had been robbed and his horse stolen, only to find its way to the Makgullane stable after Keenan's unsuccessful raid?

"That is the king's mount," Robin said, "but 'twas stolen from the king by the Grays when they attacked him on the road. Keenan stomped on his ankle and stole his clothes, so he stayed here for ten days until he could walk again. Gray rode that horse when he attacked the house, and he ran off without it."

Bretane grimaced at Robin. "Why didn't I know that the king was here?"

"We just thought him a lone traveler, not worth bothering the laird about. He had nothing with him to indicate royalty. He called himself Jamie."

"King James V stayed here?" The captain snorted. "He stayed ten days and then walked back to Stirling Palace by himself?" He burst out laughing, and his men joined in. "Ye expect me to believe this tale? Scotland's King James?"

Robin went on. "All we knew was that a young man had been attacked on the road. He had been hurt, and he stayed with me until he could be on his way. He did say that he lost his horse in the attack, but we thought him only an injured lad."

" 'Tis true!" cried Fergus unable to hold back anymore. "I found him. We played hazard together."

This brought more raucous laughter from the soldiers. "The king of Scotland played hazard with ye? Lad, have ye been dreaming? Did ye win his crown from him?"

Shaking his fist at the man, Fergus shouted, "He didna have coin! He didna even have boots! Jamie was here! I found him!"

"The king had no boots? Lad, he is the king, and a king always has boots."

Putting his arm around Fergus, Robin pulled him close. "Quiet, Fergus. You told the truth." Fergus stomped his foot in complaint at being called a liar.

"Can ye explain how ye came to have the king's mount?" said the captain.

"We already did," said Bretane.

" 'Tis not an answer I believe. Arrest him!"

As the soldiers immediately put their swords to Bretane's throat, Robin shouted, "On what charge?"

"Murder. We found five bodies in hidden graves, and we have witnesses who testified that ye murdered all of them in an unwarranted attack on their camp, and now we have the king's horse. Here we found five murders and no suggestion of theft to warrant their deaths. We will take ye to Caerlanrig, south of Edinburgh. There we will meet up with more soldiers who have captured other outlaws, and the law will be carried out in Caerlanrig, where ye will no doubt hang. Put him in the wagon."

"Nay!" cried Robin. They could not take Bretane! Not when he'd done the killing! Bretane was innocent!

"I am the one who killed them!" Robin shouted. "Bretane killed no one. I did!" He started to push the soldiers away from his guardian, but almost immediately, Robin found himself flat on his back on the ground with swords against his skin. " 'Tis me you want!"

Bretane looked down at his ward. He had safeguarded the lad from harm since the day he had found him, and he would continue to do so for the rest of his life. "Lad, 'tis no' necessary to go in my place. This is Scotland, where a fair trial will set me free. A judge will take the time to listen and will see the truth of it. No need to fear. Stay here, Robin, and take care of Makgullane."

Robin continued to struggle. "They are not listening to the truth here, and they will not listen at Caerlanrig!" he said. To the captain he called, "You cannot take an innocent man! Take me!"

Bretane raised his hand to the captain. "Let me speak to Robin."

The captain gave a curt nod.

Squatting down at Robin's side, Bretane spoke very quietly. "Robin, 'tis an *athair*'s duty to protect his son. I have lived a long life by any standards. I have done everything I have wanted to do in my life, and now I will choose what I do with the time I have left. I choose to go and answer these charges. Stay here and take care of Makgullane."

Robin's eyes misted over. "My *athair*? Your son? You never called me that before."

"I am sorry I ne'er said the words, but I always felt it in my heart. From the moment I pulled ye up on me horse to bring ye here, I have loved ye as a son."

Robin pushed against the flat sides of the swords pressing into his chest, but he could not stand to embrace Bretane as he wanted to. "And I have loved you always as a father, and today I will do what a proud son would do." He pointed to the captain. "Take me. I confess. In front of all these witnesses, I confess to the killing of Keenan Gray…and the others. Do not take an innocent man just because 'tis the quickest and easiest. Take me."

Hesitating for only a moment, the captain said, "Put the son in the wagon. He has confessed."

The soldiers hauled Robin up by his arms and led him to the small wooden wagon with barred windows stopped at the edge of the yard.

"Laird Bretane, I dinna have as hard a heart as ye may think," said the captain. "Ye should plead his case in the court at Stirling if ye can do it in time. We will be in the kirkyard at Caerlanrig in five days. There will be no reprieve after that. A confessed killer is certain to hang."

Just as the guards started to force Robin inside the prison wagon, Suann ran across the yard to Bretane with Fergus close behind her.

"I brought her," said Fergus. "She can make it right!"

"Ye canna take me guidman!" she shouted, shoving soldiers out of her way until they reluctantly stepped aside to let a woman pass.

"Guidman?" exclaimed Bretane.

By the time she reached the back of the enclosed wagon, the guards had pushed Robin on his back onto its floor and had started to lock shackles on his wrists and ankles.

"Ye canna take him!" she begged. "He saved my life. Keenan had a knife to my throat. He didna murder anyone! Defense of loved ones isna murder!"

With his hand on her arm, the captain held her back. "When it comes to reivers, self-defense is no' a defense. Otherwise the robbers could claim they only protected themselves from the ones they robbed. Any killing is murder in the king's eyes."

"Suann," said Robin. "They will take Bretane if they do not take me. I will not let that happen."

"Take yer case to Stirling," said the captain as another soldier turned the key to finish locking the shackles. To the other two manacled prisoners already inside the wagon, he said, "Is this the man?"

"Aye, he is the one," said Tinker. Ronald added in a screeching voice, "Murderer! We saw ye kill my Uncle Keenan! He just stood there, and ye killed him!"

Outside the wagon, Suann pulled herself up on the bars of the small window. "Liars! Both of ye! Ye saw what happened! Ye saw us wed. Ye said ye had changed yer ways, and ye asked for forgiveness. How can ye lie?"

Tinker smacked her knuckles with his chains, and she dropped to the ground.

The soldiers folded up Robin's chained legs and shoved him inside the wagon. The door slammed shut, and the padlock clicked closed.

Chapter Eighteen

After the last sounds of the soldiers' mounts and the clattering of the prison wagon wheels finally vanished into the wind, Suann got up from her knees in the dirt and marched back to Bretane. She replaced the utter hopelessness of seeing Robin shackled and shoved into the prison wagon with absolute determination, the kind that had served her well all her life.

"Where are they going?" she demanded to know.

"Guidman? Ye and Robin are mairrit?"

"Aye, now where are they going?"

"The captain said to Caerlanrig, south of Edinburgh."

"Then that is where I am going."

"Wait," said Bretane, stepping in front of her. "We need to go to Stirling to appeal Robin's case before the king and the court. 'Tis the only way we can save him from hanging. Robin confessed, and we have to plead the circumstances."

"Ye do what ye maun do, and I will do what I maun do. Whatever happens to Robin, I will be there. I will do whatever I can to set him free, but if that is no' to be…" Her voice trailed off.

Thalassa, who had joined the crowd just as the wagon vanished out of sight, said, "I will go to Stirling with ye, Bretane. I already told Marta to prepare food packs and for Maggy to wrap blankets and whatever else we will need. We will take the cart, and Suann will take a horse. 'Twill be easier for her to keep up with the soldiers that way." She added, "Hurry, Suann. They will get too far ahead of ye."

Suann ran to the stable with Ralf to saddle a horse.

Within minutes, Suann sat atop Bretane's best mount with bags on either side of the saddle—she refused to ride sidesaddle—that held food enough for two weeks, two water bags, two blankets, and a cloak along with a hurriedly drawn map showing the way to Caerlanrig. She also carried a small bag of Thalassa's herbs and lotions that she could use to treat a variety of injuries.

"I will come back with Robin. I promise," she said to her mother and Bretane. In a quavering voice, she added, "Whatever happens, I will bring him home." The thought that he might not be alive when she did tore a gaping wound in her heart, but she pushed it away as best she could.

Before she left the yard, she stopped and turned back in the saddle. "*A'mhàthair*, until I return, ken that I have loved ye every day of my life. Bretane, ken that Robin has loved ye the same way."

Not waiting for an answer, Suann slapped the reins on the horse and galloped out of sight.

She found it easy to follow the numerous tracks of the soldiers and the prison wagon, and soon she rode within sight of the company, although far enough back to avoid detection. Just as she turned off the road to head to the south, she spied two other travelers on foot.

"Fergus," she called out. "What are ye and Hugh doing here?"

"We are going to rescue Robin!" the boy proudly

announced. "We have a plan."

Suann's eyebrows shot up. "Oh, ye do? 'Twill be better if ye both go back and do what ye can to keep Makgullane in a good manner so when Robin comes home, he will be proud of ye."

Fergus stuck out his chin. "I dinna mean to be fashious, Suann, but we have made up our minds. Ye canna stop us. Right, Hugh?"

Hugh nodded sharply and balled up his fists to show his determination.

She sighed and rolled her eyes. The two boys looked so small and yet so resolute. These boys loved Robin as much as she did, and she couldn't deny them their quest even if it ended in disaster for all of them. On the way, she would be glad for their company, and she prayed that if it all went wrong at Caerlanrig, she could see both lads safely home. It was a dangerous journey, but true love meant risking it all.

"Well, if ye have made up yer minds, wad ye like to ride with me? Ye will wear out yer boots if ye walk all the way."

The boys looked at each other and nodded in agreement. One at a time she pulled the lads up on the horse with her, Fergus in the front with Hugh behind her with his arms around her waist.

"Fergus, does yer *màthair* ken ye are here?" asked Suann once they all settled on the horse's back.

"We wanted to leave her a message, but neither of us can read or write, so I drew her a picture."

"We made a good likeness of us walking to get Robin," said Hugh, leaning around Suann so he could see her face. "We didna want her to suffer while we are gone. I am living with Fergus and his *màthair* now. She said she is proud to have two sons to look out for her."

"Dinna ye think she will worry about ye?"

Fergus added, "We also drew a picture of a coin so she wad ken we left because we had business to do."

"Business?" She laughed to herself at the idea that these young lads knew anything about business.

"Aye, 'tis about business, mistress," said Hugh in a most solemn voice. "Robin said he would pay us each two pennies a day. I saw you there when he told us, mistress. Remember?"

She nodded, recalling her embarrassment at being found naked in bed with Robin.

"If he isna there to tell Laird Bretane, we winna get our full pay. So, we have to rescue Robin. Ye see how 'tis strictly business with us."

"I see," said Suann with a twinkle in her eye. "Ye had no choice but to take care of business. Still, I have no interest in yer business, so now that ye are with me, there will be some rules. First, ye will do as I say. If ye dinna obey, I will box yer ears." Then, knowing that a scolding from her did not make much of a threat, she added, "And I will have Robin thrash ye both soundly when we get back home. Understood?"

Both boys answered in unison with more than a little trepidation in their voices. "Aye."

"Next, did ye bring anything to eat or drink?"

Again, the boys answered in unison. "Nay."

Hugh said, "I told ye, Fergus, that we should take something to eat!"

"No mind. We will share what I have," said Suann. "And lastly, when we get home, ye will both come to see me every day, and I will teach ye how to read and write. 'Tis time ye learned. Do ye promise to study with me?"

"Aye!"

Fergus said, "I always wanted to learn. Bretane tells such fine stories about the places he has been. I think if I could read books, I could find out about all those places."

"Aye, ye could," said Suann. "Now look ahead and see if ye can still see the soldiers and the wagon." She didn't add, *And my beloved Robin.* "What do ye see?"

"They are stopped."

"Then we will do the same. We can rest the horse and grab a bit to eat. Hugh, keep watch behind that tree. If any of them look like they are coming this way, dinna call out, but wave yer hand and we will hide in the trees."

"Aye, mistress."

"Fergus, we have to get more to eat if we dinna want to go hungry now that there are three of us. Look around for some wild strawberries or maybe wild rhubarb, but dinna eat anything until ye show it to me. I dinna want ye poisoned."

Meanwhile, on the road leading east to Stirling, Bretane and Thalassa sat side by side on the cart seat in silence.

Abruptly, Thalassa said, "I slit Hubert's throat."

Bretane kept his eyes on the road. "Nay, one of Gray's men did it. 'Tis what we told Angus, and we canna change our tale now."

Thalassa scowled. "If I have to tell the true tale to save Robin from hanging, then I will. Hubert tried to kill Robin, and I winna stay silent. I winna let him die because of what I did."

" 'Twill not come to that, Thalassa," Bretane said,

patting her knee. "They arrested him for killing five of the Grays. Nothing about the death of Hubert. How Hubert died winna help Robin or make a difference to the court. I want ye to ken that no one except Angus believed what Hubert told us about how he became Suann's *athair*, and we let him believe it because the man was kin. All those years ago when I found ye in the bushes with the wee babe, I kenned 'twas no happy joining. No one hides like ye did without good cause. We havena spoken of it all these years, and we winna speak of it now." He slapped the reins against the horse's rump. "We maun get to Stirling and persuade the king to pardon Robin."

At that same moment, Robin sat on the floor of the prison wagon with his knees pulled up to his chest. With a sudden lurch, the wagon came to a halt, forcing Robin to put out his hands on the grime-covered floor to keep himself from tumbling forward.

"What did they promise you in exchange for convicting me?" Robin asked, wiping his hands on his sweat-soaked shirt.

Tinker said, "They promised us naught. If they are going to hang us for thieving, then ye might as well join us. Right, Ronald?"

The other man scratched his head more to dislodge some lice than to think of an answer. "Ye cracked Keenan's skull open with a rock. Seems like that is worth a hanging."

" 'Twas self-defense!" said Robin. "He wanted to kill Suann! All of ye tried to kill us. I have a right to protect my own, and you had no right to attack us!"

Tinker kept his distance from Robin while he tried to defend his indefensible position. "We had cause. Ye had what we wanted. We had naught, and ye had everything!"

Robin lunged at Tinker, but before he could reach him, the door swung open, and two soldiers grabbed Robin's ankles and dragged him out. He bumped down the wooden steps and landed face down on the ground with a grunt.

"Prisoner, what is yer name?" demanded the captain after Robin had been hauled to his feet.

"Robin of Makgullane," he said through his now bloodied lip.

The captain pointed back up the road. "Then, Robin of Makgullane, who is that following us? They have been behind almost since we left Makgullane. When we stopped, they stopped."

Robin stepped out of the shadows and squinted in the sunlight at the horse and three riders behind them.

Recognizing them, his heart twisted with equal amounts of happiness and fear.

Before turning back toward the captain, he wiped every trace of emotion off his face and presented a calm but somewhat curious expression. "They are strangers to me, but they do not look too dangerous."

"I am no' concerned about the danger. We picked them up after we picked ye up, so I thought ye might ken them." To the soldiers nearby he ordered, "They may cause trouble, so go back and run each of them through. Leave the bodies where they fall as a warning to others who might try to interfere with our lawful business."

Robin clenched his jaw and remained silent, although he hoped the captain didn't notice how his shoulders tensed. He had to make the man believe that those behind the troop had no connection to him or to anyone else, just unknown travelers. His effort proved in vain. Dunwoody called his bluff.

Keeping his eyes on Robin, Dunwoody said, "Step lively, men. No one kens them, and I dinna want anyone trailing us. Put each of them to the sword."

Realizing that Dunwoody's men would do just as he ordered, Robin said quickly, "Nay, stop, I do know them." It might not save them if he told Dunwoody the truth, but he had to try. They'd hang him no matter what, and he couldn't let that same thing happen to the ones following. He dropped his head to his chest.

"Stay where ye are, men. Who are they, prisoner?" asked Dunwoody.

Robin let out a heavy breath and lifted his eyes to meet the captain's. " 'Tis my wife and two young boys from the estate. They cannot possibly be a threat to these soldiers. I beg you, leave them be."

"What do they want?"

"Likely to bring my body back home with them."

Captain Dunwoody snorted. "Foolish, but I will allow it provided they dinna cause any trouble. If they get too close or if they try to set ye free, there will be no one to bring ye back home. Do we understand each other?"

"Let them be, and you will have no trouble from me."

"No trouble? So ye have no' been pounding yer fists into the other prisoners?"

"They are two-faced lying thieves!" said Robin, straining against the two soldiers holding his arms. "They beat me near to death and tried to kill everyone I hold dear!"

"Aye, they are thieves. We found them on the road carrying golden cups and crosses from a church, and from the way they cursed us, they're no' priests!" He laughed at his observation and the others joined in. "But theirs isna the only testimony to yer guilt. We found the hidden graves and stolen horses."

"I had to protect my home!"

"King James will decide yer guilt or innocence, though I dinna think it will be hard to decide. There is no proof of self-defense, and there is much to show yer guilt. The king is meeting us at Caerlanrig. He has requested a meeting with one of the more powerful Border reivers, Johnnie Armstrong, to go hunting, and the hope is they will come to some agreement to bring order and peace to the borders."

The captain pulled a face. " 'Tis about time! King James maun be strong against these brigands and any others we find. Ye may no' be a thief yerself, Robin of Makgullane, but ye did kill, and the reason why doesna matter. Take him back to the wagon."

"You will not harm the ones following us?" asked Robin over his shoulder as the soldiers dragged him away.

"Not unless they give me cause," answered Captain Dunwoody.

For the next three days, Robin knelt nearly constantly at the small barred window at the back of the wagon, grasping the bars and watching the trio trailing behind them. He ate the thick pieces of bread and drank the flagon of ale brought to the prisoners three times a day, but otherwise did not move from his spot. Once Ronald tried to push him away, but a hard fist to the man's face blackened his eye and stopped both of the prisoners from bothering him.

Over and over, he wondered what Suann and those boys could be thinking. They had no chance to change the outcome. Even if King James remembered Robin's kindness, he had to enforce the law. To establish a strong monarchy, young James could not be seen showing favoritism, especially to a man of no consequence like Robin, and killing meant hanging.

At night, he slept fitfully, waking again and again to look through the window. He couldn't see the three in the dark, but even from this prison wagon, he felt a responsibility to protect them. He admired their bravery, but to think a small woman and two young boys could make a difference against armed guards and a king was ridiculous. The most they could hope for would be to bring his body home to be buried at Makgullane. That would have to be enough for them and for him.

On the fourth night, after he awoke yet again and came to his knees to look through the bars, something appeared just outside the window. Startled by the vision, he fell back hard on the wagon floor. He came up on his elbows to see if the sound had awoken his cellmates, but their raucous snoring said otherwise. Slowly, he got back up to look out the window again. Hugh smiled back at him!

Hugh pinched his lips together to tell Robin not to talk as he handed something through the bars. Robin took it in his hand and saw the half coin with the bent corner, his coin that Suann carried with her. It had been warmed by Hugh's hand, and when Robin touched it to his cheek, he imagined Suann's touch. Closing his eyes, he let his thoughts of her wash over him. But soon the warmth disappeared, and reality hit him like a punch in the gut.

Reaching into his own pouch, he took out the half coin that he carried and handed both of them through the bars to Hugh. Hugh shook his head and refused to take them, but Robin locked his fingers around Hugh's smaller hand and pried open the fingers. He put both halves of the coin into the boy's palm, and mouthed, *Tell her I love her.*

Hugh reluctantly took both halves and mouthed, *I will be back.*

Nay! Robin mouthed, but the boy had already vanished into the darkness.

Robin slumped against the rough wall. He and Suann had been together for nearly all their lives, and he hoped that having both halves of their coin might give her comfort in the rest of her life.

He did not fear for himself. There were worse ways to die than by hanging, but his fear was for Suann and for Fergus and Hugh. If they died because of him, the eternal fires of Hell would not be enough to ease his guilt. His most damning fear, however, was leaving Suann alone. He wished she would marry again, but he doubted it. The Suann he knew would live the way Thalassa always had, alone, independent, and in the service of others.

He said another silent but fervent prayer asking the Lord to let him kiss her one more time before the noose tightened around his neck.

As soon as Hugh arrived back at their makeshift campsite, Suann hugged the boy closely. "How did he look?" she asked with her arms still around him.

"He looked verra dirty. And the smell of him was

awful."

A faraway look came over Suann. "Are his eyes still blue?" Envisioning his deep blue eyes grew harder each day. If she forgot those eyes, she didn't know if she could go on living.

Hugh said, "I could barely see him in the dark, but, aye, they're still blue."

"No one saw ye, did they?"

"Nay, mistress. The Grays taught me how to get in and out of a place without anyone being the wiser. Robin gave me these."

He held out the two halves of the coin, and in a burst of heartache, Suann's tears spilled over. She wiped them away quickly. It would do no good to let the lads see her cry. She had to be strong for them. Safeguarding the coins in her pouch, she vowed to keep these tokens together for as long as she lived.

They had to be prepared for what awaited them at Caerlanrig. She accepted that the three of them could not defeat armed soldiers, so their only chance was for her and Fergus to distract the guards by pleading Robin's case while Hugh used his wiles to help Robin slip away. A foolish plan, aye, but the only one she had. She didn't think they would hang a woman and two small boys, but if she failed to bring Robin home alive, she would wish they had.

She and Fergus rehearsed bold gestures and loud sobbing until they could bring on copious tears on cue. With Hugh, she rehearsed how to get close to Robin, how to hold his shackles so they didn't rattle, and how to move away with him as quickly as possible.

This practice was necessary so they would be prepared for anything that might happen, but also to distract their minds from their worst thoughts—Robin and the noose.

****

Thalassa and Bretane arrived at Stirling Palace, only to be told that King James and eight thousand men had left for the kirkyard at Caerlanrig several days earlier.

They had arrived too late to intervene on Robin's behalf.

They went home to prepare a place for him.

Chapter Nineteen

They called Johnnie Armstrong "The King of the Borders," and he enjoyed being the most fearsome, ruthless legend in all of Scotland and parts of England. He and his men, sometimes as many as sixty, rode where they pleased, taking what they pleased from whomever they pleased. He roamed over, across, and between the Scottish and English borders, called the Border Marches, and he built alliances on both sides. The influential Armstrong clan revered him as a hero and prospered because of his notoriety. While the rest of the clans of Scotland might fight among themselves, they presented a united front in support of Johnnie.

After a few years of riding the borders, Johnnie no longer needed to rob and pillage because of his extensive use of extortion, forcing landowners to pay what he called a "rent" or a "tax" to avoid being raided, robbed, or killed. People paid him for his "protection" without a moment's hesitation, knowing that despite the newly enacted Scottish law making these payments illegal, it could never be enforced on someone as powerful as Johnnie. When fellow looter, Adam Scot, was arrested and beheaded, Johnnie simply scoffed. It meant nothing to him! Every day, Armstrong's coffers and chests overflowed with more coin, and he became rich beyond imagining.

From his tower in Canonbie, he governed at will.

He blessed those in his favor with his goodwill, and he attacked, robbed, and often brutally murdered those who were not. To the authorities, he lived beyond the law. To his clan, he stood as a law unto himself, respected and admired.

Armstrong's domination of the border lands of Scotland incurred the wrath of many powerful men, including King James V. This didn't concern Johnnie until his arrogance led him to accept an invitation from the young king to go hunting in the forest near the church at Caerlanrig. He and twenty-four of his soldiers rode to the meeting with one plan in mind: to intimidate the youth who sat on the throne. But that youth had quite another plan.

On the day Captain Dunwoody and his troops arrived at the Caerlanrig Chapel, south of the town of Hawick, they set up camp behind the chapel in a field of tall grasses surrounded on three sides by a forest of oak, birch, and rowan trees.

The guards ordered Robin, Tinker, and Ronald out of the wagon, stripped them of their clothes, and doused them with buckets of cold water from the river.

"Ye stink!" said one of the guards giving them their makeshift bath. "This king may hang ye, but we dinna want his nose to be able to tell from Edinburgh that we have prisoners."

One of the soldiers picked up Robin's leather pouch and started to toss it into the pile of discarded clothing to be burned. Before it hit the ground, Robin grabbed it.

"He said to burn everything," said the guard.

"Not this!" retorted Robin. "This I keep!" Glad that Suann now had both halves of their coin, he still could not lose the token from his mother.

The soldier shrugged.

The guards also threw buckets of river water into the wagon in a half-hearted attempt to clean it out. After the filthy black water full of human waste and dirt poured out of the small drain in the wagon floor to the ground, the prisoners covered that sewer of mud with fresh dirt in a vain attempt to eliminate the smell.

The soldiers handed the naked prisoners discarded shirts and trews that other soldiers had worn under their uniforms and no longer wanted. The clothing was worn, torn, and lice infested, and the shirt barely covered Robin, making it not much better than nothing at all. It surprised him how the trews rubbed against his thighs after having gotten used to the free-swinging plaid. Taking a corner of the shirt, he slipped it through the loop on the pouch and tied the cloth into a tight knot. The pouch would stay with him!

Robin did have to admit that, standing in the sunlight, he felt much better, but after being forced back into the confined space of the wagon to sit in the puddles left on the floor, the seriousness of his situation came back to him. He just hoped that the king appreciated the effort made by the troops to make him presentable before hanging him.

He also hoped that the boy he knew as Jamie might remember the ten days spent at Makgullane, that he might recall the lessons on plants and on keeping proper ledgers, and that he might show the same mercy to Robin that Robin had shown to him. But kings lived by different rules and had different obligations from ordinary people. Would a king remember that for ten days he had lived as an ordinary person? Would it allow him to overrule his own law?

The next morning the guards again ordered the prisoners out of the wagon, and to their surprise, removed their wrist manacles and leg irons. Robin had only a minute to rub the raw rings around his wrists before a soldier bound his hands behind him with rope.

"Understand this," said Captain Dunwoody as he paced in front of the trio. "Ye're still our prisoners. Each of ye will have an armed guard with a dirk pressed into yer side while King James is among us. Ye will show the proper respect by standing quietly. If ye do otherwise or if ye call out, ye will be dropped where ye stand. A slice with the dirk will be a lot faster than hanging for both ye and me."

A young fair-haired soldier with a sharp chin and a straggly sparse beard stood next to Robin, and enthusiastically dug the point of his dirk into Robin's ribs.

"I will not move," said Robin. "You can hold your weapon more loosely."

"Shut yer mouth."

Robin could take out this scrawny guard with a hard shove, but he had promised not to cause trouble, and he wouldn't do anything that might put Suann, Fergus, or Hugh at risk. He wondered where they might be now.

Just then, a commotion arose as a portion of the king's contingent approached. The remaining six thousand soldiers surrounded the forest and the open meadow at the ready, waiting for the king's command.

As King James V rode through Dunwoody's troops into the center of the field, Robin marveled at how much the thin, quiet young man with the sprained ankle had changed. The red-haired youth sat on his mount with a stiff back and his head held high. His shaggy hair had been trimmed and combed, and the tam on his head bore his royal emblem. Even his blue cloak with gold trim added to his regal appearance, and he spoke to the soldiers in a strong and self-assured voice while seated astride his black stallion.

"We are here to meet with one of the worst threats to our crown. The Border reiver known as Johnnie Armstrong maun be tamed. All of ye are charged with the support of yer king! Ye are charged with preserving the rule of law!" His voice rose to a frenzied pitch. "Ye are bound to protect the realm of all Scotland!"

A cheer went up as King James descended from his mount and climbed the steps onto the platform that had been built in the center of the field. He walked over to a padded chair covered with royal purple cloth in the middle of the dais, making it clear that the king would sit above while everyone else stood below. It now occurred to Robin that all these troops and all this pomp might not be intended to make peace with Armstrong, but instead for King James to establish that, despite his youth, he was strong enough to govern the country, strong enough to be a king. Seventeen-year-old Jamie had something to prove!

Everyone waited in the sun for close to an hour before a messenger ran up to the platform. "They are here," announced the man.

"Tell them to dismount and come before us," replied King James.

Twenty-four men entered, led by Johnnie Armstrong. The extravagance of their clothing had never been seen in Scotland outside of the royal court.

They flouted all the sumptuary laws meant to establish the lines between the three groups of citizens—the royal, the noble, and the ordinary people. One's clothing told the world what class that person belonged to and thus what privileges and courtesies should be afforded them. These Armstrongs dressed as if they had royal blood, an obvious affront to the young man sitting before them on the dais.

Each man in Armstrong's group wore a long coat trimmed with ermine or fox over a colorful tunic of silk or brocade, embellished with real gold thread and sparkling jewels on every hem and collar, in the king's colors of blue, red, and gold. Johnnie Armstrong's coat of quilted brocade lined with ermine fit loosely over a velvet tunic in brilliant purple, a color reserved only for use by the royal house. Such ostentatious clothing could only have been imported from Italy or France at great expense.

These men strode into the field convinced that they could indeed behave in the same manner as the king who invited them. They soon discovered otherwise.

"Yer Majesty," said Johnnie, known as Black Jock within his clan, as he bowed to King James. "We are honored by yer invitation to join ye on the hunt."

"What wants this knave that a king should have, but the sword of honor and the crown!" cried James, insulted that these men positioned themselves at the same rank as himself. "Surround these brigands and outlaws who dare appear before us dressed as our equal!"

In short order, the Armstrongs found themselves tightly enclosed by hundreds of armed guards.

Immediately, Johnnie realized the danger and

started to bargain for their release. Previous negotiations with other enemies had always ended in his favor, and he thought the same would hold true today with the inexperienced boy king. "We are unarmed, Majesty. We meant no disrespect. We only wanted to honor ye with our finest clothing and submit to yer authority here today."

The soldier beside Robin snickered at the obvious lie.

"We are not honored!" said King James. "Ye have overstepped yer bounds for many years by yer thieving and murder, and ye choose to prove yer guilt by coming before us in this way. Ye will all be hanged as the outlaws ye are!"

Johnnie, with a stunned look on his face, recognized that the king had trapped him in a deadly snare, and pleaded his case in the only way he knew.

"Highness, we have much we can offer ye. Our lives are surely worth half of all the gold we have in our coffers. Surely the crown has fine use for such a fortune."

King James's face colored almost as red as his hair. "We have no use for a fortune obtained by theft and murder!"

Johnnie Armstrong forced a smile. He had not anticipated this situation. "If gold is no' what ye seek, then surely the king has enemies he wad like eliminated. Could our lives be exchanged for the heads of any Englishman, of any rank, to be delivered at any time ye demand, day or night?"

"We will take care of our own enemies. Hang them! Hang them all!"

The soldiers swarmed over the Armstrongs,

subduing them and binding their arms. When all twenty-five stood captured and bound, Johnnie faced the young King James, his face dark with anger and regret. "I am but a fool to seek grace in a graceless face."

"Hang every one of them," retorted the king.

The soldiers started to drag the outlaws to the trees where nooses had already been hung, when another commotion began near the platform. All turned to see soldiers trying to carry two struggling figures away from the king's dais. One of them, a woman, kicked and clawed at the arms that held her. She shouted, "King James! King James! Hear our plea!"

The other intruder, much smaller, shouted, "Jamie, 'tis me! Fergus!"

King James's head snapped in the direction of the ruckus. "Stop!" he ordered. "Let us see them."

The soldiers hauled their captives closer to the platform, not an easy task as these new prisoners continued to fight with every ounce of their strength.

Suannoch and Fergus! Robin instinctively moved toward them until he felt a weight on his feet preventing him from taking a step. Looking down, he saw young Hugh sitting between his legs. The boy pinched his lips together with his fingers like he had the night he came to the prison wagon and mouthed, *Wait*. The soldiers on either side of Robin, too engrossed in the appearance of the new trespassers, failed to notice the third one at Robin's feet.

Robin had no idea what this plan of Suann's entailed, so he waited and prayed it would not end in disaster.

"Aye, 'tis ye, Fergus," said the king. "What are ye

doing here? 'Tis no' a good time. I am about royal business. These outlaws are to be hanged."

"I dinna care about them," said the boy. " 'Tis another one. He is yer Robin who rescued ye from the road, the one who took ye from the bush and fed ye until ye could walk again."

King James said, "Robin is here? Where?"

Suann whistled three short puffs and one longer note.

Robin answered her whistle with the same pattern, and for it received a sharp poke in the ribs from his guard's dirk. In defiance, he whistled again.

"There he is!" Fergus pointed to where he spied Robin.

Suann continued to squirm in the soldier's grasp while shouting, "Yer men took Robin from Makgullane. They accuse him of being a murderer, but it isna true! We came to tell ye the truth! Not the lies told by the scoundrels with him. We are here to beg ye to set him free. Ye ken he is a good man! Ye canna hang him!"

Captain Dunwoody stepped out of the ranks. "Majesty, we have testimony that this Robin of Makgullane killed several men in cold blood and, together with others, attacked a helpless band of beggars, resulting in their deaths. He also confessed."

"Bring him to us," said King James, "and those who testify against him."

As the guards pushed Robin, Tinker, and Ronald forward, one of them noticed Hugh, who had fallen on his face at Robin's first step. "What the blazes?" Jerking the boy up by his hair, all of them made their way to the king, who with his hands on his hips, looked quite the sovereign at only seventeen years old.

Suann would not have recognized Robin had he not whistled. An overgrown beard and wild uncombed hair hid most of his face but could not hide his sunken eyes and cut lip. His clothes barely covered his chest, and his shoulders split their seams. Even then she couldn't be completely sure until he spoke.

Robin bowed from the waist. "Your Majesty." His hair fell across his face.

Hugh dropped to his knees and lowered his head until it touched the ground.

"And who is this?" asked James, pointing to the boy in front of him.

"That is Hugh," said Robin. "He once traveled with the Grays, but they mistreated him, so he came to me. He has no part in any of this. He is innocent."

"It seems that ye take in injured lads the same way another man wad take in stray kittens."

"I was once a stray kitten myself until a man took me in and saved me, so I know how it feels to be lost."

" 'Tis a worthy thing for ye to do. We are grateful when ye took us in. Now, what shall we do with ye? Captain, on what evidence do ye arrest this man?"

Captain Dunwoody spoke with the authority of his rank. "While investigating outlaw activity at yer request in the area of Makgullane, we found five graves hidden in a remote corner of the estate, unmarked and obviously ne'er intended to be found. We then found these two brigands." He pointed to the other two prisoners.

Ronald nervously danced a little jig until Tinker smacked him on the chest. "What are ye doing? He wants to hang us!" Ronald quickly stopped his feet and dropped his head.

Dunwoody continued. "These two carried goods stolen from a kirk, but quickly told us of the man who had attacked them and killed their kin. They vowed they only stole to buy food because they themselves had been robbed by this Robin of Makgullane. Several women on the road told the same story. Then while questioning the laird of Makgullane, we discovered three stolen horses, including yer mount. When we attempted to arrest the laird, this man Robin confessed to the killings."

The king's gaze turned back to Robin. " 'Tis damning evidence, Robin."

" 'Tis no' true!" cried Suann. She sank her teeth into the knuckles of the guard holding her who gave a cry of pain and instinctively released her. She ran to the dais with the guard right behind her, but James put out his hand to stop him just as the man reached for her.

"Keenan Gray tried to kill me. Robin had no weapon, so he broke his skull with a rock. He fought for me and my *màthair*. 'Twas self-defense! The soldiers wanted to arrest Bretane, so Robin confessed to stop that injustice. Now this is another one! His heart is good and strong, and ye canna hang him for it!"

"What about the testimony of these men?" asked the king, waving his hand in the direction of Tinker and Ronald. "Are we to consider them liars?"

"Aye!" said Suann. "Robin chased them off several times. He defeated and shamed them along with their leader, Keenan Gray. Isna stealing from the kirk enough to condemn them?"

King James did not answer. Instead he paced the length of the platform several times before saying, "If these Armstrong reivers are to be hanged for killing, then it maun be the same for all who kill. We are sorry to deny yer request, but as sovereign we canna do otherwise."

"Ye canna hang my Robin!" shouted Fergus. "Will ye set him free if I beat ye in a game of hazard? I have my dice." He shook his pouch. "If I lose, ye can hang me!"

"Nay!" Robin called out. The young soldier jabbed the dirk into his side, but Robin twisted away and started forward. Before he had taken three steps, the guard and two others grabbed Robin by the arms and tried to push him to the ground before King James again put out his hand to stop them. They released the prisoner but remained standing close behind him.

" 'Tis my life, Fergus, and ye will not go in my stead," said Robin. " 'Tis my destiny to face, and I alone will face it. You are noble to come here to beg for my release, but I made my choices and the consequences are mine. I would do it all again for your sake, Suann. I would do it again even knowing that hanging is how it would end. Suann, take Fergus and Hugh home."

"I winna leave without ye," she said firmly.

He expected that from her. His Suannoch had the determination of a wild boar on the hunt, and he loved that about her, but he must make her see that she had to leave him now. Who knew what the king would do if she kept up her pleading. If she angered him, he might decide to hang her, too. Robin would never let that happen.

"Please, Suann, I ask this as your husband. I will face death on my own terms. If I see your tears, it will be too much for me. If you are watching, I will die with my own tears in my eyes, and you cannot let that happen."

Then he said something he knew would hurt her. "My dignity is all I have left. I ask you to leave me now, so I can keep my self-respect as a man. Do not take it from me by staying here any longer." His voice took a cruel turn. "Let me have my dignity even in death. Make your last sight of me be as a man standing straight. Leave me with that, at least."

She winced, and he knew his words had done their deed. "Suann, take Fergus and Hugh back to Makgullane."

The wounded cast in Suann's eyes struck him like a hammer blow to his gut.

Finally, she said, "Aye, Robin. Yer Majesty, I ask that the lads and I be allowed to return home. Ye have our oath that we will leave and winna interfere any longer."

The king nodded.

"I wish to say some words to my guidman. There will be no trouble, I promise. May I kiss him one last time?"

The king nodded again.

Suann walked over to Robin, and slipping her arms under his tied behind his back, she held him around his chest.

"Ye ken I have always loved ye," she began. "I promise, in the life after this one, we will be together. We will remember how we loved in this world, and we will love for eternity." She held her tears in. She would be strong for him. He had asked it of her, and she would do it even as her heart split open.

He touched the top of her head with his chin. "I will burn down Heaven's door, and I will be there waiting for you. I promise."

He kissed her with all the longing and regret he felt, and she answered his kiss with the same longing, regret, and love of her own. Raising his head, he whistled their special signal. She whistled it back. Then she turned and walked away.

Taking Hugh and Fergus by the hand, she led them out of the field and away from the kirkyard. Fergus tried to look back, but Suann tugged him forward.

"He mauna see us cry," she said. "We will mourn when we are far away from this terrible place. Then we will cry all we want because our hearts are broken. We will remember him as he wad want us to, no' in those rags with his hands tied, but as the man who lived to make us happy."

Fergus choked back a sob. "Aye, Suann."

Hugh did the same. "Aye, mistress."

The sunset spread out orange and red across the horizon before they got to the place where they had hobbled the horse. After eating the last of the cheese from her pack, they leaned together against a tree and tried to sleep, but it would not come for any of them.

In the morning, they would go back to the field behind the Caerlanrig kirkyard and bring Robin home, just as she had promised she would.

Chapter Twenty

The sun had fully breached the horizon before Suann and the lads climbed on the horse and started back toward Caerlanrig to retrieve Robin's body. She would do her best to convince one of the soldiers to give her one of the now-riderless Armstrong horses to carry Robin. If not, then she, Fergus, and Hugh would walk back to Makgullane beside her beloved.

Just as the church, the surrounding field, and the trees that still held three dangling nooses came into sight, they met a dozen women walking toward them. A low cloud of dust from the road shrouded their feet.

"Are ye headed to find yer hanged kin?" asked a woman with a jeweled band woven through her curly hair. "If ye are, ye are too late."

"I ken he is dead. I want to bring his body home," said Suann.

"Like I said, ye are too late. All buried, every one covered over in one grave." Tears streaked her cheeks under her swollen and red eyes.

A tall lanky woman walking beside her spoke angrily to Suann. "No respect! The king has no respect! Every one of the men thrown in a hole like rubbish!" She put her arm around the first woman's shoulder and pulled her sobbing friend closer. "He didna even leave us a single thing to remember our kin by! No jacket, no jewel, not even a pair of boots! All of it in one big hole in the ground!"

A third woman, portly with a noticeable limp, moved closer and put her hand on Suann's leg. In a heavy voice, she said, "All the men hanged and dragged to the mass grave with the nooses still around their necks. No priest to say the words. We are left with nothing. Ye're left with nothing."

"I promised to bring him back home," said Suann. Her lost expression and the lifeless tone in her voice made the woman grasp her leg tighter.

"Listen to me, lass!" she said sharply. "There is naught for ye here, naught to see, naught to touch, naught to bring back. All that is left are yer memories of the man. Take yer lads home and teach them to ne'er forget what ye lost by the king's hand. Go home!"

The woman took the reins and turned the horse and its riders back the way they had come. Too shattered to resist, Suann moaned, "But I promised."

Hugh leaned around to see Suann's face. "She is right. Robin will come home with us in how we remember him. We will tell everyone all about him."

Fergus said, "We winna forget, Suann. We winna forget."

A wail leaped into her throat and had just started to sound when with great effort she swallowed it down. Those around her must not know how leaving Robin behind would be her own never-ending death. Only alone at night would she pour out her agony to the skies. Hugh and Fergus needed her to show them her courage. Robin's memory needed her to be strong.

"We will be at Makgullane in five days," she said. "We will stop at Hawick and buy food. I can sell my ring, and we will be home in five days."

"Ye canna sell yer ring," said Fergus. "Robin gave it to ye!"

"Nay, Father Bernard gave it to me. Robin gave me the coin we shared, and I will always have it." She patted the pouch at her waist. "We will be home in five days."

Five days later, the three travelers returned to Makgullane to find Bretane waiting for them in the yard. Before Suann could say a word, he pulled her off the horse and wrapped her in his big safe arms. "My sorrow is great, but I am glad ye're home."

"I couldna bring him home," she said barely above a whisper. "All of them buried in a mass grave. I couldna bring him to be buried at Makgullane. I am sorry."

"The news has traveled about how the king hanged the Armstrongs and how he showed no mercy and how one grave served for all the men. I prayed ye would be able to bring Robin home, but it couldna be." He shook his head. "Ye maun rest. I will take the lads back to their *màthair*."

With effort, Suann made her way across the yard to the room in the barn. Before opening it, she leaned her head against the door to gather her strength before entering its emptiness.

Bretane put his arm around each boy as they walked to their croft.

"Suann didna cry," said Fergus. "I cried and so did Hugh, but no' Suann, no' once."

Bretane said, "She wanted to get ye home safely. Now that ye are here, she will cry, but if I ken Suann she will do it alone. She will grieve with a heavy heart, but we will ne'er see her tears. Her tears will only be for Robin."

After pondering that for a time, Fergus said, "My *màthair* will be angry, I fear, angry that we ran off."

Hugh asked, "Even though we went to save Robin?"

"She gets angry when she is worried. I will tell her that 'twas all my fault so she winna punish ye."

"Nay, Fergus, I am yer brother now, and I will share the blame…and the punishment." His lip twitched a bit as he asked, "What will it be?"

Bretane interrupted. "If yer da still lived, I ken that ye wad no' be sitting right for a verra long time. If yer *màthair* asks me to, I will stand in the stead of yer da and do what he wad have done."

Both boys gulped but kept on walking if only a little slower now.

As her sons and Bretane approached the croft, they saw their *màthair,* Dorry, widow of Elrod, leaning against the doorway of her small cottage. She crossed her arms and scowled. "So ye decided to come home?" she said in a stern voice.

"We are verra sorry we worried ye," said Fergus. "We left ye a message."

"That scribble? A message?" She pushed herself away from the door. "Ye two worried me to the edge of sickness. Did ye even think of me once before ye went? Did ye even care that ye left me alone to cry meself to sleep every night?"

The lads hung their heads and rocked on their heels. Their sorrow for Robin mixed badly with knowing that their mother had suffered as well.

"I will make certain that ye dinna forget me again! Come inside."

Little by little, putting one foot in front of the other, the boys stepped across the threshold to a vision they did not expect. The table in the center of the room creaked under the weight of breads, candies, tarts, and a large pot of Fergus's favorite dish, cullen skink, a thick rich soup made of smoked haddock, potatoes, and onions in a creamy milk base.

Having eaten the last of the cheese on the road hours ago, both of the boys' stomachs rumbled at the sight of a meal like no other they'd ever seen. Fergus and Hugh stood stock still, unable to understand what it all meant. Finally, Fergus asked cautiously, "This is for us?"

"Aye," answered Dorry with a generous smile. "This is to welcome home my two brave warriors. Sit and eat. Bretane, ye're welcome as well."

Bretane shook his head and closed the door behind him as he left. Dorry had already told him what she had waiting for the lads, and he, of course, had no intention of standing in for their *athair* to punish them. He just wanted to make them suffer a little, so they would think twice before abandoning their mother without a word again.

"My son," he said aloud. The twelve years since he had brought Robin to the Highlands had been the most peaceful he'd ever known because caring for and teaching the lad had given him purpose. Finding that beaten boy in the rain had also taught him to love, something he vowed he would never do again for the rest of his life. He remembered the cuts and burns on Robin's back and knowing he had helped heal the lad's outward and inward scars also healed Bretane's own scars. Until Robin, he had no family to call his own…and now he had no family again.

Suddenly unable to force one foot in front of the other, he leaned into an outcropping of rocks at the side of the path. Laying his head against his arm, he did something he had not done for many, many years. He cried loud, choking sobs, pouring out the pain that he had kept inside ever since Robin's arrest. He roared his anguish.

He had no idea how long he stood there grieving until he felt a hand on his back. Then another hand, and another, and another, and lastly another. He turned to see the tear-stained cheeks of Marta, Maggy, Darby, Shane, and Henry.

"We came to walk home with ye," said Darby. "We came to take ye home."

****

The next few weeks passed with excruciating slowness for Suann. Every day, she set her mind to the tasks ahead so she wouldn't have to think about what she had lost.

The reading lessons for Hugh and Fergus went well. Fergus proved to be the better student, but Hugh kept at it despite his struggles to put the letters in the right order. The lads went home every day and showed Dorry what they had learned, until one morning she appeared at the door of the gathering room in the manor house and asked if she could join the lessons. The next day Suann discovered Henry and Maggy seated at the table with the others, eager to learn this skill of reading.

She had found her purpose, to be a teacher, and while it filled her days, it did not ease the emptiness inside. She insisted on staying in Robin's room in the barn, refusing Bretane's pleadings for her to move into one of the upstairs rooms in the manor house. Finally, she agreed to eat a meal with him every evening. Mostly she pushed the food around her plate, but she ate enough to keep his nagging at bay.

Before leaving the table to crawl into bed and cry herself to sleep, she allowed Bretane to put his arms around her and whisper in her ear, "A man isna dead as long as we still speak his name."

"I canna."

"Then I will. Tomorrow night, we will all come together to talk of Robin. It has been near a month since ye came home, and 'tis time. Tomorrow, we will tell stories about him and rejoice that we kenned him for as long as we did. We will always miss him, but we will ne'er forget him. Ye will be there with us."

"We were mairrit only three days before they took him from me," she said, clutching Bretane's shirt tightly in her fists. "We pledged our futures to each other, and I willna have the future we planned. Ye dinna understand!"

"Dinna be selfish with yer grief, Suann. My future with Robin is lost just as yers is, but we can still make a new future that honors him."

How could she make a new future without him? If she stopped thinking about him every waking moment, he truly would be gone forever. Her voice rose as she pushed herself out of his arms. "I couldna bring his body home! There is naught to bury! Nothing so others will remember he lived!" She couldn't bear it!

"The stone for the cemetery has already been carved with his name across the top and will be placed on a grave that is empty. A cemetery is not for honoring dead bodies and bones. The grave and the stone are for remembering a life, and we will always remember him. There will be a stone with his name on it, Suann, I promise ye, and everyone who sees it will ken that he lived."

The next evening just as the sun set and after all the chores, everyone who belonged to Makgullane gathered in the barn just outside Robin's room. It seemed like the best place to honor him, the place where they had seen him most often. Bretane lit a fire inside an iron ring atop a stone slab in the center of the dirt floor, and everyone sat or stood around it. Suann brought out Robin's chair, the one tucked beside his desk, and placed it near the fire. She would need it to support her in what would be a difficult time.

Darby began. "He taught me how to be the reeve, and now I ken how to do the job. He wad be proud of me."

Ralf said, "I ne'er saw a man who worked better with the horses than our Robin. He kenned each one so well, and the beasts loved him. Ye could see it in their eyes that they loved him."

Fergus put his arm around Suann's shoulder. "When I took the colt out without permission, it made Robin verra angry, and he thought his punishment wad scare me, but I wasna scared." He stuck out his chin. "I kenned he wadna thrash me. I wasna worried."

"I saw ye," said Suann, tugging him closer. "Ye were a little worried." She winked. "But Robin wadna have thrashed ye. He wanted to teach ye, not punish ye. Did ye ken that I met Robin on the day Bretane thrashed him?"

Fergus grinned at Bretane. "Really? You thrashed Robin?"

"Aye, I did," said Bretane. "He played a terrible prank on Father Bernard, and—"

Someone whistled three short puffs and a long one a note higher. Everyone looked around to see who would dare to repeat the greeting that belonged only to Suann and Robin.

All heads turned to see a tall silhouette shadowed in the open door of the barn.

From the corner, Marta reached out her hand to the figure.

The familiar voice said, "Bretane, I will never live it down if you tell that story!"

"Robin," Marta gasped.

Within seconds, all the others jumped to their feet and rushed toward the door. "Robin! Robin!"

All except Suannoch, who bolted upright out of her chair but couldn't seem to move her feet. Her mouth opened, but she couldn't form words as her heart tried to beat out of her chest.

"Why are you having a funeral for a man who is not dead?" asked Robin.

The others stepped aside so Bretane could be the first to reach him. "Lad, ye're really here!" Throwing his arms around his son, he hugged him so tightly, Robin soon struggled for breath.

"Where is Suann?" Robin sputtered. "Release me, and tell me where Suann is."

The crowd separated again, forming a path to Suann, who had not moved from her spot by the chair. Robin strode to her side, lifted her off her feet, and kissed her.

"Is it really ye?" she said in a breathless voice when he put her back on her feet.

Leaning down, he pulled her toward him and kissed her again.

" 'Tis ye, but if not hanged and in the grave, where? How?" She tightened her arms around him and pressed her face against his chest, soaking his shirt with now-public tears of utter joy.

Robin's tale came out in bits and pieces between questions from the crowd and his need to kiss Suann and stroke her hair. His eyes never left hers as he talked.

"King James ordered every Armstrong prisoner hanged on the trees where he could see them. When the commotion started, he sent Captain Dunwoody to bring me and Tinker and Ronald to stand behind the platform. We stood there, waiting for our turn. It felt like some kind of horrible dream, standing there watching, knowing we would be next. But after the last Armstrong had been strung up and the bodies dragged away, still no one came for us.

"Finally, the soldiers forced us toward the trees. We could almost feel the hangman's noose on our necks, but they ordered us through the trees to the open field, cut our ropes, and handed us shovels. They told us to dig."

"Ye had to dig the grave for all the Armstrongs?" said Hugh. To the crowd he added, "They buried all them in one big hole. 'Tis what the women on the road said."

"Aye, we dug all night long and then we had to drag the dead men into the hole. King James stood there through the night watching everything. He never said a word, just watched."

"No trial, no nothing," said Ralf. "He hanged them

all and covered them over. Our king is a cruel man."

"He is not at all like the frightened boy I knew when he stayed here," said Robin. "That boy was kind and well-spoken. He was curious and thoughtful but being king has hardened his heart."

"He is young," said Bretane in the boy king's defense. "He will learn how to handle the responsibility of being the king as he gets older, but I fear he has made many enemies with this execution of so many."

"Robin, where have ye been all this time?" asked Fergus.

"When we finished covering over the grave, Tinker, Ronald, and I sat under a tree and slept. I have never been so exhausted. When we woke, 'twas dark again and everyone had gone, all the soldiers, the king, everyone. We started for home, but Ronald got a terrible pain in his gut. We brought him some water from the river and found an onion in the church vegetable plot, but that only made the pain worse. Then he started throwing up blood."

"Did ye ken the sickness?"

"Nay, so Tinker and I carried him into the church, and we waited. Tinker left to find a physician, but he never returned, not that I expected him to, but I could not leave Ronald there alone so sick. The priest came, and he gave me food, but he could not help Ronald. Ronald had no value to anyone but himself, but he did not deserve to die the hideous death that he did. I stayed with him for two weeks, maybe more, I lost track of time. I could not ease his suffering, but at least he did not die alone. I held his hand until he breathed his last. After that I buried him in the church graveyard, the priest said a blessing, and I walked home."

"Are ye hungry, lad?" asked Bretane.

"Nay, Thomas, the tanner, fed me. His wee son cried like a banshee when I came close, so Thomas tossed me bread and a slice of mutton if I would be on my way. I must look a fright. I am covered with a month's worth of dirt, grime, and death. What I would like is a bath."

"Then a bath it is!" said Bretane. He started giving orders to prepare a bath for Robin.

Suann looked up at her man. He came back to her. She could touch his face, take his hands in hers, and suddenly she felt herself dancing and twirling around and around. At first it pleased her to be dancing in Robin's arms, but as she started to move faster and faster, she lost control. Then the barn moved in the same whirlwind. Closing her eyes, she collapsed into his arms.

When she awoke, someone had put her to bed in their room, and Robin sat up to his chest in a large tub of steaming water. Four buckets of more hot water had been placed around the tub. She sat up.

"You are awake," said Robin. "Thalassa said 'twas a faint from the shock of seeing me home. Believe me, no one is more shocked than I am that I made it back here." He laughed and rippled his hands through the water surrounding him.

She needed to touch him, so she would know for certain he had really come back to her. Sliding out of bed, she said, "Let me wash yer hair." She found two large chunks of Maggy's special soap, made from mutton fat, wood ash, and soda, then scented with lavender, on the floor beside the tub. Kneeling behind him, she lathered the soap through his tangled hair. As she did, the sorrow lifted. Touching her hands on his head and his hair made everything real, and the world within her righted itself.

Robin said, "I am tired down to my bones, and this feels so good, it may just put me to sleep."

"I dinna intend to stop for a long time, so put yer arms over the sides to hold yerself up if ye do fall asleep." He did as she told him and closed his eyes.

Her fingertips continued to massage his scalp, dislodging patches of dirt and lice nits. His curly locks straightened with the water and hung over the back edge of the tub.

"Yer hair finally covers most of your ear now," She worked the lather up around his disfigured ear, washing away the grime there and on his neck and shoulders.

"Cut the long left side and the back to about my chin level," he said, barely in a whisper.

"Are ye certain? 'Twill still be off balance."

" 'Twill look better shorter until the right side grows out all the way."

"Are ye certain?" she asked again.

He did not answer, so she retrieved a pair of scissors and trimmed his wet hair until it hung just below his chin on the left side. "Do ye want me to shave ye?"

"Nay, I have been through hell since I left in that prison wagon. It changed me. Trim my beard close to my chin and only shave the tufts that grow up on my cheeks and down my neck."

When she had finished with her barbering, he said, "What do you think?" He had not opened his eyes.

"I think ye look verra braw." She ran her hand

across his new dark beard. "Verra braw, indeed."

"The water is cooling," he said in a languid voice.

After dumping one of the extra buckets over his head, she scrubbed his arms and chest. Bruises and small cuts speckled his skin between the deep but healed scars from the beating by the Grays and those old scars from his childhood. Eventually all these wounds would fade, but when she came to his wrists and saw the raw red rings around them from the manacles, here would always be a reminder of his imprisonment. Gently, she washed each wrist and hand, trimmed his jagged nails, and kissed each finger when she finished.

"My ankles look even worse," he said as he lifted one leg and draped it over the side.

She cringed at how the skin on his ankle had been rubbed off nearly to the bone in places. "They dinna look like they are festering," she said, "but Thalassa will look at them tomorrow. She will give ye something to ease the pain." Gently, she smoothed off the rough and torn edges of the skin, working around any blisters and open sores.

He lifted the other leg, and she tended to it in the same way. Then she began to wash his body with a sponge.

She let the sponge caress him around his neck and down his chest, soothing away the aches in his body and easing the tension that he had held so tightly over the past few weeks. He snored softly until she moved her sponge between his legs. With a start, he sat up in the water, reached a hand behind her head, and pulled her into his kiss. It began gently but soon intensified into the passion they had both feared they would never know again. She inhaled his smell of lavender and warm water. He took in her familiar scent, so delicate and inviting.

"Sometimes the only thing that kept me alive was remembering your kiss and how you felt beneath me," he murmured before delving into her mouth again. When he eventually released her, he held her with a smoldering gaze. "Hand me a towel so we can make new memories of the ways you feel beneath me."

"Aye, guidman," she said with a small curtsy.

She watched him dry himself while she stripped off her kirtle and overdress and slipped under the quilt. As he padded over to the bed, his body, despite the cuts and bruises that marred it, enthralled her, and her own body prepared to accept him in his fullness.

The bed creaked as he lay down on his back beside her. Slipping under his arm, she draped her arm across his chest. While listening to his breathing, she pushed away the memory of the sorrow of the past weeks. He lay beside her. He made her whole again. Their future danced before them, and she felt safe and secure with this man she had loved since the first day she met him on the stairs twelve years ago.

Pushing herself up on her elbow to look at his face, she stretched up to kiss him, and saw that the warm bath and his exhaustion had overcome him. She would let him sleep, so she snuggled deeper beside him, knowing they had all the time in the world. She could wait until morning. He lay beside her again, and she could finally sleep.

Just before the sunrise cast its bright light over the tops of the hills, Robin quietly climbed out of bed and slipped on his plaid. He hated leaving the comfort of

Suann next to him, but he had something important to do. Reaching inside his leather pouch, he took out the circle of metal with the molded dog on it that he had carried for the last twelve years.

Quietly, he left the warmth of their room and walked away from the yard. He had no destination in mind; in fact, he wanted the place to be random, meaningless, and forgettable. It had to be a place no one would think to look, a place that even he would have trouble finding again. After walking for a time, he found such a place.

He climbed the slope of one of the many hills in the Highlands with nothing exceptional to distinguish it from its neighbor.

Even the heather that grew abundantly across it looked the same as it did on every other hill covered with heather. Closing his eyes, he walked, varying his stride and changing directions numerous times. At the site of his last footfall, he dug a hole about six inches deep with his knife.

Into it, he dropped the metal token that had belonged to his mother.

As he stared at it in the bottom of the hole, he said words that only he and the wind could hear. "I loved you before and I love you now, but the life you gave me is over. I belong to the life that Bretane and these Scottish Highlands have given me. 'Tis who I am and where I will be for the rest of my life. My heart is here. I am a Scot."

Pushing the loose dirt over the token, he covered it and filled the hole. Then he stomped it flat and pulled some of the fast-growing purple heather over it.

In a few days it would be just another tiny piece of

land, invisible to everyone, including Robin.

He went home to the warmth of Suannoch's bed.

Chapter Twenty-One

Robin awoke to another rare day in the Highlands, sunny and breezy, and warmer than it had been. The grass grew a fragrant green, and the cloudless sky sparkled a glorious blue.

A now washed and rested Robin showed Suann all the sensual pleasures a man and a woman could share. Each time he made love to her, he made certain that he completely and absolutely satisfied her before he found his pleasure in her. He spoke tender words of love with every amorous touch, but by the time the morning had passed, they still wanted each other even more.

Bracing himself over her, he stroked her lips with his finger, saying, "You may think I am done with you now, but prepare yourself to take me again. I demand it, and 'tis your wifely duty."

"If my duty is done as well as it has been this morn, I am waiting for ye with only a smile to cover me."

He gently ran his finger across her smile again just as the door burst open.

"Nay, Fergus!" said Hugh, holding back the struggling boy. "We maun wait until they say we can come in!"

Fergus said, "Why? Robin always wants to see me." When he saw Robin and Suann still in bed and hastily throwing the quilt over themselves again, he said, "The sun is high! Every time I come to see ye, ye and Suann are still abed! I dinna think Bretane wad like ye to be so lazy."

Hugh said, "I am sorry, but he is young and doesna understand what a man and a woman do in the bed."

Fergus turned to look at his friend and new brother. "What do they do?"

"Well, it isna always sleeping!"

Robin said sternly, "Hugh is right, Fergus. Listen to him." Then with a grin, he added, "Now, what do you want this fine morning?"

"A chest, a big chest, was brought here by men dressed in the king's colors. No' soldiers but dressed in fancy coats and hats. They left a chest. 'Tis all carved and decorated, verra fancy. They said 'twas for ye and yer wife. Is that Suann?"

Robin winked at Suann and said, "I will ask Suann if she is my wife. If she says aye, then we will come out and see what this chest is all about. If she says nay, then we will stay in here and I will convince her."

Hugh rolled his eyes while Fergus pouted.

"Now, Fergus, leave us so we can put on some clothes."

As soon as the door closed, Suann pushed hard against his back. "Ye will have that lad all confused. Soon, he will have to have a talk about what happens between wives and guidmen, and ye will have to do it."

"Me? Why me?"

"Because ye are the one who is confusing him! Now out of the bed."

He winked. "All right, if you insist, I will wait until the sun sets for you to do your wifely duty." She gave him a peck on the cheek and crawled out from behind him.

Just as Fergus had said, a large, dark wooden chest sat in the center of the yard. A leather pouch, bound with a ribbon and sealed with wax impressed with a crown and the words James V, lay strapped to the top. Everyone on the estate gathered to see the contents of the first chest that had ever been delivered from a king.

Breaking the seal on the pouch, Robin found a letter addressed to Suannoch inside.

"I have ne'er kenned anyone who got a letter from the king!" said Henry.

Maggy curtsied and said, "Ye are a blessed lady indeed!"

Suann read the missive aloud for all the curious onlookers who had no intention of leaving until she did.

"With greetings from James V. Robin of Makgullane took us in when he didna ken that we were king. His kindness is repaid today. We pray that ye understand how we couldna offer his freedom while others watched. Our deepest wish remained that he be released and returned home to ye. If this couldna be, then ye have our condolences and we mourn his loss. May these trinkets please ye."

"Open it!" cried Fergus. "Open it!"

"Be patient," said Robin as he broke a second, larger wax seal on the leather ties that held the chest closed and lifted the lid. Lavish gifts that only a king could offer nearly burst out of the tightly packed chest.

A hooded woolen cloak in a deep royal blue with gold embroidery along the hem and down each sleeve lay folded across the top. Several large red rubies sewn into the wool near the collar glittered in the sunlight.

"Robin," said Suann, " 'tis so lovely!"

" 'Tis for Bretane," said Robin, holding it up. "Here, Bretane, you will wear this gift proudly. No one in the Highlands has one as fancy." Throwing it over Bretane's shoulders, the smile on the older man's face told everyone how pleased he was to be the owner of such an exquisite cloak.

The next layer held cups and bowls all made of gold and engraved with the king's seal. Under that sat two golden ewers. "These are for Marta," said Suann. "Now her tables will be worthy of the food she serves."

Marta acted as giddy as a young girl as she took the tableware in her hands and rubbed it against her cheeks. "Thank ye!" she repeated. "Thank ye!"

In the next layer, Suann found deep-green silk cloth wrapped around several exquisite pieces of jewelry, two necklaces of diamonds and rubies and two brooches. An engraved likeness of the king covered one brooch, and on the other an oval studded with emeralds and diamonds.

"Every woman and lass on Makgullane will have a scarf of this cloth," said Suann. "And the jewels will be Thalassa's."

Oohs and ahhs went up from every female around the chest. Their new scarves would be the most glorious thing they owned and worn proudly at every possible occasion.

"Thalassa will be so pleased," Robin whispered in her ear. "You are a fine daughter."

Suann kissed him on the cheek and startled slightly when his new whiskers tickled her lips. In a loud voice she said, "How do ye like Robin's beard? It makes him a new man!"

"At last!" shouted Darby. "I wondered who stood

beside ye, Suann! Looking like a true Scot if I ever saw one!"

Robin gave a single nod, knowing that in his heart he finally felt like a true Scot.

The next layer of goods had been carefully wrapped in linen. Suann unpacked a saltcellar in the shape of an ostrich with a belly of pearl seated on a platform of silver gilt and green enamel. She opened a painted miniature with King James on one side of the double frame and his gardens at Stirling Palace on the other side. Last, she brought out a golden hen sitting on a white enameled egg that opened to reveal a yolk of pure gold.

"I have ne'er seen anything so beautiful," said Suann as her eyes danced over each treasure.

"The king is generous," said Bretane, "because he kens that he owes Robin a debt. Not only for Robin's care when he stayed here, but also for no' having the courage to release Robin while others watched. He may make mistakes as king, but this way of apology shows he has a conscience that will serve him well during his reign."

"There is one more thing on the bottom of the chest," said Robin. With Darby and Shane's help, he pulled out a heavy tapestry, unfolded it, and held it up for all to see.

"I recognize that," said Bretane. "It hangs, or at least it did until now, at Stirling Palace when the king is in residence there. As I recall there are seven parts to this tapestry. Let me think. The whole thing is called..." He scratched his beard as he thought. "I ken this section is called 'Coningars' or 'The Rabbit Hunt.' "

Everyone stepped closer to get a better look at the woven images of men dressed in red coats pulling rabbits out of traps and the women standing nearby ready to prepare those rabbits. Threads in vibrant reds, greens, and blues created the forest around them.

"The details are stunning," commented Suann. "Weaving this maun have taken months, mayhap even years. Bretane, this will look so fine on yer wall in the gathering room."

"But I have the cloak," said Bretane. "Ye and Robin should keep it."

"My room is too small and too plain for such a display," said Robin.

"But now that ye are mairrit, ye maun move into the manor house. That seems only fitting. I have already started plans for the addition of two rooms for ye at the back of the house. Ye can decorate them as ye please."

Suann and Robin looked around at all the smiling faces.

"Father Bernard came around," said Bretane, "to give me fair warning that ye had gone to him in the middle of the night. He said the lad who left a dead horse in his room needed a firm hand so he wad take care of that little wisp of a wife. He wanted me to provide the firm hand. In fact, he insisted I see to Robin's good behavior."

"I do not think you will have to worry about that," laughed Robin. "This little wisp has her own firm hand!"

Robin caught the twinkle in Suann's eye just before she gave a strong enough tug on his beard to pull his head down and kiss him. "Is that hand firm enough?"

All the onlookers hooted with laughter.

Robin grunted and tried to pull back from her grip. "Aye, it is! Now release me."

She ignored his request and kissed him again.

When she still didn't release her grip on his beard, he picked her up by the waist, twirled her around, and set her down on top of the trunk. Putting both hands on either side of her, he kissed her while at the same time pushing her backwards. Just before she fell off the trunk, she let go of his beard and wrapped her arms around his neck. "Truce!" she cried.

"Truce," he said before picking her up in his arms and striding back toward their room in the barn.

This brought on even more raucous laughter.

Bretane called out to the pair, "Robin and Suannoch, we give ye our hearty thanks for the gifts, and we will be on our way so ye two can have the rest of the day to yerselves. Fergus, ye are no' to bother Robin until sunset. Do ye hear me?"

Fergus shrugged, wondering why Bretane would order such a thing, and then said, "But we have our lessons with Suann."

"Not today!" Bretane grabbed the boy by the arm and led him away. Hugh trotted along behind.

Even though everyone already knew about their wedding, they insisted on a celebration. The preparations took weeks, as did the building of the rooms onto the manor house for the couple. Mae Towdy set to work on Suann's wedding outfit while Bretane commissioned Angus in Stirling to weave a new tartan to represent Robin and the beginning of his family. Angus and Glynnis, now happily wed, readily agreed to create the new tartan as a sign of their goodwill.

"Why can I not have your tartan?" asked Robin.

"Because," said Bretane, "I am the last of my line, and yer legacy is just beginning."

Robin chose to honor Bretane's sett pattern of red and yellow striping on olive green by weaving the same sett into a bright emerald-green background. Suann chose to wear the new tartan as part of her wedding outfit, draping it from her shoulders to the floor and belting it at her waist over a cream underdress. The tartan overdress had a square neckline, a fitted bodice, and opened at her hips. Completing the costume would be a yellow hooded cloak with embroidered green and red flowers and love knots stitched along all the edges and down the center of the long flowing sleeves.

Despite Robin's protests, the men of the estate refused to forgo the custom of Creeling the Groom. Shane and Darby filled a large basket with rocks from the stream, so heavy that it took both of them to lug it back to the barn, where they ordered Robin to carry it around the yard until Suann came out of their room to kiss him, thus indicating that she would accept him as her guidman. With considerable grumbling, Robin carried the basket on his back for three trips around the yard in front of the taunting and cheering crowd. On the third circuit, Suann still remained smiling and waving at him from the window, so he marched into the barn and dumped his burden at the door of their room.

"Come out, woman!" he shouted, "or I will toss every one of these rocks on the bed!"

Dashing out the door, Suann jumped into his arms and kissed him soundly on the mouth.

On the day of the ceremony, all the guests escorted the couple to the church steps where Father Bernard performed the same version of their previous nuptials. Afterward, he led everyone inside to repeat that ceremony in Latin and serve communion.

When it came time to exchange rings, the priest asked Suann to give him back the ring he had given them, so he could bless it again before Robin slipped it on her finger for the second time.

"I dinna have it, Father," she said, hanging her head in shame. " 'Tis all Robin's fault. I am verra sorry, but I had to sell it for food."

The priest's eyebrows shot up. "Did this man desert ye after ye exchanged vows? I warned ye about a man like this Robin!"

Suann maintained her solemn and regretful attitude. "Aye, he left me, but he had a good reason." She paused. "He was to be hanged."

The priest narrowed his eyes at her. "I heard the tale, and I maun admit I hoped ye wad be rid of him, but I see him standing beside ye, so I wonder why ye're so foolish to wed him twice. He is no' hiding from the law, is he?"

Robin smiled at how Suann enjoyed tormenting Father Bernard. "Nay, Father. King James freed me," he said.

The older man closed his eyes, muttered a prayer, and crossed himself. When he looked up, he said, "Suann, ye ken that next time the noose may do its work. Are ye absolutely certain ye want to marry this scoundrel again?"

She nodded. "I am as certain as I am that the sun will rise tomorrow."

Father Bernard crossed himself again. "So be it. What are ye going to use for a ring today?"

Turning to Bretane standing beside him, Robin held out his hand, and Bretane dropped two shiny silver rings into his palm. Suann's eyes blinked when he held them out to let her handle the smaller one. "These are beautiful," she said. "Where did ye get them? I thought we planned to use Bretane's ring."

"I could not let you wear a borrowed ring," said Robin. "I took our half coins and had them melted down and forged into these rings. Now we will wear our tokens on our fingers."

"I love them, but I didna think ye wad wear a ring. Most men dinna," she said.

"I am not most men," he said, slipping her ring on her finger. After he handed her the larger ring, she slid it over his finger. Then, lifting that finger to her lips, she kissed the ring and smiled at the man she had loved forever and would love forever more.

When the wedding ceremony ended, the wedding feast began. Marta, once again the center of attention, served all her luscious foods in the golden bowls and cups from the king. Dancing continued late into the night, but Robin and Suann had long before slipped away to spend their last night in the room in the barn.

Tomorrow would be soon enough to begin the rest of their lives together.

Chapter Twenty-Two

Fifty years later

It had been another wonderful day in the Highlands, warm and sunny with a breeze that as evening came brushed Robin's bright white curls off his face. He made his nightly visit to say good night to Suann.

It was peaceful in the cemetery at Makgullane. Small grave markers with names carved in them stood over the places where his loved ones rested. Bretane and Hugh had been laid beside Suann to the left while the stone that Bretane had set in place all those years ago sat on the right where Robin would someday rest beside her. Thalassa lay nearby so that her stone faced her daughter's. Suann had insisted they be able to see each other for all eternity.

Robin let the memories slide over him. For him, this place held much more than the remains of those he cherished. Here, he happily reminisced about the lives of those he had known and loved.

Sitting on the stone bench alongside her grave, he said in his now familiar Scottish brogue, "Another fine day today, Suann." For many years, when he had felt like an outsider, he had purposely kept his English accent, but ever since the day he had buried the token from his life in England, he had used and practiced a

Scottish brogue until he spoke like someone born in the Highlands. He even learned a little Gaelic, although Suann teased him saying that he spoke Gaelic like a dog with his foot caught in a trap.

" 'Twas quite a day today, Suann. Ye wad have loved it. Today our eldest, our old man, Bran, officially turned over all the duties of reeve to our grandbairn, Ian, and we celebrated with a grand party. 'Tis hard to believe that we started with Fergus and Hugh, added our own six, and now there are nearly forty we can call our own! Fergus couldna come, but he sent a letter saying that his classes are going well, but he is thinking of giving up teaching the law in Glasgow and coming home for good. Wadna that be grand, Suann, to have him back with us? I do wish Hugh could be here to welcome his brother home."

Robin leaned over and patted the stone next to Suann's that read "Hugh—Ours First, Ours Forever."

Robin got off the bench and stiffly lowered himself to the ground until he leaned against Suann's stone. He rubbed his hand over the inscription under her name: "Where I Have Chosen," the first line of the pledge they had made to each other so long ago. The words on his stone under his name finished the line: "Steadfast Will I Be."

After Suann had died of a lung ailment ten years ago, Robin had moved out of the manor house and back into his room in the barn. He felt closer to her there.

"Taran forged Ian an iron plaque representing the four seasons to commemorate the occasion, and Ian has already nailed it above the barn door. Dillon, as usual refusing to be outdone by his twin, gave Ian a colt bred from King Glory's line. I wish ye could see how beautiful that animal is."

He rested his head back on her stone. Twirling the silver wedding ring made from their shilling, he sighed. Then he fingered Suann's smaller one, which he now wore on his little finger.

"Dillon's newest grandbabe, Eileen, also gave her cousin a present. She said her first word! 'Twas *sinn-seanair*. I dinna care that Dillon thinks 'twas only *seanair*. I ken she meant me! She favors ye with gold hair and green eyes. Suann, I can still see yer eyes, how they looked just before ye closed them to sleep.

"Ye wad have liked seeing Kathleen's wee ones when they came for the party, though they wad grumble if I called them 'wee.' I was so glad they wanted to come up here with me to see their granny last night."

He sighed heavily again. "I had hoped Meara wad come and surprise us. I wrote her, but she didna come. So headstrong she was." He patted the grass over Suannoch's grave. "Just like her *màthair*." He laughed to himself, remembering all the times Suann and Meara had butted heads like two wild goats. "Quinn did surprise us though by bringing his new bride. Ye wad like her. We all do."

The view from here in the cemetery of the sunset over the hills was the most beautiful in all of Makgullane.

"Did I tell ye that Taran made an iron plaque of the seasons for Ian? Oh, aye, I did tell ye that. Sometimes 'tis hard for me to remember."

The sun dropped behind the hills, and the stars began to light the cloudless sky. That was his sign to light his lantern and head back to his room, but before he did, he said, "This is when I miss ye the most, *mo ghaol*, when the sun falls. Sometimes at night, I awake and think ye are still right beside me. I can feel yer warmth, but when I reach for ye…"

His eyes closed, and that is how they found him the next morning.

He did not have to burn down Heaven's door. It opened for him, and he saw her there, waiting for him. Just as she promised.

Historical Notes

Uncertainty and turmoil touched every part of Scotland in the years before 1530. King James IV had been killed at the Battle of Flodden in 1513, leaving his seventeen-month-old son, James V, as the country's monarch. Too young to rule on his own, his mother, Margaret Tudor, sister of King Henry VIII of England, had been expected to serve as his regent until he was grown, but instead she chose to marry Archibald Douglas, leader of the powerful Douglas clan.

Even though James had been crowned as a toddler, a variety of male regents took over all royal authority, basing most of their decisions on their own desire for personal power and wealth, and not on the good of Scotland. In 1525, James's stepfather, Archibald Douglas, seized control and had James imprisoned. All this time, the young king had only limited education. Douglas treated his stepson with the same affection one gives a family dog rather than allow him the training needed to become a king.

In 1528, at age sixteen, James escaped. The true story of this escape may never be known. Two previous attempts had failed, and this time it seemed that he just rode off the grounds in the company of two servants. Regardless, he quickly assumed his role as monarch, determined to prove that, despite his lack of experience, he could hold the throne.

At that time, vicious, cruel, and widely feared Border reivers, thieves and robbers, roamed at will along the border between Scotland and England. The young king made it one of his priorities to eliminate their influence. He invited Johnnie Armstrong, the most notorious reiver, to hunt with him at the field behind the kirkyard at Caerlanrig, but instead of negotiating, King James captured him and his followers and hanged them all without a trial. He hanged twenty-four men and burned one alive. While this mass execution did weaken the Border reivers, it also earned the king the distrust of many powerful men and clans who worried they might be his next target. This rift would never be repaired.

According to legend and song, King James V, eager to know what the common people really thought of him, dressed in rags and traveled around alone in disguise, often playing the lute and singing to entertain his hosts. People said he had a good ear for a tune, but a harsh and raspy voice. They called him "The King of the Commons." James himself wrote poems about these travels, referring to himself as "the gaberlunzieman" and "the jolly beggar."

James V died at age thirty, leaving nine illegitimate children, but despite having been married twice, he sired only one legitimate heir to his throne, a six-day-old infant girl who became Mary, Queen of Scots. On his death bed, it is claimed that he said, "It began with a girl and it will end with a girl," supposedly referencing how the Stuart dynasty began with Marjorie Bruce, daughter of Robert Bruce, and would end with James's daughter, Mary.

A word about the author...

Susan Leigh Furlong is a lifelong writer about the people who were so busy living their lives that they didn't know they were living history.

With research and imagination her favorite thing is to drop her hero and heroine into the middle of a true historical event. She has written two non-fiction books about the people and history of her hometown and co-authored a full-length play about the twelve disciples at the Last Supper.

Although raised as a big city girl, she now lives in small town Ohio with her husband and her two cats, Calvin and Hobbes.